INVISIBLE SECRETS

MARY

USA TODAY BESTSELLING AUTHOR

BUCKHAM

Cover and book design by
THE KILLION GROUP
www.thekilliongroupinc.com

DEDICATION

This book is dedicated to those readers who make it a delight to create. Thank you, each and every one of you. You rock!

ACKNOWLEDGEMENT

It takes a village to create a book and this book is no exception. A special thanks to Dorothy Callahan and Laurie Gifford Adams for copyediting, you are my Grammar and Comma Goddesses. A huge note of appreciation to my amazing Street Team, Mary Buckham's Ninjas, who, by being great Beta readers, helped so much in making sure the story held together — Gail Chianese, Kimberly Dawn and Tiger Wiseman. Thanks to them and all my Street Team members who have loved and supported these stories and spread the word. And, of course, thank you to my husband who keeps me sane — which is a full time job — but is also willing to discuss vamps, Weres and shifters even in a public venue! Any mistakes or adjustments in detail for the purpose of fiction are entirely my own doing.

CHAPTER 1

Why was it all hospitals reminded me more of death than life? Odd given that their focus was on prolonging and saving human lives. Maybe it was the antiseptically chilled air wafting against my bare arms as I entered the Georgetown Medical Center's main lobby. Outside a May day was warming up nicely D.C. style, a break from the winter slush and a prelude to the summer humidity that would make the city a ghost town.

I'm Kelly McAllister, an IR (I for Invisible, R for Recruit) agent currently recovering at our agency compound just over the state line in Maryland. I look a lot like what I used to be, a kindergarten teacher from Dubuque, Iowa, and not much like the fighter of preternatural threats I'd become in the last two months.

Was that all? How time flies when you're trying to stay alive.

That was also me, nice and clueless, or was me, before my last mission in West Africa, followed by an unexpected dust-up in Missouri. Now I was a card-carrying cynic who was tired of getting beaten, bruised, and battered — and those were on the slow days.

I was supposed to be recovering from a near-fatal experience in Sierra Leone, where I'd killed my first man. Well, technically he wasn't a man, he was an Aka Manah demon, but taking a life is taking a life. It scars a person. Then there was the fae I gutted in Missouri, literally, with a ceremonial sword. Did I mention the last few weeks have been intense?

Now I was visiting a young girl, Aini, which sounds like 'Ah-nee'. She wasn't yet fifteen but had already saved my life in Sierra Leone. Her predictions saved me, or gave me enough of a heads up to make some hard choices. As a result, I'd completed the first mission I'd led, discovered my only sister was not a saint, but a killer, and had deserved to die, and she wasn't really my sister at all. I'd been abandoned with her parents, who'd done their duty and raised me, past tense. Once they knew that I knew their secret, the one they'd kept all these years about me not being their biological child, they'd washed their hands of me and destroyed the childhood illusions that defined my life up until a week ago. They had their reasons, but that didn't mean my head and heart weren't still reeling.

Oh, and in the process, Aini fell into a coma. Leaving her in Sierra Leone was not an option. Given the available medical care there, it would have meant a death sentence. Thank heavens the IR Agency Director, Ling Mai, arranged Aini's transportation here to the George Washington Medical Center's MICU wing. That's Medical Intensive Care Unit, where coma patients are monitored twenty-four seven and kept alive.

Before you think Ling Mai is a warm and fuzzy humanitarian, she's not. While the rest of my IR team and I were slogging all over Sierra Leone looking for a rare plant we thought was an orchid, imagine our surprise when we discovered Aini *was* the rare flower. Her name means flower in Swahili and it appears she's a powerful seer. Someone who can foretell the future, though we have to wait for her to wake up to find out exactly what she can and can't do, and why she's the all important clue we need to find out more about a group of not-so-nice beings called the Seekers.

We don't know if the Seekers are human or non-human. All we know about them is that they want to change the balance between humans and preternaturals in this world and not in a good way.

Seems humans have been rubbing shoulders with preternaturals for centuries and, so far, it's mostly been a functioning arrangement. But that could easily change.

Humans currently are the beings in charge, if for no other reason than most of us think preternaturals are the stuff of legends, fairy tales and fantasy stories. If we really knew the truth, we'd either go stark raving bonkers or start eradication programs that would make the Salem witch trials seem like garden parties. Humans tend to approach potential threats as just that, with a nuke-them-first-and-ask-questions-later sort of approach.

Preternaturals, who by and large are stronger and more lethal than humans, tend to walk in the shadows and keep their secrets. According to our all-things-preternatural instructor, Fraulein Fassbinder, they don't reproduce as prolifically as humans and avoid humans as much as we'd like to avoid them.

Lately, though, some have been agitating to come out of the preternatural closet. Not necessarily a bad thing, but it is when unknown beings are pushing certain species into claiming what they've long felt denied — power, positions of authority, and acknowledgement that they are the superior creatures. The result would make America during presidential election year politics seem benign.

The Seekers have been identified as being behind a lot of this agitation, and the IR Agency's role is to find out who or what the Seekers are, and how to stop them.

Right now though, our only lead was in a coma.

I wasn't here today to interrogate doctors or nudge nurses into seeing if we could bring Aini out of her enforced vegetative state but to simply visit her. In Sierra Leone, she was an orphan, a victim of one of the recent civil wars that tore apart her small country, and that broke my heart. Every child deserves a childhood and so far it didn't look like Aini had been given much of a chance to have one.

Now she was fighting for her life and hanging on by a thread. Least I could do was visit her daily and hold her hand. Let her know she wasn't totally alone, and that at least one person cared about her, not because she was a clue or asset but because she was a person.

I walked up to the central desk in the MICU ward where all visitors had to check in. I knew the drill. Except for the two days I'd been away in Missouri helping an IR teammate track down another teen while fighting off a witch-finder and his Were and fae allies, I'd visited Aini every day. It wasn't much to do for her but all I could offer right now. Who knew when we'd receive the next call to drop everything to fight some preternatural flare-up somewhere in the world.

A middle-aged nurse with skin the color of warm cocoa was busy filling out some paperwork, so I waited, aware of the warming of the rune-incised silver ring I wore on my right hand. The ring was created to warn us agents of the presence of preternaturals. It'd work a whole lot better if it could tell us we were facing a falconi demon or a gnome. The first would rip your head off if you looked sideways at it, while the latter could help you win prizes at your local garden club.

So the nurse was some kind of preternatural. Possibly an elf, if my study of Fraulein Fassbinder's books was correct. Her sources were iffy though as most non-humans kept knowledge about who and what they are to themselves, though a number of them do update their own Wikipedia pages, which blows my mind.

Supposedly some of the elves, especially Alvor elves, were empathetic and imaginative caregivers and you could often find them in hospitals, nursing homes or childcare facilities. Maybe that's what I really was? Some kind of an elven creature?

Since my sister, or non-sister, blew my world wide apart by telling me I'd been dropped off at her parents' house like used linen, I was determined to discover who my real birth mother was. Ling Mai agreed to help me in my quest, after warning me I might not like the answers I found.

Tough. I knew I wasn't fully human, given I could turn invisible. Or, maybe I should say I used to be able to turn invisible. Not lately, not since Africa, and not since I'd received a transfusion of blood from a sexy, if dangerous, wolf shifter. Yup, part of the crazy past few weeks.

His shifter blood kept me from dying, but I was beginning to suspect it messed with my own strange genetic make-up. For twenty-five years I'd struggled with a freakish ability to disappear when stressed, afraid, or under threat — the number one reason that the parents who'd raised me had washed their hands of me. I was a freak and devil spawned, in their words. I agree invisibility isn't the most useful skill to have, but I'd been learning how to control the ability so it worked for me and helped my IR team.

Now?

Who knew how long Ling Mai would keep me on the team if I couldn't access my gift. And if she didn't keep me as an agent, she'd have no reason to help me find my paranormal or preternatural birth mother.

So for now, my *inability* to disappear was my best kept secret. Only one other knew about it, and that was Alex Noziak, my best friend and fellow IR team member. She was also sister to Van Noziak, the wolf shifter who gave me the blood transfusion.

He'd saved my life in Sierra Leone, and once again in Missouri. He also wanted to see me outside our respective jobs, his being some sort of Black Ops group that worked out of D.C. Sure, there was a crazy, wicked attraction between us, at least on my part — he made my toes curl, my pulse pick up and sucked all the air from the room when I was around him but that didn't mean dating him was a smart move.

For one thing, Alex disapproved and I didn't want to hurt her. Not to mention that, way down inside, a small part of me was angry as all get out that he was at fault for my messed up inability to wink in and out.

I must have been so deep into my own dark thoughts that it took the nurse several tries to catch my attention. At least, that was my guess as she was leaning forward, asking, "Are you all right, Miss?"

"Yes." I cleared my throat, trying for a little more certainty with my tone. "Yes, never felt better."

Which was a white lie. Outside I knew I looked like a Barbie doll's twin sister: blonde, blue-eyed, perky, but without the strangled waist and the well-endowed bust line. Or the plastic, though there'd been days lately that I'd felt very artificial. That's because I was still healing, mostly inside, where the scars didn't show.

"You wish to see someone?" she asked, still examining me with that assessing look years of nursing gave a person.

"Aini," I said, stumbling. None of us knew Aini's last name, which made filling out paperwork a bear, and there was a lot of paperwork involved in hospitals and in transporting an under-aged minor out of one country and into another. But taking care of Aini was worth all the work. I looked at the nurse who was already flipping through charts to find Aini's and asked, "How's she doing? Any change?"

The nurse cast me a brief glance and a sad smile as she shook her head. "I'm afraid there's still no response to stimulation." Her smile tightened as she added, "but we'll keep trying."

I released the small sigh of hope I'd been holding. "May I see her then?"

My expectation was to receive a quick nod before I could walk around the corner to the room I was getting to know very well, when the nurse shook her head and looked over her shoulder. "I'll have to make sure her earlier visitor has left. Only one visitor at a time."

I knew the rule. What I didn't know was who else had come to visit Aini? No one except my team even knew she was here.

The nurse walked away before I could ask the questions kick-starting through me. I tightened the grip on my shoulder bag, wondering if there was a threat to Aini? Rumors were that several different factions had tried to find and retrieve her in Sierra Leone. Could some have followed her here?

The nurse returned as quickly as she'd left. "He's gone so you may go ahead."

A male? Except for the agency instructor, M.T. Stone, there were few males with the agency so far, so who had been here?

"Excuse me." I toned down my voice so the nurse didn't feel I was verbally attacking her even as I felt like screaming. "Do you know who her visitor was?"

The woman shrugged. "I know he had some type of government ID but I couldn't tell you what agency."

This wasn't good. No one except members of the IR Agency, and Van, knew about Aini being stateside. So who was this?

"Tall? Short? Young? Old?"

"Older than you." She paused. "His eyes looked even years older than he did."

"Any thing else about him?"

"I'm afraid I didn't pay a lot of attention," she said, adding, "There was another patient needing me right then."

How convenient. See? That cynical streak raising its ugly head.

"I understand." Not. Who was this guy? And what agency? This could be bad.

Aini was our key to discovering the Seekers and no one, military or not, should know she was here.

As soon as I left Aini, I'd be calling Ling Mai to see if we could get a guard on Aini's door. She was too vulnerable as she was and our mistaken belief that her presence was a best-kept-secret might have just blown up in our faces. Or I was over-reacting and Ling Mai would let me know to chill.

On second thought, waiting to call could be dangerous. I'd call from Aini's room. Yeah, I knew cell phone usage was strictly forbidden but she was at risk. The old Kelly followed the rules. The new Kelly? Not so much. As long as I was there, Aini had protection.

One problem at a time.

"Thank you," I remembered to say to the nurse, earning a tired smile even as she turned back to her paperwork. Then I had a second thought.

"Nurse?"

"Yes?"

"Could you come with me? I'd like you to check Aini's machines. Make sure everything is functioning properly."

Confusion warred with frustration on her face, but only for a second. I guess she was used to family demands, especially in a city that used rank and position as battering rams to get what they wanted.

She set her papers down and led the way.

I listened to her shoes squeak on the highly polished floor as we walked to Aini's room all the while bracing myself. I plastered on a smile, even though Aini couldn't see me, because I had to believe she could feel my intention, and that was the important thing.

The nurse did a quick survey, then touched every machine before she turned back to me and offered a smile that was more perfunctory than real. "All looks fine."

"Thank you." I meant it. I still thought Aini needed a guard but simply knowing no one had tampered with her equipment was a relief. Though there were other ways to hurt a vulnerable, comatose girl.

"Aini? It's me. Kelly." I kept my voice hushed as the nurse left and I stepped farther into the small room dominated by beeping machines, subdued lighting and the young girl lying immobile in the single bed. She looked so alone here, her ebony black skin pale, her tightly woven cornrow hair short against her skull, accentuating the fine bones of her face, the jagged scar on her right temple looking like a lightning flash marring her face.

In Sierra Leone, she had been wary, quiet and determined. That last trait is what had her following me to a small village along the Liberian border, insisting the voices told her she must stay with me, that I was in danger, and may not want to know the truth I sought.

Boy, was that spot on.

I pulled up the straight back chair next to Aini's bed and reached for her hand. It was chilly and limp, which twisted the guilt gnawing through my stomach.

"I'm so sorry," I said, as I'd said every time I'd visited. I meant to be upbeat and positive, to reassure her that she wasn't alone, to encourage her to come back to this world, but instead, all that seemed to pour out of me was regret and sorrow. "My job was to find you and bring you back. I never meant for you to get hurt." I squeezed her hand tighter. "I'll make sure you're safe now. "

It was a vow and a promise, one I meant to keep. Ling Mai wanted Aini for her help in tracking the Seekers. Others might want her for the same reason. It's what we feared in Africa. If I was one hundred percent an agent, I should also accept that her identifying and stopping the Seekers was for the greater good. But what I really wanted was to see Aini get well, to see her smile and release some of the shadows in her eyes. To be a young girl, if only for a short time.

Blinking back the tears stinging my eyes, I talked, simply so she could hear my voice. "I've heard from contacts within Sierra Leone that Fuliwa and Moussa made it safely to Fuliwa's village." Fuliwa was a young mute boy that Aini had cared for. She had promised the boy's dying mother that

Fuliwa would make his way across the country to his only remaining relatives. Moussa was another boy, closer in age to Aini, who had also been orphaned and desperately needed to belong to someone, to someplace. "My sources tell me Moussa is now attending school and both boys are living with Fuliwa's grandparents."

So some good had come out of Africa. Small wins that might change those boys' lives. I looked at Aini, "Would you like to attend school? I'm sure Ling Mai could make arrangements once you get well."

There I went making more promises. But it only made sense. Ling Mai was gathering gifted children together to create an IR Academy. Some day, some of those students might become IR agents, but the more important part was they'd learn that their gifts, paranormal or preternatural, that made them so different from their human peers, were a vital part of who they were. Unlike myself, and all of my teammates, except team leader Vaughn, we'd all had grown up thinking of ourselves as freaks or bad people because we were witches like Alex, shifters like Nicki, psychics like Jaylene, or spirit-walkers like Mandy.

We never belonged and never admitted what we were to those around us. Even the couple who had raised me had feared my abilities as I tried to cope with my gift in my early years. Until I could hide what I was from them. Out of sight, out of mind.

"I don't even know if you'd want to go to school," I murmured, rubbing my hand over Aini's chilled one. "Or if you did, what subjects you might like." I glanced at her peaceful face, my smile real this time. "But we could find out. And I'd help in any way I could. Like a tutor if you needed one." And if I was around. "Plus, there are other teens your age at the compound now, so you could make friends and maybe do normal things with them. Movies. Going to the shore. Whatever you'd like."

I was so deep into creating this ideal existence for Aini, that at first I didn't notice the increasing warmth in her hand, that and the change in the heart monitor across the bed from me, where a small pinprick of light started pulsing stronger.

"Aini?" I whispered, afraid to hope, aware of a small buzz of energy tingling my palm. "Are you here?"

I stood, adrenaline punching through me. Not the fight or flight response, but more of a hail halleluiah bubbling up from within. I still held her hand, as if afraid my letting go might lose her.

Should I call the nurse?

"Missy Miss," Aini whispered around the tube in her mouth, which I didn't think was even possible. The nurse was forgotten as tears blurred my vision.

"I'm here, Aini. You're not alone." Where was that nurse alert button? Or should I get Aini some water? Her voice sounded so parched.

"Beware da Horned One," she murmured, freezing my movements while sending a frissure of unease racing across my skin. "Da Horned One comes."

"What?" I didn't even know what to ask. "Don't worry. I'll get the nurse, the doctor. There's plenty of time to talk. Later."

I turned to find help when her hand clutched tighter around mine, almost painfully so, holding me in place.

She moved her head from side to side as if struggling. The machine next to me was beeping like crazy. Why didn't someone come?

"Shhh, Aini. It'll be okay."

"Da Horned One is awake."

Now she was freaking me out.

"Is this something you're seeing?" I asked, clueless how seers operated, if that's what she really was.

"Learn ... learn who you are," her voice sounded so hoarse it hurt.

Where was the medical help?

"No fear da unknown." More nonsense.

I shouted, "Nurse? Nurse, I need help!"

"Fear not da unknown." She raised her head, her sightless eyes staring at me, as if begging me to believe. "Da Horned One. Too close. Beware."

CHAPTER 2

I could hear the nurse's shoes running toward the room.

But it was too late. Aini was gone again. Between one heartbeat and the next, her eyes closed and she lapsed back onto the bed.

"What is it?" the older woman asked, hustling to my side.

"She woke up." I waved one hand toward the nearest monitor, releasing Aini's hand, which was already cooling. "The machines started beeping. Aini talked, but only for a few seconds."

The nurse scooted me away from the bed and took my place, feeling Aini's pulse, using a flashlight to look into her eyes. A frown creased wide gullies between the nurse's eyes as she turned to check first one then another machine.

Only then did she turn to look at me, her expression measured as I asked, "What is it?"

"You said she spoke?"

"Yes. Just a few garbled words."

"That's not possible. Not around the tube."

"But she did speak."

"You could understand her?"

"Yes. She was clear enough."

"What did she say?"

This is where things got tricky. Was there any point in babbling about a horned one? Whatever that was. So I prevaricated. "She called me Missy Miss, just as she had in the past."

"Anything else?"

Why was she so focused on that instead of what had happened?

"The rest wasn't very clear," I said, clutching at my handbag harder. "Why? Is that important?"

The nurse shook her head then glanced back at the closest machine before answering. "There's no indication that she's revived at all. No change in heart rate, pulse or brain energy."

What? "That can't be right." It was my turn to brush past the nurse and eye the machines. All the lines, the numbers, everything showed no change. At all. "But that's wrong. She spoke. She sat up."

The nurse silently moved toward the foot of the bed. "Hope can play tricks on all of us when we want something so badly."

Now I was hallucinating? I didn't think so. But then why did nothing register on the equipment? Maybe the nurse had read them wrong and I couldn't tell.

I shook my head, knowing what I saw, what I felt. Even now the slight buzz beneath my palm still tingled as I rubbed it with my other hand.

The nurse waited, as if to make sure I didn't wig out. She cast a wary glance at Aini, as if trying to come to a decision, but said nothing.

So I said what she needed to hear. "That must be it. I wanted her to wake up so I imagined it."

Man, I was getting really good at lying. Me, who'd been taught that lies were the downfall of the weak and unrighteous.

The nurse turned to walk away, when I asked her, "Do you mind doing another quick check of her machines?" I glanced around the room. "I know I'm asking a lot, but I'm very …very worried." Now I sounded like I was babbling. First imagining things and now? Talk about digging a deeper hole.

The nurse hesitated. But why? Hospital bureaucracy, or did she know something I didn't? Something about Aini?

"I'll have someone review all the machines in this room," she said after doing another quick scan of her own that each machine was working and nothing had been unplugged. She'd done what I asked but her words and posture were stiff. Was she just humoring me until I could leave and she could call her superiors and report me as disruptive?

Best to keep things as neutral as possible, until I spoke to Ling Mai.

"Thank you." I offered a smile. "I'll step outside for a few minutes to make ... to get some coffee."

I was going to make my call, but that was IR business alone.

Did I let the nurse know that a guard might be stationed outside the room if I got my way? Probably not yet. I didn't want to have the nurse throw up obstacles to getting the room checked. "I'll be right back."

I left then, my head whirling as I made my way outside the building to call Ling Mai. But she wasn't there. Vaughn, the second in command was.

"Why isn't Ling Mai around?"

"Is there something you need to talk specifically with her about?"

"No." Not really, but then I'd noticed Vaughn hadn't really answered my question either.

Not the time to panic. Not yet. After all Aini was safe, for the time being. I normally didn't overreact but fighting preternaturals made me second guess everything.

Besides being team leader, Vaughn was the go-to person to get things done in the Agency, plus she was a whole lot easier to talk to than Ling Mai.

"You sure?" Vaughn asked after I gave her a brief synopsis of the last ten minutes.

"Positive. Someone with government ID, or fake ID, stopped off to see Aini earlier. And yes, in spite of what the equipment didn't show, I know she woke up and spoke."

"But what did she mean about the Horned One?"

I shook my head though Vaughn couldn't see me. Standing here, outside the hospital, the sun's warmth felt good on my skin after the air-conditioned interior. Watching people walking around, laughing, talking, just being alive — everything seemed so normal, so mundane. So why did Aini's words chill me to my bones?

"I have no idea what she meant, but I do know I heard her and she was very ... frightened." That's as close a word as I could pinpoint to the tone of Aini's cryptic message.

"All right. I'll arrange a guard for her room and check with Fraulein Fassbinder to see if the Horned One means anything."

"I'll stay here until you do."

"Smart." Vaughn paused, as if thinking through something before she asked, "You said she sounded frightened. Was that just being disoriented fear or as a response to what she was saying?"

I reviewed the words in my head, the tone, the intensity. "The words. Whatever this Horned One is, it was scaring her."

"Once the guard is in place, then I have an idea."

I don't know if it was her words or her almost imperceptible hesitation that had me bracing. Vaughn was not the hesitant sort. She wasn't in-your-face bold like Alex, or assertive like Jaylene and Mandy, but Vaughn carried certainty with her like one of the posh dresses she wore without a second thought. Wore and owned.

"What's your idea?" I asked, wary.

"Have you heard of the Librarian?"

"You mean that person Ling Mai mentioned?"

"Yes." The word was slow and drawn out as if Vaughn was already debating mentioning the thought. The she rushed ahead. "I may be way off base here but the Librarian might be able to help us."

"Do what exactly?" I watched a trio of young men ride by on fancy bikes. They couldn't be more than a few years younger than I was, but since becoming an IR agent I'd aged in so many ways. My first thought in seeing the bikes was that they might be a handy way to escape in a tight situation where no other transport was available. Sad, but true.

"You listening, Kelly?" Vaughn's voice washed against me.

"Sorry. Continue." Hallucinating, easily distracted, tingling skin. Maybe I should check with a medical professional instead of a librarian.

"I was saying the Librarian might know more about Aini's message."

"I thought the Librarian kept track of preternatural genealogical lines."

"Among other things."

Great, just what I needed, a wild goose chase. But Vaughn had access to intel I didn't have a clue even existed, so what was it going to hurt? Plus, and I hated to even admit this, maybe this Librarian knew something about my own birth mother. If she tracked preternaturals, and my mother was a preternatural, then two birds, one stone.

Still I asked, "Ling Mai going to be okay with my talking to the Librarian? From what the director has shared in the past, mere peons don't get access to this person. Period."

"Mandy has spoken with her, so it should be safe for you as well." I could have sworn Vaughn snorted, so not like the ex-debutante she was. "I'll take care of Ling Mai if there's a problem."

Be my guest. But I didn't say that out loud. Instead I asked, "How do I find her? Or him?" I didn't even know what sex this person was.

"The Librarian's female, at least last I heard, and you can find her at the Visitor Information desk at the Library of Congress."

Focus on the important point, not the cryptic one. "You're pulling my leg."

"Nope. First floor. Jefferson Building."

Yeah, right. The all seeing, all knowing Librarian hung out at an information desk. This wild goose chase was getting more like a bunny down a rabbit hole adventure.

"Fine," I said, trying not to sound querulous. It wasn't like I had a whole lot of other pressing engagements. "I'm going to get back to Aini now."

"Good plan. But Kelly—"

"What?"

The old Kelly, the pre-Africa Kelly, wouldn't have cut Vaughn off and a smidge of guilt lanced through me. But Aini was vulnerable until we had security in place.

"Two things."

"Yes?"

"I'd recommend you ask about Aini's message, but don't share where you learned the information. Remember the Librarian is known to sell information to others."

"Nice." My hand tightened on my cell phone at the thought of Aini's whereabouts and safety being a commodity to be bought and sold. "And the second thing?"

"The Librarian will expect payment."

Like I had two beans to rub together.

As if she'd read my thoughts, Vaughn continued, "But not in money."

"In what then?"

"She trades in knowledge."

Well, maybe this would be easier than I expected. I didn't know anything.

"Not a problem," I reassured Vaughn without giving her the reason for my sudden change of heart. If I could learn more about Aini's message, and my parentage, all for a little information exchange, piece of cake. I just hoped I knew something she wanted to know.

Too bad I'd been learning the hard way that simple rarely meant easy.

CHAPTER 3

I waited at the hospital until a burly, older man who looked like cross between a bulldog and a brick wall was stationed outside Aini's room, all life support machines had been double checked to be certain they hadn't been tampered with, and a frazzled nurse was reassured no further disruptions to her ward were foreseen. Only then did I hail a cab.

The Library of Congress is housed in three different buildings, each one named for a president who was instrumental in founding and maintaining the facilities. The irony wasn't lost on me that those presidents were three of the first four elected to office and no later presidents were included in the roster. What did that tell you about the appreciation of knowledge in this country?

No time to revert to teacher-me. I wasn't here to stand on a soapbox for reading and education. The Jefferson Building looked as imposing as I expected, and that was just from the outside. Located behind the Capital Building, the library faced First Avenue and tall, stately trees that hushed the roar of D.C. traffic and set a quieter mood for walking up the two sets of stairs and entering the building.

A tour of young students clogged the front entryway, but I'd navigated worse throngs of kids, so I kept moving forward until I broke through. Behind the information desk, several women sat, all engaged in answering questions for two different groups. I recognized that slightly dazed look of a parent volunteer from one of the factions. The other was a trio of Japanese speaking heavily accented English and waving cameras. My guess was they were trying to determine where exactly they could take photos.

I stepped over to the library gift shop to wait for a break in the bustle. After a few minutes, or I hoped it was only a few minutes, the sound level had quieted. A shop in one of the most amazing libraries in the world was a dangerous place to someone like me so, with a heavy sigh, I returned to the desk.

There was only one librarian on duty now. A strikingly attractive young woman who looked like she should be showcasing designer fashions instead of giving directions to the nearest public restrooms.

Was this *the* Librarian? And how was I going to approach her? Why hadn't I thought to ask Vaughn?

When in doubt, move forward. Tightening fingers around my purse strap, I stepped toward the desk. My jaw dropped open. Behind the desk the foyer opened into a round rotunda several stories high, filled with exquisite marble, painting after painting, and staircases that led to an arched golden dome; I'd never seen anything so take-my-breath-away grand.

"Quite a sight, isn't it?" said the woman at the desk, eyeing me and not the opulence she saw daily. I wonder if she was inured to it by now?

All I could do was nod.

"What can I do for you, Miss McAllister?"

Like a thunderclap smacking me I came back to earth. "How'd ..."

The woman canted her head to one side as if examining a big, fat, juicy worm. On first glance I'd have guessed her to be in her mid-thirties, but up close I was no longer certain. She was both beautifully young and finely hewn age, as if two very different beings inhabited one body.

My ring finger heated up, letting me know my closer examination was warranted. She was no more simply human than I was. So what was she? Fae would be my best guess because the fae were known to use glamour the most easily.

"You wonder what I am," she laughed, a soft tinkling sound that should have been melodic but instead sent shivers down my spine.

"You're not human," I whispered through a suddenly dry mouth.

"This surprises you?" That head tilt again. "No, this frightens you."

Nailed it. I didn't have any reason to feel like someone just walked over my grave, but I did. We were in a public place. With people milling about, though none were within hearing distance.

"You should not fear me," she said, which didn't reassure me in the least. "I mean you no harm."

So why did I hear the word 'yet' unspoken?

"You're the Librarian? I mean, the *real* one?" I asked the obvious but wanted to get my task completed. Now.

She simply smiled, a movement of lips only and not one that reached her eyes.

I had to start somewhere. "I have a question."

"And what have you brought to trade?"

Now we were on firmer footing. This was a business transaction. I should be able to handle that. My throat was dry though as I asked, "What do you want?"

The woman's smile deepened. "You have seen much, learned even more in a short period of time and have good connections. I'm sure we can find something to exchange."

How did she know so much? And if she was so familiar with me, why did she need to ask for information from me? I felt like an opened book laid bare.

"I do not know all your secrets, Miss McAllister." Again there was that faint echo of the 'yet' word. "But it's my job to be aware of those who are different among us."

She did say *us*, which implied she assumed she and I were of the same species, which in my mind meant mostly human with abilities. Except my gift, hopefully not my former gift, didn't activate my preternatural ring either, and whatever she was did. Being gifted, like I was, evidently made me less than preternatural, though not an average human. Complicated and messy. But this woman? She was preternatural.

When I didn't jump into the strained silence between us she spoke up, not loud, but more in a take-charge way as she straightened brochures on her desk. "Perhaps you can tell me the nature of your question, or questions, so I can tell you my fee before we continue."

I hadn't felt this rattled since my first job interview when one male principal had spent more time looking at my chest than listening to my answers. Trust me, I did not accept his job offer.

Clearing my throat, I looked around to make sure no one else was within hearing distance. "I need information about someone called the Horned One."

That had her pausing and looking up. "The Horned One?"

At the narrowing of her eyes, the breath started backing up in my lungs.

"Tell me exactly what you already know, from the person who spoke these names. Verbatim. Now is not the time to be inaccurate."

Talk about a slap of cold water. I wasn't being willfully obtuse. As I straightened my shoulders, I started from the beginning, as much as I was willing to share. "I was told to beware the Horned One. That the Horned one is close. And … " What was the last part?

"Come, Miss McAllister. The details matter."

I ignored her, pulling apart those frantic minutes; the beeping machines. Aini's voice, so raspy and frightened. That was it. I looked up, surprised the Librarian was leaning toward me. "She said the Horned One was awake."

The gasp the Librarian uttered exploded like a shot through the room.

This wasn't making me feel all warm and fuzzy.

Her gaze flittered all around before returning to rest on me. "What have you done?" Her tone made my blood freeze.

"Nothing."

"You're a fool, Miss McAllister. An innocent and a fool. Do you know nothing?"

How did one answer that?

It didn't seem to matter as she continued, her voice low and almost guttural. "Where did you hear of The Horned One?"

Prevarication time. Vaughn said not to tell the specifics, so maybe the general might work. On the other hand, this seemed an innocent enough question to answer. "I asked a young girl"

"How young?"

Why did that matter? "Fifteen, I think."

"Be precise. Is she fifteen? Or not?"

This woman was giving me the willies and she wanted to know Aini's age? "As far as I know she's fifteen but almost sixteen."

"Almost can make all the difference."

"Difference in what?" I was tired of being kept in the dark. "Tell me what has you so rattled?"

She pulled herself up sharp, her tone acidic. "Why did you ask? You speak it. You give it life."

"Give *what* life?"

"The Horned One, bringer of souls to the underworld, of course."

There was no 'of course' about it.

The Librarian fumbled with a small plaque on her desk that indicated, *Someone will be with you shortly*, then reached into a drawer and pulled out a purse.

"Are you leaving?" I whispered, each word sounding more strangled than the last.

"You have no idea what you've unleashed."

I grabbed her arm as she turned to go. "I didn't unleash anything. I need information here. What's going on?"

"Study your myths, Miss McAllister. The protectors of the Horned One may already be at work. We have little time."

"At work doing what?"

"Bringing death."

My hold tightened, which reminded me of Aini's touch, the fear behind her words. But I was an agent here, not a scared, quaking in my boots, innocent from Iowa. Okay, I was fast getting to the quaking part but ignoring it.

"What kind of death? To who?"

"To all of us."

"Like a plague? Or a war? I need details." I threw her words back in her face.

"It might start slow, depending... depending on so much."

"And then what?"

Her eyes widened as she answered. "Before cataclysmic destruction. Both humans and preternaturals will die."

Not sounding so good, which could explain the sudden cut adrift sensation washing over me. Think. There had to be more. "I need help." Urgency drove me. "Is there no turning this … this whatever back?"

The woman shook her head then paused. "There's a small chance—"

"What?" I wanted to shake the woman, rattle her as she'd rattled me.

She looked me in the eyes as she murmured, "Find out exactly how old the girl is. If she's not yet sixteen there may be time."

"Time for what?"

"To stop the Horned One before he comes. Destroy his carrier and the Horned One can not cross over."

And I'd thought Aini was cryptic.

"Ask the girl," the Librarian repeated, shaking my hand off her arm. "Return to her and ask when she reaches her natal hour. I'll see what I can do but … "

Before I could ask anything else, the woman walked away so fast all that was left was the echo of her high heels on the marble floors.

What now? Death and destruction roaring at us, and the only hope was in finding out the birthdate of a girl in a coma.

So much for thinking last week had been rough.

CHAPTER 4

As I left the Jefferson Building my thoughts cartwheeled. While I'd been inside rain clouds had gathered, chilling the air, darkening the light. If I'd wanted to conjure up special effects for a doomsday prophecy, I couldn't have asked for better.

The people who'd been hanging around only moments ago seemed to have disappeared, no doubt the smart ones wanting to avoid a sudden downpour. I rubbed the goose bumps tiptoeing up my arms and debated calling Vaughn with my not-so-good-news, or simply returning to the Maryland compound to share in person. On the other hand, maybe that was me seeking some reassurance in numbers. Right now I felt hit upside the head, as if I'd just received a death sentence.

I had. Not only for me but who knew for how many others.

Walking stiff-legged down the second set of granite stairs, I pulled out my phone, concentrating on hitting the speed dial button to the Agency when I felt it.

Instinct or recent experience, I had no idea what made me look up and turn, but that meant the first blow grazed my shoulder instead of landing solidly and snapping my neck.

I stumbled forward, tripping and tumbling down a few more steps until I landed on my back, the dark skies overhead blotted out by an even darker shape. A man. Wearing some kind of hooded jacket pulled over his face. Reaching for me.

He was one step above me. Close enough that I didn't have a lot of options.

Kicking out, my shoe caught his shin. He grunted and stumbled, struggling to regain his stability as I scooted backwards, gaining my feet, before racing down the last steps, looking over my shoulder.

The man, if that's what he was, raised his arm, revealing a tattoo on his inner forearm as he grabbed at my hair, ripping so hard I screamed as he yanked me upward.

He was still above and behind me so I didn't fight my imbalance but sagged, letting my weight pull us both down into a tumbled mess, sprawled on the pathway beside the street.

He smelled of rotten eggs, gagging me as I jabbed right and left, using nails and elbows and knees, connecting with flesh, but he was bigger and heavier.

His hand circled my throat, choking, while slamming my head back on the gravel path again and again. My screams died. I fought now for air. Air and to live.

Pinpricks of light whirled around my vision.

Where were the Library guards? Visitors with cell phones? Anybody?

This was it.

The roar I heard was inhuman, a cross between a growl and an anguished cry. But it wasn't from my attacker as he froze, straddled on top of me, hand clenching my throat.

Another body hurtled past me, tearing the man from me as I rolled away into a fetal curl, gasping for air.

Two bodies fought nearby, the sounds of flesh thudding against flesh too close.

Another scream, this one deep, rasping. Footsteps then, racing across the gravel. An oath. Then silence, except for my retching, trying to breathe, to move. And cry at the same time, though I hated to admit it.

"Kelly," a voice whispered near me. I flinched. It was instinctual even though I recognized that voice and knew I was safe.

A calloused hand gently brushed hair from my face as I quaked in a heap of misery and fear. I didn't want to uncurl, to do anything except pull my shattered self together. The suddenness, the violence of the unprovoked attack, shook me even more than the assault itself.

"It's Van," he whispered, reassurance in his voice. "You're okay now."

I couldn't speak so just nodded. That hurt too, but not as much as trying to force words past my bruised throat.

"I'll get an ambulance," he murmured, crunching gravel alerting me to his moving to stand.

My hand clutched and halted him. "No," I croaked. "No time."

Wasn't that the joke. No time to have the meltdown I so wanted. No time to warn my teammates. No time to get answers.

I tugged at Van, using him as a lever to pull me to my feet. It wasn't smooth or graceful and I moaned more than I intended even though Van, once he understood what I wanted, helped me as much as possible.

Being a shifter, he could have me standing in the blink of an eye, but he grasped that I needed to move in stages.

I struggled to make light of what just happened, no matter what I felt. "Must be some crazy."

"Yeah, right."

"I mean it." I even managed a strangled laugh. "Don't they say three Super Moons open the doors for the ancient demons to leave hell?"

"And steal the soul of a human," he all but growled the old adage. "How the hell could you be attacked here in broad daylight?"

I shook my head, but stopped because it hurt too much. "I don't know. Lunch Break?"

"Or someone was awfully lucky to strike when he did." Van redeemed himself by adding, "Come here."

So I did something I never thought I'd do. I leaned my head against his chest. That rock hard, mile wide chest that made me feel anchored to something solid and real. I didn't touch him with my hands, just my forehead, breathing in deeply of his scent, listening to his steady heartbeat, and inch by inch, pulling my shattered composure around me.

And he let me. Didn't rush, didn't pressure, didn't question. He gave me the gift of a moment before both of us were back in the world of threats and stalking danger.

Only when I was mostly standing on my own did he speak. "Damnit, Kels, every time I turn around you're putting yourself in danger. You're not invincible."

And the moment was over.

Wasn't that just like a guy, chewing my head off before I even had a chance to explain that none of this was my fault. A small sound escaped me, caught between a laugh and a snort. If I'd been more like his sister, Alex, I'd already have taken his head off — not literally, because I don't think even she could do that.

I didn't bother to look up, knowing what I'd see. Van was all muscle and power, his Native American ancestry clear in the angles of his face, the coal darkness of his hair, the deep brown of his eyes. If I'd looked, I'd have sighed. He did that to me. My first glance melted me, made me a gooey puddle of hormones and sheer appreciation, and now wasn't the time for either.

Then he threw me for a loop, changing his tone and his movements as he gently raised my chin with his hand to look at my throat. "Lucky that bastard wasn't any stronger or you'd have more than bad bruises."

Except that it'd take words I didn't want to waste I longed to point out to him that what to a shifter might look like a *bad bruise* was a whole lot worse to this human, or mostly human. Oh, tarnation, I didn't even know what I was and that, along with being attacked and choked nearly senseless made me want to lose it. Something I wasn't going to do in front of Van Noziak. He was too protective as it was and we barely knew one another.

Which had me looking up at him. He wasn't tall, less than six feet, but I always felt small next to him. Fragile and needy, which was not what one agent should feel around another. "Why are you here?" I whispered, all I could manage.

He paused, making me wonder if he'd been following me. If so, why?

He had the sense to look sheepish, then spoiled it by saying, "You haven't been answering any of my calls."

"Seriously?" The word escaped before I had a chance to corral it. But it gave me a chance to step back, to stand on my own and to feel something other than fear washing through me. I bent to pick up my purse, glad to see it'd survived better than I had, no rips or tears, though canvas wasn't easy to destroy. Not like I was. "I saw you in Missouri, too. Though I have no idea how you found me there?"

Again, not what I meant to share. He'd appeared just when his sister and I needed his help the most, and then disappeared before I could thank him or ask him how he'd known where to find us. Which I latched on to now. Horrible, awful, stinky attack guy pushed to the side, though trust me, I was keeping an eye out for him. Now.

"You want to know about Missouri?" Van ran one had through his short, military-style hair, looking like he was the one who'd just gone a few rounds with a deranged assailant. Except he appeared more confused than frightened. "You and Alex needed my help. I came."

That wasn't the whole story by a long shot. "How'd you know we needed help?"

He snorted. Yup, cool, sexy, controlled to the bone Van Noziak snorted. "Every time I turn around you're in trouble. I expect it from Alex, though she has enough experience and magic to mostly get herself out of predicaments. But you?" He waved his hand in the direction the man he'd chased off had disappeared. "Case in point."

Sure, there might be some validity to his argument, and it kept me from dealing with his earlier, more personal comment about avoiding him, which I was, but wasn't ready to admit to him, yet. So I offered a grumbled, "Thanks."

"For?"

I glanced at him, gauging his tone. If he was poking fun at me I'd take back my words and tell him where to vamoose. Okay, maybe more than a vamoose, but he was still looking more perplexed than anything.

"Thanks for Missouri, and for here." I glanced again in the direction the man had raced away. Who was he? And what did he want?

As if reading my thoughts, Van asked, "Any idea why he ... why he ... " His expression tightened, shadows of his tightly leashed wolf side peeking from behind his dark brown eyes.

Enough to make me rub my arms to get rid of the goose bumps and grip my purse tighter. As if it'd protect me against a wolf shifter. But Van wouldn't come after me, not that way. Soul deep I knew this, but it didn't help lessen my jangling nerves.

I shook my head, swallowing past the painful and sudden lump in my throat. "No idea at all why—" I reached one hand toward my throat then let it drop. "No idea at all."

"Did you recognize him?"

"No."

"Any identifying features? Something you could give a sketch artist?"

"Not really." Another head shake, this one more in frustration. "He was wearing some kind of hoody or jacket with a hood. Covering his face." I shrugged. "Only thing I saw was a tattoo."

"Every person under the age of twenty five has a tattoo." Van's voice sounded barely leashed.

"You're right." Even I had one, small, discreet, and not any place I wanted to share with Van, just yet. If I needed to describe the shape of the attacker's tat I'd seen, I could, but there really wasn't enough other identifying information to call the cops on.

Van turned in a full circle as if gauging something, which also gave me a few seconds to catch my breath. "Maybe he was just a mugger hoping to score easy."

We both knew that wasn't likely. The man had been too determined. If he'd meant to rob me he should have grabbed my purse the second I was down and vulnerable. Not hung around, in a very public venue, and try to choke the life out of me.

Van stood shoulder to shoulder with me, both of us looking in the near distance toward the Capitol building as if it had all the answers. He lowered his voice before speaking again. "Noticed you didn't turn invisible." I could have dealt with that observation, until he added, "Which might have saved your fanny."

Now that was choice. Even if he didn't know what I was hiding as my new best-kept-secret, did he think I was too clueless to wink out in broad daylight? In downtown D.C.?

Yup, anger worked much better than fear to give me a backbone.

Van wasn't finished pushing my buttons though. "So what's up with that?"

"You mean not becoming invisible?" Who was he now? My keeper? Holding on to a temper I didn't realize I had, I bit off a non-committal reply. "Can't say. "

There, that was better than 'mind your own business,' which is what I wanted to shout as I brushed off my pants.

"Can't or won't?" Van's voice took on a low-timbered growl.

"Same thing." Obviously I wasn't the only one with a temper percolating too close to the surface. I brushed so hard on my pants I was going to add to the bruises I'd already earned.

"You've been avoiding me."

Now we'd come full circle. It was said as a statement, not a question. But it struck me the same. Besides, I was looking for a way to release some of the emotions churning through me. I turned to look at him so he couldn't avoid hearing me. "You do know the world doesn't revolve around you?"

A deep V appeared between his too intense, too darkly lashed eyes. "Where's this coming from? A few days ago, we were right as rain. Now?"

That wasn't the whole truth. A few days ago I was barely out of physical therapy after Africa. I was vulnerable, and I owed him for saving me, more than once, in Sierra Leone, so when he'd suggested we get together, as in a date, I'd been okay with that. Plus there'd been that toe-curling kiss that still made my skin heat.

That was before I discovered that the one ability I'd had, the one that had made me an IR agent, was missing. Gone, as if it'd never existed. A gift I didn't appreciate until I needed it in order to remain an agent, at least long enough to find my birth mother. The reason it'd disappeared? The only thing I could pinpoint was the transfusion of blood Van had given me to keep me alive. Shifter blood.

Now I was a mess, in more ways than one.

"Well?" he asked, looking me straight in the eye. "Why've you been avoiding me?"

"It's complicated." Which was the truth, just not the whole truth.

Van took a step closer, invading my space. Gone was the caring man who'd let me rest my head against him. Now he was all pissed-off male who wanted an answer. He wouldn't hurt me. I wasn't afraid of that. No, I was more afraid of what I might say, might reveal, that could hurt Van more than he deserved.

He was a good man, an honorable man. And if it was his blood that was screwing with my life, I didn't know if I could ever forgive him. Something he'd once said indicated another woman had scarred him emotionally because she couldn't accept what he was. I didn't want to layer more guilt on that old wound.

The sudden ringing of my cell in my purse caused both of us to flinch. I'd never been so happy to step back and grab my phone, recognizing Vaughn's number.

"Kelly here."

"How far away are you from the hospital?" No hello, no preamble, just a cut to the chase, slam-adrenaline-through-my-system question.

"I can be there in fifteen minutes," I croaked out the words, hoping Vaughn could hear me.

"Good. I'll meet you there."

I thought she was going to hang up before I had a chance to ask, "What's up?"

"There's been an attack."

Time screeched to a halt. Vaughn cut the connection before I could ask anything else. Aini? Oh, please don't let her be ...

"What is it?" Van was at my side, his tone all military-precise and focused. I had no doubt he heard Vaughn's side of the conversation, enhanced hearing ability being a side benefit to his shifter genes, but worry was quickly morphing into outright fear. Aini was vulnerable. I'd left her alone. With a guard, but alone.

"I've gotta go. There's been an attack."

I wasn't being rude as I stepped past him to flag down a taxi. Thank heavens this was D.C., where the one thing you could find easier than a politician was a cab. One was already rocketing to a halt along the curb.

Van's hand caught my arm as I reached for the door. "Alex?"

I shook my head, having no idea if Alex was involved or not. "I don't know. Not yet."

"If Alex is involved, I deserve to know."

I eyed him. He, being an agent of some hush hush, intelligence para-military group that worked for the government, should know and understand more than most. I spoke the words that should have been enough through gritted teeth. "It's IR business."

His eyes narrowed. "Alex is an IR agent."

Van had his priorities — his job first, his family second and maybe, just maybe, if the other two were okay, time for a life outside his job and career. That's where I might or might not come in. Not much left for that last category. I yanked the door open and slipped into the back seat of the cab.

Van blocked the door. "Kelly? I need to know."

Agreed. But he was wrong in asking me what I couldn't give. Even if I knew what he wanted.

"You'll have to ask Alex yourself. I've got to leave." I tugged the door closed, calling to the driver, "George Washington Hospital. And hurry."

I didn't look behind me as the car peeled away from the curb.

CHAPTER 5

The MICU wing of the hospital was a mess. Or maybe it was just me, nerves drawn tensile tight, heart pounding, mouth too dry. I made it to the entrance of the ward where a uniformed officer raised his hand to stop me.

"No one's allowed entrance at this time, Miss." His gaze appraised and then dismissed. I'd been deemed as non-threatening. Not that I blamed him. Looking like a cross between a Barbie doll and a kindergarten teacher, I got that low-level threat assessment a lot. I glanced around him as opposed to barreling through him. It might come to that but maybe not as my first move.

It took only seconds to spy the nurse I'd seen earlier, away from her desk, standing between two burly officers who looked like cracking a smile was a felony. Not that I wanted levity, not until I knew Aini was okay.

With a little more effort, I caught a glimpse of Vaughn, giving her a chin nod rather than a hey-hi wave. That would have seemed way out of line given the faces set in stone around me.

Vaughn walked my way, speaking to the officer still barricading me. "She's with us," she said, already moving away, not waiting for a response.

I don't know who was more surprised, the policeman or me. Vaughn was never that curt.

With a quick nothing-personal nod at the officer, because I'd been raised to respect all law enforcement personnel, I did a two-step to catch up with my team leader. My very focused, bad-stuff-was-happening-under-her-watch, leader.

"Is Aini okay?" I didn't care if I sounded breathless.

Vaughn eyed me. "What's wrong with your throat?"

"Long story." I brushed off her question with a wave of my hand, nerves racing like mice on crack beneath my skin. "Aini? Is she okay?"

"Yes." A tight pause, followed by, "Officer Packard isn't."

Who was … oh, fud-a-stick. "The man who'd been on duty here?" It'd been a rough morning already, which could account for some of my confusion.

Vaughn's abrupt nod indicated how unhappy she was. "Aini's doctor is in with Aini now."

"What happened?"

Vaughn cut her gaze toward the nurse whose head hung low, her hands wringing one another. "She happened."

I glanced at the woman I'd spoken to only a short while before. The one who'd been kind, who had tired eyes. "I don't understand?"

"She tried to kill Aini. Packard stopped her but was killed in the process."

Some words were not going to register, no matter what you did to them. Unfortunately, I didn't have a lot of time to put the pieces together as Vaughn and I stepped inside the door of Aini's room.

I gave a what's-up look at Vaughn who stood beside me, offering me nothing except a tight smile as I stepped deeper into th,e room, not sure what I'd see, but it appeared they'd removed Officer Packard's body already. Everything else looked much like the last time I'd been here, except for the chair I'd been sitting on. It was crumpled into one of the corners as if violently thrust there and forgotten, plus looking like it'd been made of tinfoil, not molded metal.

A man, in an expensive-and-it-showed suit, not a law enforcement suit, stood on the far side of Aini's bed, looking serious and pissed at the same time, every line of his body tense, the vein along his left temple pounding hard.

"I can assure you, Ms. Monroe," he spoke to Vaughn in a voice that clearly indicated he was used to being the man all deferred to. "There's no need—"

Vaughn raised one hand and he sputtered to a stop. "Miss McAllister here," she glanced at me, sort of like having a stun gun on full blast, "indicated that she spoke to Aini earlier."

"But that's not possible," the guy in the suit, who must be Aini's doctor, barreled ahead, barely tossing a withering look toward me. "There's been no change on the monitors."

"That's what the nurse said, too." I spoke only to Vaughn.

"Which nurse?" she asked.

I nodded toward the hallway. "The one out there."

"Interesting." Vaughn looked at the girl, the only point of quiet and stillness in the room. "And yet you still believe Aini woke up?"

No believe involved. I knew.

"Yes. She spoke and squeezed my hand." I swallowed at the thought of how defenseless Aini had been here. How close she might have come to dying. Both Vaughn and I ignored the doctor whose face was growing redder and redder.

"This has never — we've done everything to care for this patient — there's no—"

Vaughn looked over my shoulder and spoke to a uniformed officer who'd followed me in and was now standing silent in the doorway. "We'll be moving Aini to a more secure location in Maryland. Please make the arrangements."

He said nothing, just turned and walked away. I wished I could join him.

Vaughn appeared to have finished with me as she turned back to the doctor. "What happened here is not a reflection on your level of patient care," she said, no doubt bringing the poor man's blood pressure down a few notches. "However, it is a reflection on the dangers to this young woman's life. I'm sure you…" she smiled at the man and I wanted to warn him not to trust it. Didn't sharks smile right before they attacked? She continued with a gracious angling of her head, "I'm sure it will be better for Aini, and your staff, to remove the patient to a facility less…" she looked as if she were searching for the correct word, which I didn't believe for a minute. "It will simply *be* better."

With that, she dismissed the doctor, who looked at me as if for a translation. No doubt he was used to being the one to make unilateral decisions and not being in the position of having no say.

Poor guy. Welcome to the real world. My world. My own attention was only on Vaughn as I asked, "What about the nurse? Why would she try to hurt Aini?"

"We'll ask her that and a few other pressing questions as soon as we have a chance. So far, she hasn't said anything. For now I'd like you to contact the rest of the team and have them all report to the Compound."

Good. Too many unrelated, but connected things were going down. I didn't say about time, but felt it. With a last glance at Aini, and a small thank you for blessings received that she wasn't hurt, I turned to leave as a tussle erupted outside the room.

I reached the doorway in time to see two police officers calling for back up as the nurse who'd been between them, looking so lost and docile, now lay in a motionless heap on the floor.

"Let me past," the doctor bit out as he thrust me aside. This type of emergency he could handle as he quickly knelt beside the woman. Several more officers appeared, every one coiled tight, ready to act, but there was nothing to do. Not until the doctor looked up, not at me but at Vaughn who'd joined me.

He shouted orders and several nurses fetched equipment. The Doctor continued working on her though the slow dive of my stomach told me he wasn't getting the results he wanted.

At last, his expression stern, his tone belligerent. "She's gone."

As in dead.

I glanced at Vaughn, who didn't seem surprised in the least.

One of the officers who'd been guarding the nurse spoke to two of the other officers. "I swear, she was fine one minute and the next she just crumpled."

"She didn't ingest anything?" a voice demanded.

Both guards shook their heads, one said, "No. No movement. Nothing."

That made no sense. Unless the poor woman had a heart attack or something. Funny that I was still thinking of her as a victim and not the one who tried to kill Aini and managed to kill Officer Packard. But how?

Packard didn't strike me as an easy man to disarm, unless he took the nurse at face value, got too close and … and what?

"How was the guard killed?" I spoke out loud, forgetting for a second I was in full view of everyone circling around the nurse.

Vaughn stood beside me, her voice low and controlled. "They'll be performing an autopsy later as the cause of death wasn't immediately apparent."

Just like the nurse before us, now all but obscured by the huddle of people around her. The doctor was barking orders in a terse tone. He wasn't loud, aware the last thing the patients on this ward needed was even more of a crisis. One attack and the death of Officer Packard might be contained, but a second suspicious death? Heads might roll.

I remained where I was, in part to avoid crowding the hallway even more, when they brought a gurney and placed the nurse on it, quickly covering up her body with a white sheet.

But not soon enough, as I caught a glimpse of her inner arm. And the raw looking tattoo there.

My breath backed up in my lungs as my hand instinctively went to my bruised throat.

I must have released a sound as Vaughn turned in my direction. "What is it?"

"Her arm. The tattoo. I don't remember noticing it earlier."

"What tattoo?"

I pointed to the lower half of my own inner arm. "About here."

"What's it got to do with anything?"

With a wary glance at her, I hoped I wasn't opening a huge can of worms. No way to avoid the issue now. "It's the same tattoo I saw earlier today on the man who attacked me."

CHAPTER 6

Vaughn and I had returned to the IR Compound located in rural Maryland almost an hour ago. She'd immediately disappeared with M.T. Stone, team instructor and so much more, so I'd been left on my own, waiting on the arrival of Mandy and Jaylene who were caught up in the D.C. beltway, aka jammed parking lot.

I'd stopped by the gym where two of our new, younger additions to the Compound were sparring. Sabina was an untrained witch with some wicked powers, including the ability to fly short distances. Since she was about the same age as Aini, with the proper training, she could surpass even Alex in her use of magic, except Alex had her additional shaman skills. Working with Sabina was Hercules, who preferred to be called Herc and couldn't look less like the Greco Roman son of a God than the geek he really was. Though barely older than Sabina, Herc was a wiz at creating gadgets and weapons, both offensive and defensive, against preternaturals. Only challenge was, most were still in the prototype stage, which wasn't doing us agents a fat lot of good in the field. As a result, most of us were recovering from broken bones and other injuries. It'd only be a matter of time before one, or more, of us were killed.

Right now Herc seemed to be working on some sort of web that could stop the forward movement of Sabina who gamely was launching herself in the air time and time again to see if Herc's invention could catch her. So far Sabina was winning hands down.

"You're trying to shoot the thing where I was, not where I'm going to be," she pointed out, one hand on her slender hips, the other still in a sling. Her foot tapped as Herc was hunched over his hand-held launcher.

"Not helping," he muttered with that tone men can get when the obvious is pointed out to them while they're trying to focus on a solution.

"If you just try—"

"I am." His head snapped up, a frown digging grooves in his forehead and revealing what he would look like as an old man. If he lived that long.

"Fine," she sighed.

Herc went back to fiddling and Sabina to toe tapping. I could have tried a few of the rudimentary spells Alex had been teaching me since our return from Missouri, but since my magic wielding contained about as much finesse as Herc's weaponry right now, I figured some more private sessions on my own in the woods might be a better option.

Since nerves were jitterbugging beneath my skin, I changed into my shorts and an old tank top and took off running along one of the trails winding from the Compound's property line. Yes, it was a risk, but I'd stay close, and wary. I wasn't stupid as much as desperate to release the pressures building inside of me.

Surrounding our thirty plus acres were several neighboring small farms and isolated residences. A bucolic setting where the worst thing that could happen was a mosquito bite or skinned knee if a buried root tripped an unsuspecting runner. Running was also one of the new pastimes I'd taken up as a way to beef up my response time to preternatural threats. Magic and speed could be lethal assets, especially if I didn't regain my ability to disappear. Maybe a marginal spell casting ability would keep Ling Mai from booting me off the team. A big maybe.

Right now I wished I'd learned a disengage spell, something to keep my mind from spinning in useless circles. Until the team gathered and we had a plan of action my hands were tied. I didn't even know what was threatening us. I had a name, and a few scary descriptive phrases, but not much else.

Concentrating on the rhythmic pounding of my feet against packed earth helped, but only a little. I knew where I was headed, toward a small speck of normality I'd discovered a few weeks back. I focused on my breathing, not the zillion what-if questions jangling in my head, and the image of Van's disappointed face as I jumped into the taxi, front and center in my thoughts. Right now I craved normal the way an addict craves his next fix.

Rounding a bend on the path, a quick yapping pulled me up short. A brown and white puppy, with feet larger than its head, was tugging on a leash held for dear life by a little girl of about eight or nine. Fang, a dog as aptly named as Herc was.

I skidded to a stop, so as not to frighten the poor dog or struggling girl any more. Gabby was about seven or eight, a guess based on my years teaching, with one skinned knee, grass stained shorts and a wrinkled t-shirt that looked like it'd bathed a dog recently. She also possessed the most gap-toothed smile I'd seen in what felt like ages and spoke with a lisp.

I kept my voice low as I reached out my palm to get licked by the ferocious Fang. "How's the training going?" I asked, knowing this guard dog was about as deadly as I was. Only thing he might do is love someone to death.

"Okay," the girl said, "I guess."

The puppy was licking my hand, wiggling its furry butt so hard I was surprised it didn't topple itself.

I caught sight of an older sister standing on the edge of a cleared space and a double-wide trailer. It made me feel better, that someone other than the fur baby was looking out for Gabby.

"Is Fang going to an obedience training course?"

"Nah," came the mumbled response, quickly followed by, "he won't eat you."

I bit back a smile. That wasn't my worry. Silly puppy might get himself in trouble though if his only deterrent to running off was Gabby restraining him.

"Papa says he's still a baby, but he's supposed to grow big right away."

From the tone of her voice I could tell this was good news. I cast another quick glance at the trailer home, the rust spots and faded paint, the beater truck listing to one side of it. Professional dog training was a luxury to some.

"You think your mom and dad would let me pay to have Fang trained?" I offered, wanting to be careful not to overstep the fragile friendship I'd made with this child and her dog. Sometimes pride was the only thing that kept people going. I know it had for me on more than one occasion. "If he were trained he could fetch things for you and watch your house when you're away."

She lifted one shoulder and let it fall. Not a yes, but not a no either. Baby steps. For now, I could live with that.

"I like your hair." She shifted the conversation in that straight-to-the-point-way I missed from my former kindergarten students. Then pushed a handful of fly-away hair that was almost the same shade of reddish brown as Fang's fur. "Can I have hair like yours when I get as old as you?"

"I think that's very likely." Feeling like I was on the far side of my eighties, I still couldn't help grinning as Fang rolled on his back and all but begged for a belly rub. "But my hair isn't as pretty as yours. You're lucky."

"That's what Mom says."

"You believe your mom, don't you?"

"Yeah." She looked at Fang again and added, "'Sides, my hair's just like Fang's and that's good."

Sometimes life could be that simple.

Giving Fang one last chin scratch, he suddenly jumped to his feet and started barking wildly, peering around me as if the hounds of hell were arriving. Given the morning I'd had I snapped to my own feet as fast as I could without frightening the girl, or her pet anymore than it already was. I turned, bracing myself for who knew what, when Wyatt, one of the newer recruits jogged into sight.

Wyatt was some type of Bada-demon, one of the exceptions in the demon world for not being nasty and ugly. Actually, he was kind of cute, and so sincere in wanting to be a hero. He had a lock of blond hair that kept falling over his forehead, the kind you wanted to brush back for him. Somewhere along the line since he'd joined the IR training program he'd decided he had a crush on me. A shy, tongue-tied idea that I walked on air, and he was content with thinking only the best about me. It was actually kind of nice that someone felt that way, because I sure didn't, not about myself any more.

"There you are," he said, then did a double take seeing my defensive stance in front of the girl and her growing-up-fast pup. "There a problem?"

I eased my shoulders. "Nah, just saying hi to Gabby and Fang here."

With a smile again at the furry ball of love, I nodded at Gabby. "Thank you for sharing your dog with me." And I meant it. For a moment or two I'd pushed the Librarian's words, an attack, two deaths and one attempted murder out of my mind. Or at least behind a closed door.

As if reading my thoughts, Wyatt cleared his throat. "Vaughn wants you back at the compound. Everyone's there now."

A weight thudded in my stomach, I knew my reprieve time was over. As I turned to run back with Wyatt I gave a wave to Gabby.

"Will you come see me again?" she asked.

I nodded. "As soon as I can." It might be a lie, but little girls still need their illusions.

I know I did.

CHAPTER 7

After a light jog that barely made us sweat, Wyatt and I reached the main Compound building, where the conference room was located. But before we entered a low growl stopped us. That and a high-pitched shout from Sabina.

"Don't move."

We froze, my muscles locking as I scanned the area for a threat.

"What—" Sabina cut off Wyatt's question with a raised hand, her good hand, her eyes wide, showing too much white. The finger she used to point with was steady though, as I followed the line of sight to where she was jabbing.

I couldn't see anything. Not right away. Nothing except, near the gym, an over-sized bush badly in need of trimming, shivering a bit in the breeze. Only there was no breeze.

Goose bumps danced across my skin as I peered closer.

What I thought was dusky shadows wasn't. Mottled tawny fur and two deep golden brown eyes stared between the green leaves. Very serious, lethal eyes.

"A lion?" I didn't realize I'd said the words aloud until Sabina shushed me with a hissing sound, her whole body as frozen still as mine.

When she did speak, her voice was so quiet I had to strain to hear her. "A Were lion. Herc's experiment backfired."

Was nothing going to go right today? Then a dark thought slammed into me. "Where's Herc?"

"Still inside," she whispered. "Trying an invisibility cloak."

Now was not the time to give a lecture on how lions, particularly African lions, hunted by smell. A fact the teens might know if they ever played Lions and Tigers and Bears. Invisibility would only give the illusion of security.

"What now?" Wyatt muttered next to me.

As if I had tons of experience fighting Were lions. Weres tended to be large, dangerous and stupid, a combo that made me very, very wary of them.

"Can you do anything?" I asked, not sure of what a Bada-demon could do, but it was worth a try.

"I don't think giving it a rash or a bad case of the hives would help," Wyatt said, his tone dead pan. "Boils won't help either."

Got it. Plan, zero. Knowledge of Bada-demon abilities, one.

"I know." Sabina's voice raised on the last word as she angled her gaze in my direction. "You could wink out and go get help."

Not a good idea, even if I could.

"He'd track me by scent." I kept my own words calm and slow, nothing like my racing pulse. Could big cats scent fear like dogs did? If so, we were goners. We were also in deep trouble if someone came barreling out of the main house and startled the beast into attacking.

Think, Kelly, think.

"Sabina," I smiled, as if the lion was going to be appeased by that movement. I didn't think so, but it helped keep my words less hysterical, "Did Alex teach you her freeze spell?"

Sabina paused even as the bush started rustling more. Not a good sign.

"You know the one. She used it on a couple of Weres in Paris. To stop them." I was not going to panic. Yet. But I was getting close.

"I think I do," came her less-than-sure response.

I wasn't sure I remembered all the words in the exact order, but if Sabina and I could both say them, then maybe, with her magic and my apprentice magic, we could contain the kitty-from-hell long enough to find a tranq gun to stop it.

"How's it start?" Sabina asked.

Not good.

"Something like … air to earth, dirt to dust—"

"No. It can't be," she cut in, focusing more on the spell now than the movement behind the bush. Movement that revealed one humongous paw, which was a good foot and a half across. I knew Weres were larger than their pure animal counterparts, but knowing and seeing were two different things. One swipe with that weapon and there'd be no surviving.

My mouth bone dry, I tried to listen to Sabina's mumbling.

"Air to wind, Earth to dust.
By water and by fire."

That was it. Now I remembered. My voice joined with hers in a low chant.

"Trouble to heed and trouble to find.
Compel. Coerce. Constrain.
I thee call. I thee command.
Threat be gone. Power be bound."

Nothing.

CHAPTER 8

Why did magic look so easy when Alex did it?

Sabina shot me a wild-eyed look, evidently as clueless as I was. The only one who looked like they were totally in control was the lion who emerged from behind the bush in a near silent side step.

Dear Lord, it was huge. In the wild, male lions could be nine feet in length and up to four hundred pounds. This one looked twice as large. How'd it ever hide behind that bush?

I know, not the most pressing question, but easier to latch on to that than the fact there were three of us smack dab in front of this beast. Appetizers in jeans.

"Sabina, if he attacks, levitate."

"But—"

"Do it." There was no time for arguments. "Fly and warn the team. Conference room."

I couldn't even talk in full sentences. There wasn't enough air in my lungs.

The lion stood less than fifteen feet away, one easy leap. If Sabina listened to me she might be safe. Wyatt? No way was I going to let him get killed just for being in the wrong place at the wrong time.

Channeling my inner Alex, which felt a lot like heartburn, I raised my hands, earning a slanted eyed golden glare.

"Slide away from me," I murmured from one side of my mouth,

"Not and leave you."

Didn't he know heroics could get him killed? "Both of us dying won't prove a thing." My shoulders were so tight I was surprised they didn't crackle and pop. "Move. Now."

I blocked him from my periphery vision. One problem at a time.

Except the door to the gym squeaked open right that second and all hell broke loose.

Sabina screamed and lunged forward.

Wyatt tackled her, pulling her to the ground and rolling away.

Herc froze.

The lion pounced. In his direction.

And I started shouting, putting every ounce of desperation behind my words.

"Air to wind, Earth to dust.
By water and by fire.
Trouble to heed and trouble to find.
Compel. Coerce. Constrain.
I thee call. I thee command.
Threat be gone. Power be bound."

I wasn't sure who was more shocked — Herc, the lion, or me. Time slammed to a halt, just as a door from the main house slammed open to my left and a half a dozen people ran forward and skidded to a stop. Someone growled low and deep in their throat. Probably Nicki. As a shifter cat, she liked Weres even less than the rest of us, which was saying a lot.

Hoping Alex was among them, I called out. "Were lion. Think I have it frozen but could really use your help, Alex."

I wasn't sure but I think she snorted. "Damn beginner's luck," she mumbled then added, "I've got him."

Wait? Did that mean she did the magic? Not me?

Her voice and a rush of magic wafted over me as I was still too scared to lower my arms.

"Power of darkness and of light, I call upon you.
Make me a barrier between those here be.
Between dark and light.

Between good and evil.
Protect me as I am willing to pay the cost.

To the light, better things.
To death, watch over.
To struggle and emerge, advance as I follow.

Going on forever, light shines in the darkness.
Dispel those who seek to harm your one.
Circle round and protect. Let it be!"

Alex's second chant did the trick. Only then did I start breathing. Good news — the lion looked fully contained. Bad news — Herc was in the same boat.

"Explain." M.T. Stone came up beside me, which was the only thing keeping me standing upright, sort of like getting an electrical jolt from a cattle prod. My arms now hung limply at my sides as my shoulders dropped.

"Far as I know, one of Herc's experiments went cattywampus. Wyatt and I walked into it. Sabina and I tried to freeze the cat but first time it failed." Second time too. I could have killed us all playing at magic. I cleared my throat and finished, "Thank heavens for Alex."

It wasn't the best after action report, but I'd had a rough day. Besides it seemed to be enough.

Wyatt had scrambled to his feet, ignoring a grumbling Sabina as he crossed to stand beside me. "You were amazing."

I looked at him, feeling a million years older than him. "You ever disobey a direct order from a superior team member again, and your ass will be out of here so fast you won't know what happened."

Stone ducked his head to hide what I think was laughter. Not that there was any mirth anywhere in the situation.

Wyatt looked gob-smacked, which is exactly what I intended. Heroics held no place in this business. Not even well-intentioned heroics. Especially that kind.

On the other hand, he had kept Sabina from making a bigger mess of things. "Nice tackle, though," I added, turning to walk into the main building while I could still move.

Stone barked a few orders. "Terringen and Baxter, dart the Were and transport to a holding cell until we can determine what to do with him."

"What about Herc?" Sabina demanded, having more balls than I did taking that tone with Stone.

"Leave him be. The spell will wear off soon enough."

"That's not fair," the young witch whined.

If she had any more complaints, they were quickly cut off, not by Stone, but by Vaughn. "Fair would be sending him packing," she said, her voice as cold and precise as I'd ever heard. "Only an idiot would let a Were lion loose in the compound, and idiots get others killed."

Sabina pulled herself up into a statue of indignation but she kept her mouth shut. So the novice witch could learn. Good news. We needed all the magic users we could get. Especially since I just proved I wasn't going to be one of them.

Vaughn wasn't finished though. "If I find out you were involved in activating such a stupid stunt, you'll be punished, too." She nodded toward where Herc remained statue-still. "When he comes around, have him report to me."

She pivoted on her heel and marched back inside.

Bravo Vaughn.

The rest of the team and I followed her lead until we were all seated around the conference room table. Ling Mai, who usually presided at the head of the table, was missing though.

I leaned toward Alex. "Thanks for the help back there."

"No problem. Van would tear my hide off if he knew I let you get as much as a scratch."

Not what I wanted to hear. I was not Van Noziak's pet project. I didn't know what was between us but no way did I want to be his Lois Lane, always getting into scrapes and then waving my hands around and hoping like all get out that he'd save me. Not that it wasn't nice in some ways, but that also made me a weak-ninny victim and I so wasn't going for that.

So I changed the subject. "Where's Ling Mai?"

The furrow of my brows added enough umph to my question for Alex to whisper, "Some hush hush crap with the Council of Seven."

The Council was the preternatural governing body, made up of seven members of the most powerful of the preternaturals. Their primary goal was to keep their world a secret from the humans, and their decisions were law. The fact they tended to kill their own kind first, at the least breath of impropriety, made them a group to walk warily around. It's better to avoid them altogether than cross their path. Alex knew that firsthand so I let my curiosity drop.

M.T. Stone, our instructor and so much more, sat to the right of Ling Mai's empty spot. Across from him, to the left side of the table, was Vaughn, sitting in the position of power. Good role.

Then there were the rest of us. We currently active agents, spread down both sides of the table, three on one side, two on the other.

Next to Vaughn came Jaylene Smart, a tall, black woman whose face and body belonged on a photo spread in a glossy fashion magazine. She was our resident psychic with her tarot cards that, unfortunately, usually spelled doom and gloom, so as a team we tended to ignore her predictions. Next to her sat Mandy Reyes, a Latino, whose exotic looks reminded me of some movie star I remembered from an action flick that Alex made me watch. Mandy and Jaylene were best buddies, not so much Mandy and Alex, who was next to me. Both being intense, stubborn to a fault, and unwilling to back down, they butted heads more than played well together. Mandy was also a Spirit Walker, someone who could cross over to the other side as Alex called it. That wasn't an offensive or defensive ability as far as I'd seen, but maybe we just hadn't seen her use her gift much. So far.

Next to Mandy was the newest recruit, Nicki Yarblanski, our resident shifter; a cougar and the reason my ring was heating my finger even from across the width of the table. I didn't know a lot about Nicki, but it was nice to have someone on the team who could hold her own in a physical battle with some of the preternaturals we kept coming up against.

Beside me was Alex Noziak, part-witch, part-shaman and, thanks to being attacked by her brother while crazed on designer drugs that had been forced on him, she now possessed some shifter abilities. She was still figuring out how to deal with this new twist to her genetic make up, but even before that event, she was our ace in the hole when it came to dealing with a lot of the non-human beings and situations. Nothing like that quick spell to freeze a threat she just used or a cloaking spell to get out of a tight situation.

She was also Van Noziak's little sister and none too happy with the idea of Van and me becoming an item. Which, given his last glance at me outside the Library of Congress, might not be much of an issue any more. The two of us I mean.

I wrapped up the members of the core team, and only Alex knew my secret of not being able to turn invisible any more. She might not approve of my dating her brother, but she'd keep my confidences, as long as doing so didn't put the rest of the group in jeopardy.

And that was a huge question. Van had already pushed that button, wondering why I hadn't used invisibility as an escape tactic while being attacked. I'd side-stepped the issue but if I needed to call on an ability I no longer had, someone could get hurt. Besides me.

Somewhere in the Compound, which was what we called the former posh residence of a 19th century industrial magnate, there were more recruits being trained, like Wyatt and the two tasked with containing the Were lion, but for now there were only the six of us experienced agents, plus Vaughn and Stone. Though the term 'experience' and 'three months' was an oxymoron. Who learned their job totally in three months? Especially a life and death job?

We'd been baptized by fire, fighting infiltration of the agency by a doppelganger during early training days, destroying a power-hungry Grimple, stopping a nasty djinn in Rwanda, minimizing Weres and a druid bent on changing the status quo between preternaturals and humans in Paris and, for Alex and me, eliminating a witch-finder who'd been trying to skin Alex alive in Missouri. Events that changed us all.

And that didn't even include my first taking of another's life, an Aka Manah demon in Sierra Leone, that still gave me recurring nightmares. That was compounded by my killing yet another, a fae, in Missouri.

Yeah, we'd already been through a lot in a short time and it didn't look like the pace was about to slow.

Vaughn, with no preliminary words of greeting, announced, "Aini has been successfully transferred from the George Washington hospital to the infirmary, a previously vetted nurse and doctor available twenty-four seven here now. She's as secure and stabilized as possible."

Which left a back door open. Sure there was a cyclone fence surrounding the property, with security lights and cameras and enough land around us that the casual person would think twice about infiltrating. But someone who wanted to approach the series of buildings that made up the Compound, probably could without a whole lot of extra effort. This wasn't a stronghold, it was a living and training facility.

"With that taken care of..." Obviously our team leader wasn't going to dwell on the indefensibility of our location as her gaze shot to me. "Kelly, please tell us about the attack on you earlier today."

Interesting that she started there. Not with a focus on what had happened to Aini, which is where I'd start, but then maybe that's why she was in charge while Ling Mai was gone. Since it wasn't that long ago that the Director warned me that any extra-curricular activity outside of agency-mandated would result in immediate dismissal — and going home meant no help in finding who or what I was through my unknown birth mother — I ignored my sweaty palms and pasted a sure-why-not smile on my face that felt very wobbly around the edges. I hadn't done anything wrong and visiting the Librarian *was* on agency business, but once called on the carpet, twice shy. Even if I trusted Vaughn a whole lot more than I trusted Ling Mai.

Since only Vaughn was aware of my fun and games at the Library of Congress, all gazes shot to me. Alex leaned forward, scowling. Her normal approach to a threat, especially on someone she saw as under her protection. A Noziak trait, whether you liked it or not.

In as precise, if dry-mouthed a way as possible, I explained leaving the library, the skirmish, and what I could recall of my attacker. Which wasn't much, except for his tattoo. I didn't mention Van because … well because his presence added more complications than I was ready to go into.

Leave it to Alex to not let me side step that point though. "How'd you break away?" she asked, like picking at a healing scab.

"Someone came to my help." I know, I know, I was glossing over who that someone was, which would come out eventually, but one challenge at a time. Time to shift focus again. My team's focus. "Thank heavens."

I received head nods and smiles. So far, so good. I kept my gaze averted from Alex's, like a kid playing if-I-can't-see-you-then-you-can't-see-me.

"You're sure it was a man who went after you?" Jaylene scooted forward in her seat. I wanted to hug her for wrestling the conversation more in the direction I was willing it to go.

"Yes."

"Even though you didn't see his face?"

I nodded. "I had no doubts he was a male, not so sure that he was human."

"Because?" Alex prodded.

"His smell." I couldn't help the face I made even recalling it. "Rotten, sulphur stench."

Mandy raised a brow as if wondering why, in the heat of battle, I was aware of his stink, but couldn't recall his face.

Vaughn cleared her throat. "Tell us more about the tattoo."

"What tat?" Nicki glanced around the table.

Instead of answering directly, I grabbed a small paper pad from in front of Alex then nabbed her pen and started drawing. I'm no Picasso but the image was so specific, so branded on my brain, that it took only seconds to sketch what I saw.

"Like this." I held the paper up. "A crude face without features, colored in blood red, thick black outline, and two horns."

I knew it looked like a crude child's drawing but its very starkness leant it power, even before Vaughn nodded and spoke. "The Horned One," she said, her voice somber in the closed room. "You're sure?"

Why was she asking? She'd seen the tattoo on the nurse, too. "Absolutely. It's the same image that was on the nurse's forearm."

"What?" Jayleen's voice crackled through the tense room. "You're telling us that whatever attacked you is connected with the nurse who went after the kid in the hospital?"

"She's hardly a kid." I grasped at the most inconsequential point first because the bigger issues scared me silly. "She's almost sixteen." Which reminded me as I glanced over at Vaughn. "That's what the Librarian told me is important. We need to know Aini's exact age. Her birthdate."

"Because?" Jayleen drew out the single word.

I gave a tight shrug. "She didn't give me specifics, only that the Horned One was associated with carrying dead souls to the underworld and Aini's exact birthdate mattered."

"Sounds like a really creepy kind of guy." A deep frown bit into Nicki's face as she pointed out the obvious.

"Still doesn't explain why it's important to know Aini's age," Vaughn said.

"The Librarian indicated that if Aini is not yet sixteen, that there might be a small window of time."

"To do what?" Jayleene demanded.

"To stop cataclysmic destruction of humans and preternaturals."

That sucked all the air out of the room.

"You forget to mention this before?" Mandy gave me a why-is-that look to match the sharpness of her tone.

"Maybe 'cuz she's been running from pillar to post," Alex waded in, "dealing with a comatose girl speaking when she shouldn't be, meeting with the Librarian who's scary enough all by herself, fending off attackers, being in the middle of our chief suspect suddenly dying, and facing a Were lion with barely a smidge of magic experience. Gee, I wonder why Kels hasn't been laying everything out point by point to get you up to speed."

It was like being back on the playground with the looks being tossed around.

"Ladies." Vaughn picked up the role of play monitor. "This isn't getting us anywhere."

Alex and Mandy pulled back, not all the way, but there wouldn't be blood spilled because of me. This time.

Vaughn continued to speak as if words hadn't been slung back and forth like weapons. "Be specific Kelly. The details matter."

Funny how Vaughn sounded so much like the Librarian. Tarnation, I'd barely thought of the Librarian's words since I'd been attacked, which showed me how wild the morning had been.

"She didn't really tell me a lot." Except for calling me a fool, and an innocent, which still wasn't sitting well. "When I told her Aini said the Horned One had come, the Librarian became very rattled."

Alex whistled, but that wasn't what had the hairs along my arms standing up.

When she didn't say anything, though, I continued, "She also said the protectors of the Horned One might already be at work, but she wasn't clear about who they were, or where we might find them."

"Still don't get why knowing the kid's age matters?" Jaylene eyed me.

"I'm getting to that." Sure I sounded a bit tetchy, but Vaughn wanted the details, and it took a little time to straighten out all the threads. Jaylene leaned back in her chair, crossing her arms, as if I were the problem here.

I ignored her and shifted my gaze to Vaughn. "The Librarian mentioned something about speaking of the Horned One giving it life. Then she kept asking about Aini's exact age and if she hadn't yet reached sixteen there might still be a little time."

"And that's when she mentioned cataclysmic destruction?" Alex clarified.

"Yes. That and the fact there might be time to stop whoever or whatever this Horned One is."

"Did you ask for specifics on how we're supposed to do that?" Jaylene was back to poking at me. Who'd pissed her off?

"I would have except the Librarian hustled away as if her house was on fire."

I caught the quick glance Vaughn shot to Stone before she spoke, "The Librarian left you?"

"Yes."

"Did she extract payment for the information she shared?"

I shook my head. "No. She wanted to know the nature of my question before she determined what she wanted in return from me." I looked across the table at Mandy and Jaylene. "Which is also why I didn't have a lot of time to ask as many details as I would have liked. One second she's asking what I came to see her about and the next, she's closing up shop and disappearing."

"That doesn't sound good." Vaughn's frown didn't bode well for whatever was going on.

It was Stone, though, who jumped in. "Did the Librarian mention the Seekers?"

A logical question, since finding Aini was tied with her being a lead to the Seekers, creatures who were determined to change the relationship of our closed society. Closed meaning humans not being aware of non-humans, except in a few isolated situations. A situation both those humans in the know, and preternaturals, wanted to keep as it was. Unfortunately, we didn't have a lot of intel about these Seekers. We'd been waiting for Aini to wake up to ask her questions, a whole lot of questions the more she remained comatose.

"Neither Aini nor the Librarian mentioned the Seekers at all." I glanced at Jaylene to cut her off before she got all in my face, as she was already uncrossing her arms and leaning forward. "And no, I didn't ask either of them specifically about that issue. As I said, there just wasn't time."

Jaylene sat back. Score one for me.

I decided to go on the offensive instead of only being defensive as I glanced at Vaughn. "Have you had time to ask Fraulein Fassbinder about the Horned One? Did she share anything that might help?"

"Only that in the Wiccan Book of Shadows, the Horned One is associated with an unknowable supreme deity called Dryghtyn."

She pronounced it dry-tun, which didn't help me a lot.

I felt more than saw Alex stiffen next to me. Alex was a blood-born witch as opposed to a practicing Wiccan and I knew, to her, that made a difference, but wasn't sure of the particulars. Guess I should pay more attention.

"So this Horned One is supposed to be what? A god?" Nicki's tone indicated how unlikely she thought that was.

My parents, dyed-in-the-wool Baptists, who were firm believers in good and evil, also strongly believed in not worshiping false prophets, which included the idolatry of gods. Even mentioning the possibility of another 'god' was blasphemous. If they had heard this discussion they'd shake their heads, knowing full well I was going on the express train to hell.

But then they'd assumed that the first time I disappeared from sight in front of them.

It was Alex who broke the dark spiral of my thoughts as she answered, "It's more that Wiccans believe The Horned One is the Lord of Death. He's seen as their comforter and consoler after death and before reincarnation. "

That didn't sound so bad. Not as horrific as the Librarian was making things out to be.

"So you're saying this Horned dude is the devil?" Nicki jumped in.

"No." A quick glance at Alex showed her deep in thought, as if trying to pull from something learned a long time ago. "Though he's supposed to hold a powerful position in the Underworld. "

"Sounds like the devil to me." Jaylene pressed her lips into a tight line.

"He's also only supposed to be able to leave the Underworld on rare occasions. Mostly he hangs out in the other Realm and lets humans wreck havoc on one another here," Alex said.

I thought of the words I spoke to Van about ancient demons leaving hell to steal the souls of humans and shoved away the shiver of fear crawling up my skin. Probably not related at all.

"We're going up against devils and demi-gods now?" Jaylene all but snorted in a just-our-luck tone.

"Given we dealt with the not-so-nice brother of Christ in Paris, this surprises you?" Alex did call it as she saw it.

Maybe I wasn't the only one dealing with lessons of childhood. I was still grappling with knowing shifters, Weres and demons existed. But now? Going up against a possible god? Or the devil himself? Not buying it. Not wanting to buy it.

"It is not yet clear what we are dealing with," Vaughn interjected, as if reading my thoughts while bringing the fear factor down by a dozen degrees. "Alex, I want you to speak with Fraulein Fassbinder, compare your knowledge of what the Horned One is with her intel. Any information is important."

Alex nodded as Vaughn turned to Stone. "You and Nicki return to the hospital. Review their security tapes and see if you can get the autopsy reports of the nurse and Officer Packard prioritized so we'll know exactly how they died."

"Oh," I said, earning a whiplash of attention once again focused on me. No one interrupted without a darn good cause. Which I think I had, though it could be a wild goose chase. "Some time this morning a man visited Aini."

"Who?" Stone snapped.

I was getting very tired of having no answers. "The nurse," I raised my hands before the next question was asked, "Yes, the same nurse accused of attacking Aini and killing the guard and who is now dead, she indicated a man with government ID had visited Aini."

Several voices broke out at once.

"She telling the truth?"

"Why would we believe her?"

"What government agency?"

I cleared my throat to finish what I'd been about to say. "No, she couldn't recall the agency or even what the man looked like except he had dark, short hair and old eyes."

Jaylene snorted.

"At the time," I spoke to her and the rest of the room, "I was more focused on making sure Aini was okay and that her room hadn't been disturbed." Only then did I realize the person I'd trusted to have the machines checked for possible tampering was the person who tried to kill Aini. How stupid could I have been? How naïve?

My face must have betrayed me as Vaughn asked, "You okay, Kelly?"

I swallowed and looked up. "I should have never left Aini alone. I should have guessed that nurse wasn't what she seemed to be. I should—"

"You called me the minute you left Aini's room," Vaughn's voice was meant to soothe, but the way I felt right then I didn't deserve it.

"A call that led to an innocent man's death."

"Don't be an idiot," Jaylene snapped. "So you're human. Your ability is not to see and know the future. None of us suspected the kid to be in danger. Hell, we didn't even know anyone else knew where she was."

"I think what Jaylene is trying to say…" Vaughn smiled. "Is there's a lot more going on here than we originally suspected. Aini is safe, in large part because you suggested we bring a guard in. Yes, he died, but that's a risk he took in accepting the job."

Alex slapped her hand down on the table. Not mad as much as determined — not that she had any other method of approaching a problem. "I say we get back to finding out exactly what happened to the nurse and why Kelly was attacked. Someone must have followed her from the hospital to know she'd be at the Library of Congress."

That had my stomach knotting. Again clueless. How many times could I get away with being too naive?

Vaughn looked at Mandy and Jaylene. "As I started to say, I'd like you two to follow up with the Librarian. See if you can get more details on who or what we're facing and if there's a connection to the Seekers."

"You think that's a possibility?" Mandy asked.

"I think it's best if we are prepared for all possibilities."

"And if the Librarian isn't at the library?" Mandy asked.

"Find her," came Vaughn's whiplash response.

Ouch. Glad I didn't ask that.

When it appeared that I'd been overlooked as everyone started to stand and head out, I raised my hand, a leftover action from my days in a classroom. "And me?"

Vaughn's gaze whipped to me, her expression once more enigmatic. "I've got something special for you to do."

Now why did that sound like the worst of all options?

CHAPTER 9

Vaughn was speaking with Stone as I rose to my feet, feeling every bruise on my body. Alex leaned in close to me and whispered, "So you met with Van?"

She might have said it in as neutral a tone as she could manage, which wasn't all that objective, but I could tell she was trying to approach the subject of her brother in a way that didn't have me calling for immediate back up. Sheesh, why now? And how did she know? I don't think I mentioned his name.

"How'd—"

"He called me." She shook her head. "Needing to check on his little sister. Criminey. When's he going to realize I'm no longer a kid."

She didn't say it as a question, so I left it alone. Besides I didn't want to admit that it wasn't likely to ever happen. Good part was she wasn't coming down on me like a ton of bricks.

Then she looked at me and I knew my reprieve was over. "So you met with him?"

I nodded, aware my throat was still very sore.

"And?" she pushed.

"And what? Technically we didn't meet. I was at the library and he showed up."

She released a sigh indicating she'd be patient but not for long. "Pretty coincidental that he just happened to materialize when you needed his help."

Now that she mentioned it, she was right. "He did the same thing when assistance made the difference between dying and walking away in Missouri." She'd been there so she understood. Yes, I was deflecting, but I had too much on my plate to deal with a complicated non-relationship, too.

"And how'd he find us there?" Alex's eyes narrowed, letting me know she'd spent more time thinking about this than I had.

It was an automatic reflex that had me looking at my cell phone. GPS tracking. Duh! "Guess it's time for a new cell."

How many lessons did I need? Enough to stop thinking like I was still a Dubuque kindergarten teacher and more like a trained operative.

"Look, Kels." Alex ran her hand along the back of her neck. "I just don't want you to get hurt."

"By Van?" We were talking about her overly protective brother who'd saved my life several times even though we'd known each other for little over a month? Van who I'd trust with my life and had, several times? That Van? Sure he could be an overly protective, macho male, but I didn't think he'd ever hurt me. Except there were several kinds of hurts, weren't there?

Alex cocked her head at me as if trying to find the way to say something I either didn't or couldn't understand. "Yes. Van." She paused then glanced away before continuing. "He's damaged goods. In the relationship department."

My brow rose before I was aware of it. She'd mentioned this before, but I hadn't pressed for more details. The time was coming though, when veiled references just weren't going to cut it anymore.

Alex pushed on. "I know, I know, not my business, but there's a lot of backstory you don't know."

"Don't you think that's something Van should tell me?" I wasn't sure if it was temper or wariness coating my words. "Besides, you're assuming a whole lot more is going on between us than really is. Van's an adult. I'm an adult. If we want to meet for coffee or dinner, where's the harm?"

I was going for the we're-all-experienced-women-of-the-world approach without spelling out that if Van and I wanted to have hot, sweaty sex and lots of it, then it was none of Alex's business. Not that I even allowed my thoughts to go down that path, except late at night when I needed something really intense to keep my mind off my nightmares. Plus I didn't need to put any graphic images in Alex's mind; Van was her brother after all.

She looked at me, really looked before asking, "Is that all it is? Just friends?"

I could honestly answer. "I'm not sleeping with your brother. We haven't even gone on a normal date, which is almost impossible to arrange, given what we both do." All sore spots. "So there's nothing to worry about."

I watched her shoulders ease as she offered a rueful smile. "Yeah, maybe I'm overreacting a bit."

"You think?"

"I just ... I just care for you both. I don't want to see either of you hurt."

"I'm supposed to be capable of hurting Van?" Him being the most self-contained, the most assured, the least likely to be caught off guard no matter what he did person I'd ever met? And Alex was worried about me nicking her big brother's self-esteem? "Not going to happen."

I meant it, which more than anything else was probably what allowed Alex to ball her fist and tap my shoulder. "You're right. Forget I said anything."

Not likely. It wasn't every day I was accused of being a femme fatale. I wasn't sure if I should be shocked or pleasantly surprised. Maybe, if Van and I ever got together for that cup of coffee or glass of wine, I'd share with him and we could both have a good laugh. Not that we would. Get together. So not going to happen, and now I had one more good, rock solid reason to avoid that. Even casual dating with Van meant putting my friendship with Alex at risk. I'd already lost one sister, no way was I going to lose another.

Alex started to walk away then paused and looked over her shoulder, her expression once more intense, her voice pitched low. "Make sure that's all there is connecting you two 'cuz I don't want to have to choose between you and Van."

A threat? I had no doubt whom Alex would choose. Blood came first for her, always. Just when I thought we could return to best buds. Was nothing going to go right today?

"Kelly?" Vaughn called me from near the doorway.

Guess I got my answer.

CHAPTER 10

I waited for Vaughn to turn her back and start to walk away from the conference room before I double-timed it to catch up with her, heading down the hallway toward her office. She didn't pause until we reached Ling Mai's inner sanctum. Not for the first time I felt like a student being called before the principal.

Vaughn waited until we were both seated, her behind the Director's formal desk that spoke volumes about power and prestige. Probably to make the folks, like me, sitting in the chairs opposite it, feel even more exposed. It worked, too.

"I need to speak to you about what you heard Aini say," she began, crossing her hands before her on the desk.

I waited.

"Did you *truly* hear that conversation?"

Back to this again. Now she was doubting me? My doubting myself was one thing, but if Vaughn started doing the same thing I was knee-deep in quicksand. Combine losing my ability to turn invisible with a poor performance as an agent and I'd be booted from the team quicker than I could say *gesundheit*.

"Yes, I did." My tone erred on the side of neutral when what I wanted to do was scream 'Why won't anyone believe me?' So I added, "I have no reason to have made up that conversation."

She briefly raised one hand. "I am not doubting you, Kels. You and I both are aware that there are creatures with an enormous range of abilities."

She'd lost me. "Meaning?"

"Meaning that there are creatures capable of creating illusions so real it's hard not to believe them. They can manipulate our thoughts without our being aware we are being victimized."

And I'd thought I'd reached rock bottom in the doubt department. I threaded my hands in my lap, mostly to have something to hold onto as I absorbed Vaughn's words.

"I was aware the nurse was preternatural," I started slow, choosing each word carefully, "and maybe, if I'd only heard Aini speak, it'd be easier to believe I'd been controlled by someone else. But—" I looked at Vaughn straight on. "I was also holding her hand, watching her struggle to get her words out. Aini was terrified. So if the nurse was a powerful being who could manipulate what I heard, what I saw, and what I felt, all at the same time, there's a chance I'm wrong."

A slim to none chance but I didn't think I needed to beat a dead horse.

A slight smile played around Vaughn's mouth before she resumed her usual powerful-woman-on-a-mission face. "Then we may have a bigger issue that we're dealing with."

"Such as?" Wasn't murder and mayhem enough?

She spoke as if thinking out loud rather than talking to me. "It is difficult to believe the attack on Aini and the attack on you have no correlation."

Just like that my stomach took a dive as my skin grew cold. I'd come to the same conclusion but that didn't mean I liked it, or liked my boss making the same connections.

Vaughn continued, "On the other hand, the two different events occurred close enough to one another in time that it'd make it hard to be instigated by the same individual."

I hadn't thought of that. "So are you saying we might be up against two different threats, the individual who attacked me and the other who attacked Aini?"

"That's one possibility."

I only needed to hear her tone to understand she wasn't leaning toward that theory.

"What else can it mean?"

Her gaze locked with mine, appraising, debating, deciding, before she spoke again. "One possibility is that the Librarian

was correct in her assessment. That the followers of the Horned
One have been activated."

Which meant a threat multiplied. Not good. Not at all.

She added, "And they're not only targeting Aini. They're
also targeting you."

CHAPTER 11

There are some words a person never wants to hear: we're sorry to have to tell you: there's been an accident, ma'am; it's terminal, there's nothing we can do. I just added a new phrase to that collection. *You're being targeted by a demi-god whose function it is to drag souls to the Underworld. Ready or not.*

I listened to the beat of my heart work against the sudden chill in my body before I raised my gaze to Vaughn's and swallowed around the rock in my throat. "Why would anyone have a reason to come after me?"

"They might be under the impression Aini told you something important."

Made sense. Not that she did. Not really.

"Or that you were a witness to something at the hospital, something you don't even know you saw or heard."

Also made sense.

"Or..."

Her voice trailed off until I looked up. "Or?"

"Someone fears your connection with Aini."

What connection? "I watched out for her in Africa," I admitted. "And I've visited her a few times in the hospital, but that was just being nice. She's so alone here."

"Is she?"

"Yes."

"And yet she spoke to you. Not to the doctors or nurses who have been around her daily since she was admitted."

"They were strangers to her."

"Exactly."

"So she knows me. That's all. Is that enough to have a bull's-eye on my back?" Okay, that sounded whiny and scared. Which I was, the last part for sure. Vaughn was grasping at straws, or trying to terrorize me. Which she was doing very well.

I tried to keep an open mind, even as I wanted to dismiss this last idea as preposterous. I was no more connected to Aini than ... well than Van was. He'd been with Aini and me every step of the way in Africa, so why wasn't he being targeted?

Maybe he was? I just didn't know it yet.

"You've thought of something?" Vaughn asked.

I cleared my throat. "I was thinking of connections." Vaughn's eyes opened fractionally larger. "And the fact Van Noziak knew, or was connected with Aini as much as I was in Sierra Leone."

"Yes?"

"So if I'm in danger, he could be, too."

There, that didn't sound like I was personally worried but professionally worried. The first would not be deemed a worthy reason to react. The latter option might warrant a heads-up call to him. Which is all I wanted. I didn't even have to make it, as long as someone checked that he was okay and aware that knowing Aini might be hazardous to his health.

What a mess.

"I'll make sure he's informed of developments, as much as he needs to know."

Which wouldn't be much. Secrets and spooks were more than kissing cousins. Good thing I knew that Van was the most capable person to translate vague hints into keeping himself alive warnings.

That's all I needed.

I started to release a breath I hadn't realized had backed up in my lungs when Vaughn asked, "Is there anything else you need to tell me about?"

Shadow boxing. That must be what she was doing, focus me in one direction then slide in something totally unrelated to keep me on my toes. "I'm sure I've told you everything I know."

Just to make sure, I mentally ticked off the day.

Awareness of Preternatural nurse? Check.

Unknown visitor to Aini? Check.

Aini speaking with no verification by a second party? Check.

Visit to Librarian? Check.

Attack on me? Check.

Noticing similar tattoo on nurse before she suddenly died? Check.

I shook my head as I looked again at Vaughn who'd been patiently waiting as I reeled through the day. "Nope. I'm sure we covered everything."

"If you think of anything else you'll let me know as soon as possible, won't you?" She rose to her feet.

I guessed our little chat was over so I stood too, my body stiff from even the few minutes sitting. Movement would help until I could take a nice soak in Epsom salts or find a luscious bottle of wine and a dark corner retreat.

"—is that clear, Kelly?" Vaughn's voice broke through to me.

What? Only an idiot spaced hearing the person in charge. Vaughn was not Ling Mai, thank heavens, but she was running the show in the meantime. Maybe I was suffering from a concussion after all. "I'm sorry, I didn't catch that."

That sounded as lame as 'my dog ate my homework.'

Vaughn's quirk of a smile told me she was thinking along the same lines, even as she repeated, "You'll be sitting by Aini's bed."

"Now?"

That made no sense. If Aini was safe and everyone else was searching for intel on the Horned One, or following up leads, to have me twiddling my thumbs on the off chance Aini might wake up again was a waste of limited resources.

"Yes, now." By the tightness of Vaughn's expression she'd made up her mind. Should I protest? Or suck it up and do as ordered?

Like I had a lot of choice. Raising a stink about duty assignments wasn't worth the risk of Vaughn's ill will, even temporarily. The way I saw things, the minute she discovered I could no longer turn invisible she'd report to Ling Mai, and I'd be booted as an agent. The clock was ticking. Best to keep on everyone's good side as long as possible.

"We need to speak to Aini," Vaughn continued, making me scramble to catch up. Again.

"Are you saying you want the doctor to bring her out of her coma if possible?"

"No." Vaughn gave a slight shake to her head. "They've already indicated that would be too dangerous for Aini."

Should have known Vaughn would have already covered the most direct option for finding answers.

"Then what are you saying?"

She glanced away for a second before answering. "For now, I'd like you to remain at Aini's bedside. Since she roused herself once and spoke to you, perhaps she'll do so again."

Talk about a miniscule hope.

The smile I gave Vaughn as I hobbled toward the door was real.

"Oh, Kelly?"

Just when I thought I was safe. I turned part way, making it clear I was on my way to do what I'd just been ordered to do. "Yes?"

"There may be more to this situation than what's apparent so far."

Every achy muscle in my body clenched. "Do you know something I should know? Something more concrete than a hypothesis?" The words sounded raspy even to me.

Vaughn smiled at my verbiage. Came from being a teacher. Words held nuances, as did threats. "We'll make sure Aini is truly safe. Let's do the same about you."

My own smile froze in place. Be thankful for small favors or pissed off that I couldn't speed along the search for answers? Where was the threat coming from? Why? And was my being eliminated part of someone's solution?

And to think, it wasn't even noon yet.

CHAPTER 12

"Come in Noziak." Commander Lucius Kincaide's voice revealed no hint as to why he'd called Van into his office.

Not that Van expected otherwise. Kincaide was old school style from the knife-edged pressing of his uniform to the high and tidy cut of his dark hair, silvering slightly near the temples. The man had come up through the ranks as a Navy SEAL, winning a boatload of medals including the Navy Distinguished Service Medal, a Silver Star, two Bronze Stars and a Legion of Merit commendation before a sniper cut his career short in Mogadishu.

Stopped one trajectory but created a new one at EMA, also known as Elite Mission Alliance. EMA started as the U.S. government's strongest provider of translators and interpreters but quickly branched out to deliver a number of operational solutions for high-consequence missions. You name it, EMA was on speed dial for the Department of Defense, diplomatic corps, the Alphabet intelligence communities, law enforcement customers, as well as a select few multinationals and friendly foreign governments. Counter terrorism was a booming business, and EMA filled a very specialized niche.

They weren't grunts on the ground like some of the better known para-military organizations that blossomed under the Bush administration. Nothing so flashy or mercenary. Which is why Van had been happy with his position within the tight EMA ranks.

Sure his last mission, working with a contingent of NATO officers, went Fubar, but from everything he and his superiors had learned, Van had been the right operative in the wrong place.

Seems the druid and Weres who had abducted and tortured him were looking for any preternatural being who served in a U.S. military capacity with distinction. They had needed a test subject who would act against his nature, and his training, with the right combination of a designer drug and auto-suggestions.

Being preternatural in the military was the ultimate don't ask, don't tell approach and had been since George Washington's time. Rumor had it that Francis Marion, also known as The Swamp Fox, was a shifter. No doubt Benedict Arnold was a Were, the only type of preternaturals who'd betray their responsibilities for their own interests. Bottom line, only fools wasted good assets and Weres and shifters were damn good assets. They also tended to be the most populous of the preternaturals to serve, though there were a few Sisimites, Baldor and some types of fae in the Intelligence divisions, and maybe a vampire or two, but only as covert operatives.

Once captured in France, Van had been meant to die, but he'd proved tougher, or more stubborn, than his captors. A Noziak trait that had served him well more than once.

Technically, he was not yet back to full duty with EMA, not until the shrinks signed off on him. His shifter abilities made sure his body healed, though it'd taken longer than usual. The a-holes in Paris used a combination of designer drugs to saturate his system. Combine that with the amount of silver they used to restrain him, and he was damn lucky he wasn't dead. Use enough of that metal against a Were or shifter's skin and disability and death were inevitable.

The scars that were proving more problematic were the mental ones. Mind rape, which is what he'd been through for weeks, took a huge toll. Coming back from that meant Van was still regulated to light duties assigned from EMA's company headquarters off M Street in the capital.

Van had taken some leave to shadow Kelly McAllister in Sierra Leone. Another mission that went tits up almost immediately, but there'd been some good to come out of it, too. Kelly, who was too damn nice to be anything more than the school teacher she once was, had proved to be made of stronger stuff than he ever imagined.

He could appreciate that as he could appreciate a lot about Kelly — sweet, sexy and a smile that put the sun to shame. But that didn't mean she should be an IR operative. He had huge reservations about his sister Alex being one, but at least she had a very good reason to see her commitment through, and she was a witch, with enough magic to keep her mostly safe. But Kelly? Hell, the woman was a walking innocent waiting to die. He had no idea how Ling Mai coerced Kelly into working for the IR Agency, but it was wrong on every level; only her stubbornness kept Kelly from realizing that.

In less than a week he'd had to counter two different attacks on her, but at the rate she was getting into trouble with creatures she shouldn't even know about, it'd be sooner rather than later that he'd be attending her funeral. A thought that had his gut in knots and kept a low level burn of anger spiking through him.

Shoving the emotion behind a locked mental door, Van braced himself to find out what his Commander wanted. Kincaide was new to the squad, squeaky new, less than a week or so. As a result, Van was feeling his way with how the man worked and what he expected. Scuttlebutt was Kincaide expected a hell of a lot but backed his operatives to the hilt and didn't ask anything more from his men than he hadn't already done himself. A good starting point as far as Van was concerned. Besides, as soon as his appointment with the shrink, scheduled for the following week, took place, Van expected to be assigned back to the front lines.

Exactly what he wanted.

And Kelly?

Not going to think about Kelly.

Like that was possible. School teacher had gotten under his skin, badly. Didn't mean she had to sidetrack him. No woman had since, hell since Amber, and she'd been in high school. His dad said that shifters, once they'd chosen a mate, mated for life. Too bad the old man hadn't explained what a living hell it could be when the chosen mate didn't reciprocate. With Van's mom ditching the family, and his dad, when Van was about eleven, his dad had to have known first hand what it meant to have your heart ripped out and pulverized.

Like father, like son. Once destroyed, forever wary. Van only had to remind himself of that around Kelly and it should work. The fact it hadn't so far was an aberration, nothing more. Might even be a lingering side effect of whatever the hell drugs the druid had pumped into him in Paris. Once the last of that was flushed out of his system, Kelly could become just a friend of his sister's. Nothing more.

A friend with benefits?

Not that rule-follower Kelly was the type, but if she quit denying the sparks between them, who knew.

He was actually smiling as he grabbed the straight back chair in front of Kincaide's desk, sat down and waited for the man to finish signing documents before spearing Van with a cut-to-the-chase gaze.

"You clear for full duty yet?" the man asked, though Van had no doubt he already knew the answer.

"Physical docs have signed off. One more visit to the head docs and I'll be fit to go."

"Good." Kincaide anchored his elbows on his desk, steepling his fingers like a church roof.

Van waited. Whatever the man was thinking about, no amount of rushing was going to push him to act, or speak until he was good and ready. Another tidbit Van had learned from his fellow operatives, mostly Mick Sweringen, a pal from way back.

Mick enjoyed his duty station being stateside and the nightlife D.C. offered. It'd been good to connect with his bud and also fun to josh the other guy into considering getting back into field ops. The man was a natural; he just needed enough of a nudge to remember that.

Kincaide cleared his throat and Van sat up straighter.

"I might have a small diplomatic op tailor-made for you," the older man said, his eyes narrowing, eyes a cloudy shade of grey that made Van feel like he was peering into deep, dark shadows.

"You took your leave in Africa," Kincaide stated, changing the conversation — a standard tactical maneuver when getting the feel for another. But again, not new intel.

"Yes."

"And it appears you know a bit about this new agency Ling Mai has started up."

Nerves heated Van's skin but he simply nodded. The IR Agency wasn't that old, or well known, so what was up? "Some."

"You know the director herself?"

"We worked some ops together in the Far East, years ago." Hell, Van had been a raw recruit with a facility for languages. Veteran Ling Mai taught him how to navigate the nuances of a foreign country where he stood out like a bull in a herd of sheep. He owed her and, except for her asking him to keep an eye on Kelly recently, she'd never called in any favors. In fact, she allowed her team to help extradite him from the druid in Paris. As if Alex gave Ling Mai any options. But she did lend support to take down the druid and stop a dangerous preternatural predator from materializing. Van wasn't about to hang Ling Mai out to dry. From Kincaide's tone, that might be exactly what he wanted.

"I see," Kincaide murmured, though his eyes said otherwise. "And you have a relative working for this agency."

A statement, not a question. This man held direct command of one of four subcommands with maybe two hundred active duty personnel and at least half that of support and reserve personnel. He had six to eight direct tactical commanders under him whose duties were to handle day-to-day operations, training, deployments and actual field operations. Van would expect his direct duty commander to know who he was and the details of his background, but not the guy behind the desk. The fact Kincaide did set off some alarms. But not red flag go-to-ground alerts. Yet.

Van kept his response even-toned. "Yes."

"A sister."

"Yes." What was Kincaide fishing for?

"How close are you to her?"

What the hell kind of question was that? Close enough he'd die for her and she'd almost died for him. The fact he'd been the one to nearly kill her he'd have to live with for the rest of his life, in spite of her blowing that detail off. Alex was far quicker to forgive him than he was to forgive himself.

"Close enough," came his non-committal answer.

"Know anyone else on their team?"

Kelly. No way was he going to pull her into the Commander's sights.

"Not well." An evasion, but until he knew better he'd err on the side of caution.

Kincaide opened a folder squared with the angles of his desk and pulled out a photo. He pushed it toward Van, waiting for Van to glance at it before asking, "You recognize this girl?"

How closely had Kincaide been monitoring Van? Of course he recognized the image. It was the girl, Aini, that Kelly had befriended, protected and, when the girl had a seizure that left her in a coma, arranged to have brought back to the States for medical care. If Aini was involved in trouble, it meant Kelly was, too.

Why wasn't he surprised?

"I've met her," Van offered. Then, in case Kincaide thought Van was trying to hide something, he added, "Name of Aini."

"Only one name?"

"Far as I know."

"Do you know where she is currently?"

Van shrugged, back on safer ground. "She'd slipped into a coma. Last I heard, she was at Georgetown Medical Center. I haven't kept tabs on her any more than that."

"Do you know what caused the coma?"

Van shook his head. "No idea."

"But you were there when it happened." Statement again, not question and the commander knew way too much for this to be a casual conversation.

"Yes. We were all taken by surprise."

"We?"

"There were several of Ling Mai's agents on hand." Don't single out Kelly. Bringing her name up would only muddy already murky waters. "A few Sierra Leone locals, one CIA contact."

"I see."

If he did then he was alone, because Van was in the dark. Still, he waited. It never paid to volunteer too much information, even when you were on the same team.

"If I asked you to find out where this girl is now, would you be able to do that?"

"She's no longer at the hospital?"

That explained the call Kelly had received. Might also explain who was attacked. Van's shifter hearing had caught that much, but he'd been more focused on what new mess Kelly had stumbled into than in listening until it was too late to catch more than a few words.

The older man cracked a half-smile, one that changed the symmetry of his face, made him almost charming. Van didn't trust charming. Give him a chew-your-ass drill sergeant any day over a senior officer hiding an agenda behind a hail-thee-well smile. "My apologies. I haven't been forthcoming."

So Van wasn't the only one who noticed that.

"This girl was removed from George Washington earlier today."

Van still waited, even though he was tempted to ask if that meant Aini had recovered enough to leave. Otherwise, there had to be a pretty good reason to shift a comatose girl from the GW facility.

"She's still in a coma," Kincaide answered Van's thoughts, though he knew he'd kept his face blank. So blank most of his fellow operatives wouldn't play poker with him anymore.

Interesting that Kincaide had no trouble reading him, or made an assumption that was logical. So where was the girl? Ling Mai had most likely secreted her somewhere. But where? And who knew?

The Commander opened the folder again and pulled out another image. This one of a young man, probably early to mid-twenties, narrow face, skin the deep black of some native-born Africans, especially those of the equatorial countries. Between the grainy image and the expression on the man's face, Van would have guessed this was a surveillance photo taken without the man's knowledge. Still, it managed to capture personality as well as a physical likeness. Wariness, cunning, a hint of brutality lurked behind the eyes of this stranger.

"Do you recognize this man?" Kincaide asked, his own gaze direct.

Van took a second look to be sure then shook his head. "No."

"His name is Haroun Keita."

Meant nothing to Van.

The Commander looked at the photo again as if waiting for it to speak. When Van held his silence the older man continued. "Haroun Keita has ties to several known terrorist organizations, including working closely with Al-Shabab's leader Ahmed Godane."

"He's Somalian, right? Involved in the mall attack in Kenya?"

Kincaide nodded. "Yes. His recent attacks have shown he's willing to export his crimes to a larger transnational audience rather than limit his activity to his native country."

Van still wasn't sure what any of this had to do with Ling Mai, Alex, the IR Agency, Kelly or Aini.

Kincaide proceeded. "Haroun Keita started as a courier in his early teens. More recently his name's been linked to planning several events throughout Africa, especially through the Sahel-Sahara region."

The man paused as if waiting for Van to pick up and run with what he's just shared. "Sorry, Sir," Van admitted when the silence stretched thin. "I'm not seeing the correlation between Ling Mai's Agency, Aini and this..." He pointed to the last image. "This Haroun Keita person."

Kincaide flashed a shark smile before answering. "Did I neglect to mention this Haroun Keita is your Aini's brother?"

The trap door opened and Van had walked right into it. *Bend over, here it comes again.*

First off, the girl wasn't his Aini at all. If anything she was Kelly's kettle of worms, and a sticky mess it was.

Van kept annoyance out of his tone. "News to me."

"Understood." Kincaide leaned back in his chair. "But we seem to have a problem."

"Being?"

"Homeland Security suspects that Haroun Keita has entered the U.S."

SSDD. *Same shit, different day.* This Keita wouldn't be the first to slip through the nets, nor the last, so what was up?

"He's here and is suspected of operating toward two goals."

Van waited, expecting the boot to drop at any moment. Drop and ass kick him in the process.

"The first is a possible attack against a soft target but one taking out as many civilians as possible."

"Any idea where or what kind?"

"Markers point to the greater D.C. area."

No big surprise.

"An attack on the mall, a parade, who the hell knows what." Frustration coated Kincaide's words. Van didn't blame him. Since nine-eleven, most of their missions involved reactive assignments. Multiple intel agencies shoveled through an overwhelming mass of information to pick out minute pieces of a larger puzzle. They'd then pull the information together and try to stop some bastard or bastards from killing for a cause that was as vague as the leads produced. Dancing with the boogieman and the boogieman always had the lead. Always.

"How does this involve me?" Van asked, figuring that tracking and neutralizing a target was just up his alley. Even if he hadn't yet been cleared for active duty. Shifter abilities helped, but so did experience and Van had a boat load of experience doing just this kind of assignment.

"I haven't mentioned the second target Haroun Keita has in his sight," Kincaide said, closing the folder.

Van waited until he wanted to reach across the desk and shake his superior officer. Not a great approach to remaining with the EMA agency.

Kincaide cleared his throat. "We suspect Keita's also after his little sister."

Which meant this douche bag would be headed directly toward Ling Mai, Alex and Kelly.

The solution was easy enough. He just had to convince Ling Mai, with or without Kelly's help, to remove Aini from under the IR Agency's care.

Piece of cake.

CHAPTER 13

Van should have seen this coming. Even in Sierra Leone he'd warned Kelly against mother-henning a trio of abandoned kids. But would she listen? No. Stubborn and foolish. A sure recipe for disaster. In spite of what she'd like to think, she wasn't experienced enough of an operative to leave her bleeding heart at home, and it was going to get her killed one of these days.

If Van was smart he'd take this as a red flag warning and keep his distance. Too bad it might already be too late to heed that thought.

Kincaide tapped one finger against the closed file on his desk before looking up at Van. "I want you to use your connections with Ling Mai and any of her agents to locate this girl."

Something was off here, but Van couldn't put his finger on it. That, or he no longer trusted his hunches, given the last one led him into an ambush. So he asked, "Shouldn't this be handled peer to peer, Sir? A quick call to Ling Mai?"

The look Kincaide shot him was deserved. Who the hell was he to suggest an alternative to a superior officer's direct order. Instead of taking his head off, which is what the darkening of the man's eyes threatened, Kincaide uttered a casual laugh. Casual but forced. "We all know that Intelligence Agency heads can be ... territorial."

That was the truth, and it wasn't unusual for that defensive instinct to filter down through the rank and file. Calling Ling Mai territorial was spot on, though she was no more protective

of her turf and her missions than any other person in her
position.

"I'm looking for two things. " Kincaide leaned forward,
adopting a man-to-man tone. "I don't want to raise Ling Mai's
hackles. Elevate what can be a quick in and out operation to a
level of Commander to Director right off the bat. That doesn't
give us much room to maneuver."

True that.

"Plus I'd like you to approach the girl directly. Feel her out
on her relationship with her older brother, where he might be
headed, anything to flesh out the scant picture we have."

Van hesitated, then took the plunge. "Not causing waves
here, Sir, but even if Ling Mai knows where the girl is…" most
likely but not proven, "there's still the matter of Aini being in a
coma. That and Ling Mai allowing me, an operative from
another agency, to interrogate her—" What the hell was Aini?
Not a guest. Not a prisoner.

The girl supposedly knew something about the Seekers,
which sounded like a plot from some comic book of the 50's. If
the druid who'd held Van hadn't been the one mentioning this
unknown threat, Van would have discounted them totally. He
had mentioned them in his after action report though, even if he
glossed over the fact they might not be human. A threat was a
threat. Forewarned meant more survivors. So was that the tie in
here? The Seekers?

With his shifter ability to scent out preternaturals and
identify almost all of them, given they'd crossed tracks more
than once, Van was sensitive to threats most humans didn't
even know about. Kincaide was clearly human. Being human,
did Kincaide even know of the alleged preternatural threat?
Not likely.

Better bet was to take Kincaide at his word. This op might
be just what Kincaide indicated; a terrorist seeking the
whereabouts of his sister. Whether Keita might do this before
or after wreaking ruin on hundreds was unknown. Only known
element was the tie between Aini and Keita.

"I'm counting on your connections and your experience to
finesse a way to speak to this girl as soon as she is awake."
Kincaide's tone sounded calm but his nostrils flared. He

obviously was not as even-keeled as he wanted to appear. "Talk to your sister. Use the contacts you have. Just get as much intel as possible."

"Yes, Sir." Van knew when a direct order was etched in stone. He stood, pausing. "Anything else, Sir?"

The Commander looked away before answering. "Yes. Find out anything more you can about this Aini. All we know is her name and approximate age. Any other relatives? Here or back in Africa? And family friends that her brother might tap into, you know the drill."

"Yes, Sir."

"Act as quickly as possible." Kincaide was already directing his attention back to other papers on his desk, dismissing Van.

"Yes, Sir. Right away, Sir."

What had Kelly done this time? And how was he going to keep her safe from her own actions?

CHAPTER 14

I paced the twelve steps between Aini's bed and the room's only window, a barred one looking out to a courtyard which might have been charming once upon a time but now looked pathetic and neglected, especially as the evening shadows deepened. Go figure. There wasn't enough time to do everything, and gardening wasn't high on anyone's agenda. Pick and choose your priorities as my mom, or my ex-mom, would have said. Who had ex-moms?

Losers.

Swallowing a sigh I glanced back at where Aini lay so still. If it wasn't for the beeping of the monitors which kept her breathing, fed and alive, it'd be easy to believe she wasn't there at all. Not dead so much as like a princess at rest. Sort of a modern day Sleeping Beauty.

Had I really gotten to the level of fanciful thinking about fairy tales? Much more time trapped inside these sterile white walls and I might start howling, just to break the monotony.

I'd been sitting next to Aini for hours, talking to her, holding her hand, asking her questions as if she could answer, and a big fat nothing. How long did Vaughn expect me to stay here? Out of sight, out of mind.

Now, why didn't that make me feel easy?

Just then my phone vibrated, startling me. I was glad I'd muted the ringer or I'd be peeling myself off the ceiling.

A quick glance had me wondering if I should just let the call go to voice mail.

Van.

Which reminded me I needed to ditch this phone and get a new one. Ready for another lecture on safety and being naïve? Or, and this had me even more wary, about the two of us getting together. The date he'd asked for and I'd been avoiding.

'Scaredy cat.

So what was new?

On the other hand, if Vaughn hadn't contacted him yet, I could let him know to watch his back given his tie-in to Aini. One as nebulous as mine, but if I was a target, he might be, too.

I punched answer and squared my shoulders. If I was fighting to stay an agent I'd better get used to acting like one. "Van?"

"Kelly?"

"You called me. Isn't that who you were expecting?" Yes, that was testy, but testy beat being a quaking mouse, which is what Van could easily reduce me to in minutes.

He paused. "Is something wrong?"

"No. Why should there be?" Except for the whole being attacked thing earlier in the day.

"Fine. Forget I asked." So two could do testy.

"Has Vaughn called you?" I asked, aware of my pounding heart.

"Yes. Tempest in a teakettle."

Not that I expected any other response from him. I was supposed to run and hide according to him, but him? Business as usual.

I waited, catching myself tapping my shoe on the floor, knowing full well that Van called for a reason. But which one?

"Where are you?" he asked at last, and I could see him running his hand through his hair. Something he didn't do often, except when he was holding on to his patience.

"Why?" I knew he wasn't fully back on active duty with whomever he worked for — Alex had shared that much. I wasn't either for that matter. Not until I'd finished PT for my hand, but regardless, he should know, speaking agent to agent, that asking even the simple questions could be out of bounds.

"I want to know you're okay. See if I can meet you."

"Why?" Now I was sounding like a cranky toddler, but in spite of what Van had indicated before, about wanting to get together as a couple, I was sensing something else going on. Plus that whole he got to worry about me but there was no reason for me to worry about him issue.

"Kels, why the third degree?" His tone pushed.

And he was right. I was acting like he was one of the people gunning for me when, if it weren't for his earlier intervention, I might not even be here to be having this conversation.

"Sorry," I murmured, glancing away from the window to look at Aini again. He'd helped her too, protecting her for my sake. "What do you need?"

"To meet."

"I'm not in a position to really leave."

"Thirty minutes. That's all."

Vaughn had said to sit with Aini to see if she'd wake up. She hadn't said I couldn't walk away for a short period to eat or take a breather. But last thing I would do was leave Aini vulnerable, especially for a relationship rendezvous.

Van must have heard my hesitation. "I need to share something. About Aini."

That kick-started me into high alert. "What about her?"

"Not over the phone."

Could he have intel to share with Vaughn and the team? A strong possibility. But why hadn't he said as much to Vaughn if he'd spoken to her?

"If you have something to tell Vaughn about Aini, why didn't you?"

"Didn't know what I know now when we talked." He dismissed my question that easy before continuing, "Are you at the Compound?"

What harm was there in answering that. It wasn't a closely guarded secret. "Yes."

"Good. There's a small diner down the road a bit."

"The Delaney?"

"Yeah. I'll see you there in fifteen minutes."

He hung up before I had a chance to answer. Arrogant? Yes. Or he was that certain that I had no choice. If he knew anything behind the attack on Aini, or the attack on me, it made perfect sense that I meet with him. Doing so in person meant no one monitoring one or both of our calls. Which meant what he had to share mattered.

A quick call to the nurse monitoring Aini so she could stand in for me for the time I'd be gone, a message left for Vaughn as to my whereabouts, and I was in my Jeep Rubicon gunning down the road, hoping that I wasn't making a big mistake.

CHAPTER 15

The Delaney was one of those neighborhood institutions that changed hands every few years, probably since it was first built in the thirties when the back roads were the main roads. The one story building sprawled, chunks having been built on as needed, with the busiest and largest section being the bar with several big screen TVs. I doubted Van was there, as trying to talk over the noise, especially if there was an important game on, was impossible. For some guys that was every game. Like a sliver festering under the skin, I realized how little I knew about Van. Was he one of those guys? Into sports? If so, what kind? How could I know so little about him and still feel like I knew him. Or did I?

Since those thoughts weren't getting me any closer to figuring out what he knew of Aini, I stuffed them into the deal-with-later part of my brain, a part that was getting more and more compartmentalized and scooted through a rabbit warren of rooms until I came to the back patio.

It was not yet full dark out and, with strategically placed propane heaters, the patio seating was nice. And private. Which is why I wasn't surprised to see Van sprawled in one of the far wrought iron chairs, his back to the building.

At first glance he looked casual, but I could tell he was anything but relaxed. He'd pushed his chair at an angle so that he could quickly launch himself if necessary, one hand tapping on the tabletop, the other loose at his side, no doubt a concealed weapon handy. His gaze was sharp, especially as he spotted me.

I was glad it'd take me a minute to wend my way through other empty tables to reach him. Enough time to get my head into the game, the agent game, and forget the way just seeing him made my breath hitch, my pulse pick up its pace. And that's before my gaze collided with his.

Man, he packed a punch. Sexy dark bedroom eyes only showing brown, which meant his wolf self was well controlled.

Not that I feared his wolf. I'd been with Van in a number of life or death situations and, while his wolf might have wanted to be released, Van had way too much mastery over both sides of himself to allow that to happen.

I nodded at him as I grabbed the chair opposite, glad to see a glass of ice water in front of me. Something to keep my hands busy.

"Thanks for coming," he said, waving the waiter over. Two civilized adults meeting for a casual get-together.

"Did I really have a choice?" So I wasn't that casual. Pinch me.

He managed a wry grin that revealed one dimple and softened the planes of his face, though his was not a gentle appearance at any time. His Shoshone ancestry was evident, in the line of his bones, the tilt of his eyes, the tan of his skin. But there was more. He carried the honed and hardened look of a true warrior, as if all the softness had disappeared from him, as if his being had been forged in fire.

It made a woman look twice, a wary woman to hesitate, and a smart woman to pause and consider before getting involved with him in any way. Like a predator animal, this man would never be easy to be with, but for the right woman, he'd be as solid as they came, true and consistent, and a man you could trust to the end of your days to watch over you.

Was I that woman? We hadn't even begun to explore that possibility, for a number of reasons. From what his sister Alex had said, he was damaged goods. By another woman? Yes, compounded by what he'd been willing to do for his country and for the greater good. That required a toll that isolated those who chose that path.

I'd been an agent for only a few months and already I knew my world-view would never be the same. Taking things like security and the kindness of others for granted was a part of my old life. Not anymore. And that didn't factor in knowing now how many *others* lived among us. Preternaturals and those humans with extra abilities. Like me up until a few weeks ago.

Sweet and innocent me was long gone. Which is why I waited for the waiter to take an order for two burgers. Van insisted I eat, though I didn't feel all that hungry. But it wasn't worth winning the small skirmish when I was already bracing myself for a larger battle.

Only one of the reasons it'd be hard to discover if what sparked between us was worth fanning rather than ignoring.

"You have information?" I jumped in first, making sure no one was close enough to hear.

"I need to know where Aini is." He kept his gaze on his one hand resting on the table. Less threatening than a direct scrutiny.

I caught myself wanting to physically pull back, so I held myself still. "Why? Who wants to know?"

"Her life may be in danger."

He hadn't answered my second question. Plus I already knew she was in peril, but how did Van know?

"She's safe."

Two porcupines warily dancing around one another.

He released a sigh and sat back, a shadow casting sharper angles across his face, making it harder to read than usual. I expected him to push — it's what he did best — but instead he threw me when he nodded his chin at my throat. "How is it?" he asked.

I raised fingers to touch my bruises before I realized I'd done so. "Fine." Both of us knew it was a lie. It hurt like all get out, but we weren't here about my health.

"Tell me what you know about Aini," I said.

A corner of his mouth quirked up. A reluctant smile that winked his dimple so fast it had come and gone before it changed his expression. An expression that was all business as he spoke. "Did you know she has a brother?"

"She said she was alone." I recalled a very brief conversation we'd had back in Sierra Leone. Should I have pushed then for more answers? Not really. She'd said she had no one. Why should I interrogate her?

"Alone can apply to a lot of situations."

Was he talking about her or us now? Us here — together but growing further and further apart as the seconds ticked past. There was a tension in him that hadn't been there earlier in the day. What caused it? What or who?

I cleared my throat, focusing back on the reason we both were here. "Are you saying Aini has a relative? Alive? Looking for her?"

"There's a strong possibility," came his noncommittal response.

Thankfully the burgers arrived before I could lean forward and smack him for being so obtuse. This was Van, the agent. The side of his personality I hadn't seen a lot of so far. His wariness, caution and control were by-products of his chosen career and were as much a part of him as his coal black hair and his toned body. Even as I was saying my mental thank yous for us currently not navigating the murky waters of our *relationship*, I wasn't so sure I liked being on the end of his interrogation, either.

He waited until I'd taken a couple of bites of my burger, nibbles that felt fist-sized and closed off my throat. "I need to talk to Aini."

So Van knew about the attack and the fact we'd moved her to the Compound? Or maybe he was just fishing? And how'd we jump from see to talk to Aini? "I can't arrange that."

"You can try."

What was going on? He knew what Ling Mai would think of this request, absent or not. I doubted Vaughn would feel otherwise. His sister was an agent. Why not ask her? Alex would be in the same boat I was, the no-power-or-authority boat, but he should know someone higher on the food chain than Alex or I needed to give permission to even consider such a request.

"Ignoring the whole Aini's in a coma bit, why are you asking me?" I'd set my burger down, knowing I'd choke for sure if I ate any more. "Why not go to Ling Mai? There are proper channels."

"Yes," he nodded, looking no happier than I was, "but we also know that the higher up the food chain you go to take an action, the more ways and means people have to say no."

"Why should Ling Mai say no, unless there's something more at stake here?"

I might be a relative newbie as an agent but I'd dealt with people and their agendas, clear and hidden, for a long time. You didn't attend parent-teacher conferences semester after semester without learning a whole lot about tactics and strategies.

Van flattened his hand along the tabletop, the same as a fist slammed by another, before he glanced up at me. "There's a strong chance Aini has this brother."

So he'd implied. That should be good news. She wasn't alone in the world. But Van wasn't smiling. He simply looked at me as if waiting for something.

"What's wrong with having a brother?"

"He's a suspected terrorist."

And that fast my stomach took a swan dive. "Suspected or known?"

"Known."

Okay, not good. There had to be more though. "Where is he?"

"We don't know."

I picked up on the plural 'we.' So Van *was* on an operation.

"In the U.S.?" Which could explain his hesitation.

He gave a silent nod.

I sat back, wrapping my arms around me, aware of the sudden chill creeping through me.

"The attack on Aini in the hospital might have been her brother," he said, as if I couldn't connect the dots.

"There's no way this brother can find her where she is now. She's safe."

"For how long?"

"What do you mean?"

"Get real, Kels. After Aini collapsed back in Sierra Leone, arrangements were made to bring her here. How many people knew she was coming to the States? To D.C.? Even to which hospital? How many forms have been filled out with your or

Ling Mai's name attached to them? And when she left the hospital, how many people were aware who she was last seen with? We live in a world that makes it very hard to hide a paper trail. Or a person."

The temperature plummeted another ten degrees.

But I wasn't ready to concede defeat yet. Besides, there was a big speed bump in his logic. "You think he ... this brother would go to such lengths to find her after leaving her on her own in Africa? Just to kill her? That makes no sense."

Sure, he was thinking like an operative, I was thinking on a more human scale. If Aini didn't mention this sibling it was probably because they weren't close. Someone who left for a cause didn't necessarily keep solid tabs on family members, otherwise he'd have helped her after the death of their parents. But he didn't. So why now? Coming to a strange country and expecting to navigate the technological pathways to track her down? What were the chances? Besides, the nurse had been the one who attacked Aini. Why did Van know about the attack but not about the nurse?

Van glanced away. "Let's say this brother did want to find her. With his connections and agenda, he could, not worrying about who he'd take out in the process."

The hard whomp of my heart alerted me that now we were getting closer to the real issue.

"I'll repeat," I said, surprised I could keep my tone as level and calm as I did. "Aini's safe. I'll relay your concerns to Ling Mai." When she returned. I'd share with Vaughn in the meantime. "Meanwhile we'll take the necessary precautions to protect our charge."

He sighed, not a patient sound. "I still would like to see her. Talk with her when possible."

"I'll run it pas—"

"Damnit, Kels." Van sat up straighter, the gloves off. "Don't you realize the danger you could be in? That you're putting Aini, Alex, and yourself, as well as everyone at the Agency, at risk?"

I leaned forward, my voice lower. "What do you want me to do here, Van? Roll over and say, by all means, walk all over the IR agency, please waltz in and interrogate a traumatized coma patient? Ignore my chain of command so your superiors will be happy?"

He shook his head as if I was the one being difficult. "Just tell me where she is then. That's all."

"If the positions were changed, Van Noziak, and I was asking *you* to reveal someone secreted away for their own protection, what would you be doing? Throwing open the doors and sharing everything because you liked someone's sexy smile and their dimple?" I was practically frothing at the mouth, until I saw the gobsmacked expression on Van's face.

"What'd you just say?"

"I said no." What part of this didn't he get?

He scrubbed his hands over his face before he eased his shoulders down and took a new tactic. "I don't want to fight you, Kelly. I want to help you."

"You want to help yourself more." I so was not going to be sweet talked by this man, even if his new approach made me aware how close we were sitting to one another, how so much between us was unresolved, and how easy it'd be to lean in and taste those lips of his again. A taste I hadn't forgotten since our first, and only kiss, a little over a week ago.

The shift of his gaze from my eyes, to my lips, told me I wasn't the only one struggling on several levels.

I rose to my feet, bracing my legs to keep from shaking. "Thank you for the meal." The one unwanted and half-eaten, left on the table. "But I've got to be getting back."

"To Aini?"

"You want to know about Aini, you ask Ling Mai." I didn't tell him he'd have to track her down first. Good luck with that.

"It won't stop here," he said, rising to his own feet. "Don't make this a pissing contest, because you won't win."

I had no doubt he was right. Just as I had no doubt this was an opening salvo, not a battle won.

What I didn't know as I walked away, my spine rigid, my mind whirling, was if Van was warning me? Or threatening me?

CHAPTER 16

When I returned to the Compound I debated reporting to Vaughn immediately or returning to Aini's side.

I didn't choose either of those options as I saw a familiar figure slip between the shadows heading from dorm to cafeteria.

Hop-skipping to catch her, I called out, "Alex, wait up."

She paused, her look wary as I joined her on the graveled pathway.

"What's up?" she asked.

"You talk to Van lately?"

Even in the half-light I could see one brow arch, a very effective look Noziaks must have learned in the cradle. "Why?"

"Good grief, what is it with you two?" I snarled. "Is there some rule about not answering a direct question?"

"Us two? As in Van and me?"

"Of course, who else would I be talking about: stubborn, thin-skinned, think-you-are-the-only-ones-who-can-protect-the-world Noziaks." I sounded like a raving lunatic but I'd been pushed to my limit.

"I hope you're only describing Van and not me," came Alex's measured response.

"Just tell me. Has Van talked to you about Aini?" There, I couldn't be more direct.

She shook her head. "No." She paused then cocked her head as if studying me before adding, "Do I get to ask why you're asking without getting my head bitten off?"

"Sorry." The word escaped before I could rein it in. Part of the old Kelly response, even if I meant it. "Didn't intend to go postal on you. Just had the strangest conversation with your infuriating brother."

Alex went still, as if I'd just told her I'd been skinny-dipping with Van after wild monkey sex.

"Trust me, there was nothing personal about the conversation." All the undercurrents, yes, but technically we'd only talked business.

Guess that's what Alex needed to hear, as her shoulders slid down from around her ears. "About Aini?"

"Yes." Then I thought about it. "Mostly."

"You want to speak in full sentences and let me know what's going on?"

"That's the problem. I don't know." It was the truth. "Van was pushing to talk to Aini—"

"Aini? In a coma Aini?" Both Alex's brows angled up now. Which made me feel better. If she was as confused by the request as I was, then I wasn't alone in wondering what Van's real agenda was. "Tell me exactly what he wanted to know?"

I ticked off on my fingers. "He wanted to know where Aini was, if he could talk to her, and if we knew she might have a brother who's a suspected terrorist who's searching for her."

Alex whistled. "Sounds like we need to talk to Vaughn."

"I'm supposed to be staying with Aini," I mentioned, already bracing to explain to Vaughn why I'd left my duty station to meet with Van.

"Later." Alex was already striding toward the Director's office.

She was right. Hiding out in Aini's room was not going to help the girl or the team. Plus Alex's response to my short summation of the conversation let me know I wasn't alone in worrying. Something was up. Until we found out what, we couldn't help anyone. Especially ourselves.

CHAPTER 17

We'd lucked out. Vaughn and Stone were in Ling Mai's
office talking when Alex and I knocked on the door.

It took a few deep breaths for me to repeat what had gone
down between Van and me, which led to a lot of sharp looks
being passed between Stone and Vaughn.

"What's going on here?" I said, tired of being kept in the
dark. I knew I wasn't on the same level as the three of them,
but my gut told me that whatever was happening involved Aini
and me. I just didn't see the connections.

"I'll call the rest of the team in," Vaughn said, rising from
her seat.

It was an answer, of sorts. There was something bigger
developing.

Less than fifteen minutes later the entire core team was
assembled in the conference room. Sitting in basically the same
seats we had been earlier: Jaylene, Mandy, and Nicki ranging
down the left, Stone, Alex and me on the right, with a very
somber Vaughn at the head of the table. It was getting late, but
not a hair was out of place on the woman. Not fair when I felt
like a wilted sun flower. Getting attacked might have explained
some of it, but more was caused by the unanswered questions,
the doubts, the worry, even if I wasn't carrying half the
responsibilities Vaughn carried while Ling Mai was away.

Vaughn nodded toward Mandy and Jaylene. "Can you tell
us what you discovered from the Librarian?"

Jaylene glanced at Mandy and then shrugged her shoulders.
"We got squat." Then before she got flack for not doing her

job, she quickly added, "because we couldn't find her. Neither hide nor hair."

Mandy jumped in. "And we looked. Just returned. No one we spoke to had seen the woman since—" Mandy jerked a thumb toward me, "since you spoke with her earlier today. Seems she abandoned her shift and hasn't returned phone calls."

"And you checked where she lives?" Vaughn asked, her tone indicating it wasn't an attack on the thoroughness of her operatives, just a T being crossed.

"Damn straight we did." Jaylene nudged Mandy. "Took a lot of hunting to even discover where her home was: a townhouse in Georgetown. No one there, and her nearest neighbor said the woman had come home in a flurry in the middle of the day, run into her place and left minutes later with packed bags."

Silence greeted Jaylene's words until Vaughn spoke. "I was afraid of that." She turned to Stone. "What do you have to report from the hospital?"

Stone shot a quick glance at me. "There were no other reports of a man, military or otherwise, visiting the MICU ward before Kelly did this morning."

That had me sitting up straight. "What? But—"

Stone raised one hand. "So I checked the security tapes."

Amen. First no proof that Aini spoke to me and now this? I was beginning to doubt myself.

"There was no visitor on the tapes either." Stone deflated my hopes.

Lord love a peanut, what was going on? I glanced between Vaughn and Stone, waiting for them to tell me they were joking, in spite of the seriousness of their expressions. Vaughn subtly shook her head as if saying, sorry Kels, we tried.

Then she threaded her hands together as if not trusting them to behave if she didn't. "Stone had a good idea to check the date time stamps of the video tapes."

"Meaning?" Alex beside me asked what I was afraid to ask.

"We could assume the nurse lied to Kelly, deflecting attention off of herself and on to a phantom person."

"Which would make sense if…" I looked around the table as I hit the one snag in the logic, "if Aini was dead before I entered her room."

"Which meant the mysterious stranger killed her and left." Alex followed my logic route.

"But since Aini was still alive, why bother?" I asked.

"Exactly." Vaughn jumped in. "Unless the nurse could point to something having been injected into one of Aini's IVs or a malfunction of one of the monitors being set up by this unknown stranger."

"And I'd be a witness to the fact someone had come and gone." Very plausible and very calculated. Which I had a hard time aligning with the woman I'd spoken with at the nurse's station. Then a thought struck me. "Except, if that were the case someone could quickly prove just what you did. That no one had, in fact, been there."

"They might have if they looked close enough." Stone cleared his throat. "It wasn't what we found as much as what we didn't find."

Don't do cryptic on me I wanted to shout as nerves jitterbugged through me. But I held my tongue.

Vaughn nudged Stone or he might have remained Sphinx-like indefinitely, or at least long enough to have me lunging across the table to shake him.

"There were several seconds of missing video footage," he said.

"The tapes were tampered with?" Jaylene asked.

"It'd take a lab technician to verify that, which we haven't had time to arrange." Vaughn glanced first at Jaylene then at me. "We have another theory."

I guessed she meant her and Stone.

Alex broke the strained silence. "And your theory is?"

Vaughn's gaze moved to Alex. "Aren't there cloaking spells, or magic, that can make a person appear invisible?"

Jaylene whistled. "You're thinking this visitor hid himself? Like Kelly Blue-eyes here can?"

I didn't say a word though I felt Alex stiffen beside me, the two of us thinking along the same lines. *Like I used to be able to do.*

"Another speed bump," I mused out loud. "Why tamper with the tapes if he could be invisible?"

"And why could the nurse see him if he was able to cloak himself?" Mandy asked.

One more good point. Vaughn glanced at Stone before speaking. "Here's exactly what we saw. The nurse raised her head and spoke as if to someone—"

"But no one was there," Stone broke in.

That had goose bumps skittering down my skin.

Vaughn continued. "A moment or so later the curtain to Aini's room rippled."

Stone added, "As if pushed aside."

"And you'd only have noticed it if you were closely looking for it."

"So you think someone really did go into Aini's room?" I rubbed my hands along my arms, though the chill I was feeling wasn't going to go away that easily.

"Yes." Vaughn and Stone spoke at the same time.

"Because there was another ripple about ten minutes later," Vaughn said.

"At about the same time there was a break in the time sequence on the tapes. And just a few minutes before Kelly arrived."

I was missing attackers right and left today.

"So someone really didn't want to be seen," Jaylene spoke up. "Even if they could do some creepy disappearing act."

Guess I now knew how Jaylene felt about my ability. As if reading death portents through her tarot cards wasn't just as creepy.

"What I don't get is—" Nicki broke through my petty thoughts, thank heavens. "—if there was actually a person in the room with Aini, and was a threat, why didn't he kill her then? No one would have been the wiser."

"Except for the nurse," I commented, then realized what I was saying. "The nurse and me, once she told me."

"Is that why she was killed?" Alex said. "And Kelly attacked?"

Something wasn't quite tracking here, but I couldn't put my finger on it. Maybe one too many Gordian knots to unravel today.

"Still doesn't answer Nicki's question." Mandy was playing devil's advocate, a role that suited her well. "Why didn't the intruder eliminate Aini?"

Alex spoke up. "Maybe he wasn't a threat to Aini as much as checking in on her, to make sure she really was in a coma or something."

"So the visitor might not have had anything at all to do with the later attack." Vaughn looked around as if waiting for someone to refute her idea.

Nicki jumped into the opening. "And the nurse took advantage of the stranger's arrival, and Kelly's stopping by, to use it as a smoke screen for her own attack."

"Part we're all forgetting here that matters —" Stone's tone dashed cold water on all of us. Which is probably just what we needed before we concocted too many more tangled theories "—is that whoever this visitor was, it's clear he was preternatural."

Jaylene whistled which Stone ignored as he continued. "If the nurse saw him—"

"When the security cameras could not," Vaughn finished his sentence.

Stone nodded. "Then he could both appear as a human, while not appearing substantial enough for detection by the video equipment."

Vaughn looked at me. "How had the nurse described the visitor?"

"Dark, short hair. Military ID and old soul eyes, like vets who'd returned from combat action." At least I think that's what she said. Said or implied. Which had me thinking. "Why choose that disguise?"

Mandy nodded. "As opposed to being a nurse or doctor or an orderly. Hell, lots of people walk around a hospital daily. People the nurse wouldn't have thought twice about seeing. Why bring attention to himself by stopping at the desk?"

"And flashing ID," Jaylene said. "It's like he wanted to be seen while he didn't want to be seen."

"Maybe he had no choice." I glanced around. "You know how sensitive hospitals are these days. Especially ones that handle a lot of VIP patients."

"Like George Washington." Jaylene was nodding now.

"The president?" Nicki asked, earning a groan around the table.

"No, like George Washington hospital." Jaylene didn't roll her eyes but I could tell she stopped with an effort.

"Exactly. So to find out exactly where Aini's room was or..." I was thinking about the first question I'd asked of the nurse, "or how her condition was, then someone would have to find a way to get that intel without drawing a lot of unnecessary attention to himself."

Nicki pressed her lips together. "Couldn't he have just called up and asked?"

I shook my head. "No. That kind of update isn't given out over the phone. But, what's more natural than asking if there'd been any progress in her coming out of a coma? It's exactly what I did this morning."

"Couldn't he have remained invisible, waited for the nurse to step away and then checked Aini's charts?" Nicki wasn't about to concede easily.

"Maybe he had," I mused out loud. "No telling how long he'd been waiting around, but we all know that in an Intensive Care Unit there's usually someone coming or going."

"Very interesting feedback," Vaughn summed up, pulling our attention away from the what-if possibilities to the here-and-now. "Let's combine what happened at the hospital with what Kelly has since learned."

I summarized Van's vague hints, hitting on the high points — Aini and a possible terrorist brother who might or might not be in the area — and sort of rushed over Van's wanting to talk to her. I didn't leave it out, but the bigger issue, to me, focused on the security, or lack of, for Aini here at the Compound and for all of us.

"How serious a threat did Van see this brother being?" Vaughn asked, obviously thinking along my same lines.

"He seemed pretty upset when I told him I couldn't arrange for him to visit Aini without Ling Mai's knowledge or permission." Then, before Vaughn could ask, I looked straight at her and added, "I didn't tell him she was away from the Compound. I figured he'd find that out if and when he contacted you."

"You sure it was Van Noziak you met with?" Stone's gaze suddenly locked with mine.

What kind of — oh, yeah, disappearing guy from the hospital. Didn't matter. Like it or not, it was Van. "No doubts that it was Van," I answered, aware my hands were knotted in my lap and several of my teammates were looking at me with questions in their gazes. Relationship questions, not threat assessment questions. "Besides, all it would take was a phone call to Van from me or Alex or Ling Mai, when she returns, to verify what he'd requested."

Vaughn looked at both Alex and me. "Did either of you make such a call?"

I shook my head as Alex mumbled, "No."

Talk about feeling like idiots in front of the whole team. Except we didn't know there was a possible Doppelganger wandering around. If that's what the man at the hospital was. Our first weeks of training Alex had to fight one, but she'd said they were pretty rare, too. They were some kind of death omens or something. And I don't think any of us had heard of a preternatural who could both assume another's shape *and* turn invisible.

"I called him," came Vaughn's next words, giving only one of the reasons she was left in charge. Figured she'd not take anything at face value.

"And?" I couldn't stand too many more unanswered questions.

"There was no answer and he hasn't returned my call."

"Would he know why you called, and not the Director?" The words slipped out before I could corral them.

"I indicated I was calling on behalf of Ling Mai," came the death knell response, the chance to go up the chain of command with Van's request, if it really was a normal request and not something else.

I told myself to breathe normally. There could be perfectly natural reasons he hadn't returned a call yet. It was late. He could be busy, or poor cell phone reception. Anyone who had tried to use a cell in D.C. quickly learned it was a hot-zone of dropped calls no doubt because so much monitoring of calls went on. The really amazing fact was that any communication happened at all. Yes, I was becoming more and more cynical by the minute and was also grasping at very thin straws.

Alex nudged me. "Van didn't say *not* to tell anyone what he asked?"

"No."

She looked at Vaughn. "He had to assume Kelly would bring back what she learned to us immediately upon returning."

"Your point?" Stone interjected, using his clipped someone's-in-trouble tone.

Leave it to Alex not to be fazed. "Maybe Van was using his request to visit Aini, who he knew was in a coma, as a smoke screen to share intel that he couldn't otherwise pass along."

"That the kid's brother was a fanatic and hunting for his little sis," Jaylene summed up in her straight-to-the-point way. "So we'd increase our security measures."

"Which we'll need to do regardless," Stone said, "given what you learned about the autopsies."

He was looking directly at Vaughn, who looked like she wanted to release a sigh but had been raised otherwise. Which she probably had been.

When she did speak, it was to the whole group. "The autopsy results have come back."

"That was fast." Jaylene's expression suggested she hadn't meant to speak out loud.

"Yes." Vaughn paused as if waiting for anyone else to speak before she continued. "Like the security tapes at the hospitals, the autopsies on both Officer Packard and the nurse revealed more by what wasn't there than what was."

"So what killed them?" Alex asked, her patience as tensile thin as mine.

"An embolism."

"Like a blood clot?" Nicki asked, while the rest of us just looked at each other.

"Yes." Vaughn's tone didn't change at all as she continued. "Usually an embolism occurs when one or more pulmonary arteries in a person's lungs become blocked. Usually, but not always, it can be caused by blood clots that travel to the lungs from the legs."

"But how likely is it that two different people suffer an embolism so close together?" Now I was the doubting Thomas.

"Exactly." Vaughn offered one of her well-done smiles. "Most humans have four pulmonary veins that emerge in sets of two from and toward the lungs."

And this mattered because?

Vaughn wasn't finished with her anatomy lesson. "Some people are exceptions and may have two to five veins leading from their lungs. The two left pulmonary veins can be united as a single pulmonary vein in about 25% of humans; the two right veins may be united in about 3% of the same population."

Waiting. Not patiently, as I caught myself chewing my lower lip.

"What was found in both the detective and the nurse was not only extreme blockage of all pulmonary veins but both victims were among the 3% of the population with a right vein union."

"What are the statistical chances of that happening?" Stone asked.

"Extremely rare. Both total vein blockage and the right vein issues." Vaughn glanced around expecting a response, but we all were digesting her news.

"Was Officer Packard preternatural?" I asked, remembering my ring heating when I approached the nurse that morning.

Vaughn cut her gaze to Stone who answered. "Yes. He was a shifter. It was felt that we needed preternatural protection in case the threat to Aini came from that direction."

Sound reasoning.

"But aren't shifters very hard to kill? Even in their human forms?" Mandy asked all of us in general, but looked at Nicki, the only shifter among us.

Nicki nodded. "Shifters can heal quickly, more quickly in their animal form, but we aren't invincible. Stop our brains, our hearts—"

"Or your lungs," Alex inserted, and she'd know, having four shifter brothers as well as a half-shifter father. "Which could explain why the damage was done to all four veins. A single vein and a shifter could morph into his animal self to heal if he had enough time."

"There was no indication that Officer Packard changed." Vaughn's words dropped like weighted stones in the room.

I broke the silence. "When I spoke to the nurse this morning, my ring heated, so she was preternatural, too."

"Any idea what kind of creature?" Alex asked.

I offered a partial shrug. "I assumed an elf, being a healer, but she could have been something else."

"If she was an elf, she might have been slightly more vulnerable than the officer, but elves are known to live long lives, centuries even, as they're not susceptible to a lot of the issues that kill humans." Vaughn was obviously much more on top of her preternatural studies than I was.

"Issues such as?" Nicki asked.

"They don't have heart attacks, cancer, catch communicable diseases. More elves die from releasing themselves than anything else."

"Which means what?" Mandy asked the question that was on the tip of my tongue.

"Elves tend to be very sensitive creatures, though there are exceptions. On the whole, though, they feel deeply. Living several generations and experiencing the deaths of others, the changes in society, wars and catastrophes, year after year, it eventually can become too much for them and they let go of life, allowing themselves to fade away."

Wow. Who knew?

Stone gave her a let's-get-back-on-task look. "So we have two preternatural deaths. Two unexpected, and statistically improbable, deaths linked by their proximity to Aini."

I was going to ask if there could be any other common threads, something, anything, except a teenage girl who couldn't defend herself, when Vaughn stepped in. "And then there are the tattoos."

That had me straightening in my seat.

"Both Officer Packard and the nurse bore the same unique symbol that Kelly drew for us earlier today."

All gazes slammed into me. I wanted to raise my hands to deflect them, even though there was little hostility, only confusion.

"So what do we have?" Vaughn grabbed the reins of the conversation, giving me a breather. She raised her hand to tick off on her fingers. "An attack on Aini." One finger down. "Two deaths that are tied to common threads — proximity to Aini, improbabity as to their cause of death, both victims were preternatural, and possessed the same tattoo."

"Did the autopsy show if the tattoos were administered pre or post death?" I asked, then added, "I don't recall the nurse having one when I saw her in the morning, but only after she died."

"Good point." Vaughn glanced at Stone. "I don't think we asked the coroner to specifically look at those tattoos. Will you follow up on that tomorrow?"

Stone nodded as Vaughn continued, three fingers still raised. "We have an unprovoked attack on Kelly by a man, and I'm using the term loosely, with the same tattoo as on the dead victims."

Made me realize how lucky I was to be alive right now, even if tired, battered and aching.

"The invisible, non-invisible visitor to Aini." Vaughn was down to one finger.

"And Van's sudden interest in Aini's whereabouts and safety," I added, not daring to glance at Alex.

Vaughn's last finger disappeared.

"Have we forgotten the appearance of Aini's supposed brother?" Nicki asked. "And could he be preternatural given that Aini is a seer?"

"No, we haven't forgotten him," Vaughn said, "which is why I've increased security patrols at both the front gate and along the perimeters, as well as outside Aini's room tonight. By tomorrow Stone will have drawn up a rotation schedule with every one taking a turn on duty, two at a time. We are under-staffed for this type of situation, but enough of the new recruits have abilities, which will make up for our limitations, at least in the short term. Nicki, I'd like you to make sure our newer recruits are tuned into the possibility of preternatural as well as human threats until we know what we're up against. We must find some more answers. We can't fight what we don't know or understand."

"Will you be calling Ling Mai back to the compound?" Nicki asked, saving the rest of us the trouble.

Vaughn paused, that split second before one plunged off a cliff. "No." The single word slid into the room like a blast of chilled air. "We're on our own until you're notified otherwise."

She rose to her feet, effectively ending the gathering. Not that there was a lot to say. What was Vaughn doing? It wasn't like we were a bunch of inexperienced agents, even though it felt like it at times, and we did have a contingent of new recruits and training teens. But still. If there was a terrorist hunting Aini, or this Horned One doing the same thing, shouldn't the Director be on hand? Or was that scaredy pants Kelly coming to the fore? Long day. The attack. Van pushing at me. Yeah, probably stress layered on concern. Tomorrow I'd have a better perspective.

Or not.

As if echoing my thoughts, Vaughn spoke. "Everyone get what sleep you can tonight, and be prepared to report in immediately after finishing breakfast tomorrow."

A general marshaling her troops.

As I walked past her, she cut a quick glance in my direction. "At first light, I want you to report to Aini's room, Kels. Remain there until I say otherwise. I'll have your meals delivered to you."

Wonderful. I understood needing to watch over Aini, but surely I wasn't the only one who could do that. Unless I was being kept isolated. But why?

Then I heard Vaughn direct Alex. "Try and reach your brother, Alex. Verify that he did indeed speak to Kelly and see if you can ascertain the level of threat against Aini, or more details about her brother."

Neither Alex nor I spoke as we headed down the hallway, both of us lost in our own worries. Her brother, Van, being the most immediate.

And he thought I caused problems.

CHAPTER 18

Van received the summons from Commander Kincaide at first light. It wasn't unexpected.

"Well?" the older man asked the minute Van reported to his office. Since there'd been no offer of a chair, Van stood at attention before his desk, aware of an increase in tension from yesterday. The grooves in the man's face were deeper, his frown clear.

"I contacted one of the IR agents but made little headway, Sir."

Kincaide slid a photo across the desk. One that had been resting beneath his clasped hands. "This the agent?"

Van cast a quick glance, recognized Kelly and was aware of the increase of his pulse. Kincaide wasn't holding back. "You had me followed, Sir."

There was anger beneath the question. A question that was out of line but not unwarranted.

Kincaide's eyes narrowed, two thin, small slits. Whether Kincaide responded to the tone or realized that Monday morning quarterbacking his agents, especially before they'd had a chance to fulfill orders, was not the way to build team loyalty.

The older man pointed to the chair still front and center to the desk. "Sit, Noziak."

Van did, his posture no less stiff than when standing at attention.

Kincaide's gaze lasered into Van's. "Look, son. You don't know me. I don't know you. So no need to get ruffled feathers until we learn how the other operates."

Van could accept that, easing his shoulders, but only by a bit. "Understood, Sir."

"You weren't being spied on," the man continued. "I had another operative doing preliminary reconnaissance on Ling Mai's compound in case your forays didn't produce results."

Things were more serious than Van suspected if the commander was going to such levels to scope out a fellow Agency. Ling Mai's agents worked directly for the U.S. Government, while EMA worked in a private capacity. Still they were kissing cousins in the Intelligence Community, so why the hell didn't the man just contact Ling Mai and discuss his concerns?

"You think this terrorist, this Haroun Keita, is that imminent a threat?" Van asked.

His boss looked confused for a moment before his face cleared and he waved one hand. "Were you there, son?" he asked.

"Where, Sir?" What was he talking about? The diner last night? The Compound?

"The Pentagon. Nine eleven."

Now Van could track the dramatic shift in the conversation, if not the reason for that shift. "No, Sir."

"I was." The man's voice sounded decades older. "Bad day. Really bad day. Lost good people that day. Good friends."

Van could understand the sentiment but wasn't following his superior's thought trajectory. Yet.

Then Kincaide murmured, "Only way to deal with a terrorist is to kill them before they kill you."

Van held his tongue. He wasn't here to debate approaches to terrorism containment. Plus he understood the power of lessons learned firsthand. Not only in war but in matters of the heart. Hadn't he spent years protecting himself given Amber's response to discovering his being a shifter?

Back on task, Noziak. Threat assessment, nothing more.

Kincaide cleared his throat and continued, "I don't want another Pentagon situation on my watch."

Van was tempted to give himself a swift kick. Where was his sense of focus? Of duty before all else? Get your head into the game, Noziak. "You think Haroun Keita will escalate to that level?" he asked.

"I have to think that." The man released a near-silent sigh. "That's my job, and yours. Plan for the worst. It's easier to reel back our response once we know where this chicken-shit coward is hiding."

"Yes, Sir." Van waited, knowing more was coming.

"Which is why I want you to push your contacts faster and harder. We're losing time."

Then why didn't the old man go directly to Ling Mai? Probably the same reasons Van hadn't. If she said no, and got her hackles up, that line of approach would be sealed off. Plus it could earn dire repercussions if Kincaide ordered a secondary, more direct approach. But if Van had only talked to Kelly or Alex, there was always the fall-back save-face reality of communication errors made by underlings. Van was being hung out to dry if this op went tits up.

Good to know. His gut didn't have to like it but better to know who your allies and who your enemies were, and right now Van held no doubts Commander Kincaide was not on the side of Van's supporters.

Wasn't personal. Even if it was, it didn't matter. Van was committed to follow direct orders and minimize the fallout to the Commander as much as possible.

"Anything else, Sir?" he asked, surprised he could sound so calm and level. The side benefit to working under more than a few a-hole leaders.

"I'll give you till eleven a.m. today, Noziak. If you can't find a way to prove this girl is holed up inside Ling Mai's compound I'll find another way to get the intel I need."

"Understood, Sir." Van rose to his feet and snapped a salute, though both Kincaide and he were no longer in the military. They might not wear regimental uniforms anymore but they both understood they were at war.

Only question was, were they both understanding which war they fought?

CHAPTER 19

I was considering shaking Aini to see if that might help break the sheer monotony of sitting in a silent room with a silent patient for hour after hour when my phone buzzed.

Not recognizing the number, I jacked my voice up to sound like just-another-day-being-a-super agent. "Kelly McAllister here."

"We must meet."

Why was that phrase getting a little old? Only this time it wasn't Van. It sounded like a ten-year old boy. As if I didn't have enough plates to juggle. "Who's this?" It was less a question and more demand. Only my team, and Van, had my number.

A pause on the other end told me the listener might be a little surprised at the response, or more likely the tone. Then he said, "The Librarian."

Yeah, right. I ignored the jumpstart of my heart as a way to treat this like the joke it probably was. At least I hoped it was.

"I'm hanging up now," I said, mostly because I'd been trained to be nice on the phone — to everybody, which was a pain in the backside when dealing with telemarketers.

"No, wait. It's imperative I speak with you."

What child spoke like that? I paused before I asked, "And I should believe you because?"

"You came to see me. Yesterday. And I left before we could finish our conversation."

So how many people knew that? Except for the team, and the Librarian herself. On the other hand a total stranger had followed me there, so he also could know.

"I need something more." Talk about walking through quicksand. Yes, the Librarian scared me down to my toes, but if I made a mistake, no telling what the consequences could be. "Can you tell me what you did after you left the Library? When you returned to your home?"

"When I—"

I could tell to the second when the person on the other end of the line realized that for me to even ask that question meant she or he had to have been followed.

The boy's voice sounded more wary when he spoke, probably realizing that if the IR agents tracked his whereabouts, others could, too. "I returned to my townhouse. Packed a few items and drove away."

In spite of my doubts about what kind of creature the Librarian was, given the change in voices, I had to give him the benefit of the doubt, if for no other reason than he had intel the team needed. That I needed.

Still, after one attack I was understandably skittish. "Can't we talk by phone?"

"No. It's too dangerous."

For whom? I glanced at Aini, realizing I was being asked to abandon my post, again, but this time Vaughn would know up front where I was going and why.

"What do you suggest?" I was happy I could keep my voice from shaking. Meeting with the Librarian last time hadn't worked so well for me.

"Bring the shifter. Second floor. Jefferson building. African and Middle Eastern Reading room. That's usually fairly quiet."

"What shifter?" I was already feeling out of my element from his first demand.

"The wolf, of course."

There was no 'of course' about any of this. Nicki was a shifter, a cougar, so it wasn't as if there was only one shifter hanging around. Still, better to be clear than to screw up what might be the team's only chance to get enough intel to protect Aini. "You mean Van Noziak?"

"Don't be slow-witted, Miss McAllister." I swore I could hear his sigh. "Do you know any other wolf shifters?"

No. But how'd he know that? I caught myself shaking my head, then realized he couldn't see me. "I'll try and contact him."

"Don't try. Do."

That yanked me back to my childhood home and my mother's voice lecturing me on how to stop turning invisible. Fat lot of good it did then. Or now.

"Be here in two hours," the Librarian continued as if I'd answered.

"I don't know if I can. Or if Van can. If I left right now the timing would be tight."

"Every moment is precious, Miss McAllister. Do not squander them."

Now he was just pissing me off. I was mulling over my options, which left a strained silence stretched between us.

"If you want to find the connection between the Horned One and the Seekers, you'll make every effort to be here. Two and a half hours. That's all I offer," he/she said and rang off.

Great. This kid had better really be the Librarian, and he had better spill the beans enough to justify dereliction of duty to Aini.

Saying a quiet "I'll be back" to Aini, I hustled down the hallway to summon the nurse to sit with the girl, find Vaughn, and track down Van. So much for today being less intense than yesterday. On the other hand I hadn't been attacked.

So why did I hear the echo of the word "yet" following that thought?

CHAPTER 20

Vaughn took the news like I expected — pragmatic to the core. She did suggest I take another agent with me but that would pull someone off sentry duty or research — tracking down more information on Aini's possible brother, the tattoos, and anything we could find on the Horned One. We could have used double the number of agents and agents-in-training we had, which I'm sure Vaughn and Stone were feeling way more keenly than I was.

So after swinging past the dorm room to pick up a Taser that was totally illegal to use, I went alone, hightailing it into D.C., for once not caught in Beltway gridlock. As soon as I could, I cut through Rock Creek Park, popping out near the Watergate and skirting George Washington University as I angled toward the Library.

I'd left a message for Van, telling him I'd meet him at the Union Station parking lot and would wait for him as long as I could, which wasn't long. It was a half-mile walk from the lot to the Library, but I was sure I could nab a space.

Pulling into the lot, I realized I was breathing fast, as if I'd run most of the way. A quick glance at my dashboard clock told me I had a few minutes to cool my heels for Van, but if he wasn't here pronto, I'd go without him.

No calls on my cell. No idea if he'd received my message, was blowing me off, or … yeah, it was that last unnamed worry, that something might have happened to him, that had me rubbing my hands against my jeans. But the repetitive, soothing movement wasn't going to tamp down the concern boiling just beneath the surface. Concern for Van.

Should I ring Alex to find out if she'd tracked him down? Or was that opening a can of worms I'd best avoid for now?

Assume the best.

Besides, last thing I wanted to be doing was explaining to Alex that it was the Librarian, not me, who wanted Van in on this meeting. A meeting I wasn't even sure was legit. Vaughn had questioned that fact, too. Except the moment I mentioned the Librarian sounded like a young boy, she seemed reassured. Who knew?

I got out of my jeep, hugging the backpack containing my sole defensive weapon, should I need it, handy. I glanced around. No Van.

He was fine. He was busy. He was angry because I wouldn't help him last night.

The squirrels in my brain were on overdrive as I wandered toward the edge of the lot, seeing no one that remotely resembled Van.

His loss.

Please let it be nothing more.

Straightening tense shoulders, I headed south on First Street, a straight shot to the Jefferson Building. Was it only yesterday I'd been here? Trust me, I was keeping a wary eye on my surroundings and every person in the area. A few were preternatural, judging by my warming alert ring. Not surprising. Preternaturals and power often went hand in hand, at least in my recent experience. I bet at night the vamps would be out in full force, as they seemed to enjoy the game playing of politics.

It took a little over ten minutes to reach the granite steps leading into the Library. Good time as I still had five minutes left to get inside and upstairs.

Still no sign of Van, so I hit speed dial. Getting his voice message again, I kept my tone all business calm and professional. That was me. Not nerve-jangling McAllister, but consummate, professional agent.

"Van, Kelly here. I'm at the Library and about to go in. Second floor. Middle Eastern Reading room. I hope you can make it."

What I wanted to say but didn't was, "Call me back. Don't leave me worrying. If you expected tit for tat, least you could do was show up when I shared the best lead I have with you. Where are you?"

Swallowing frustration, and other pesky emotions that had no place on a job, I headed inside.

Yesterday I'd only seen the vast ornateness of the main rotunda from a distance. Today it was all I could do not to drop my jaw as I stepped beneath the dome, aware of the coolness of the interior compared to outside, listened to the soft scuffle of shoes against the marbled floors, and murmurs of hushed voices. The place created awe, which explained, in part, the nerves sliding down my skin. But only in part.

Exactly who was I meeting? Was the voice on the phone truly the Librarian and not an imposter baiting a trap? And why had he/she called me instead of Ling Mai?

Maybe because the Librarian had been doing hush-hush-behind-the-scenes-business that might have forced her to fall back on contacting me, especially with the Director out of pocket. But why not call Van directly? Maybe he didn't have Van's number, but he seemed to know a whole lot about me, which was disconcerting to say the least.

The silver lining? If he knew who I knew, and how to track me down, maybe he knew where I came from? Who my birth mother was? And exactly what I was?

Good, something more to focus on than a missing wolf shifter.

I hated to admit it, but those questions, as much as seeking answers to Aini's predicament and the threat of the Horned One, were what drove me up the two flights of stairs and toward the northwest corner, each footstep a little less assured than the last one.

Call me callous and shallow, but I really, really wanted to know at least what I was. The only way I could do that was ask someone like the Librarian, the font of preternatural knowledge, or find my birth mother. So I was here, he/she was here. What could asking one or two small questions hurt?

By the time I reached the doorway of the room, my heart was beating hard and sweat made my cotton shirt sticky against my back. I so was not playing the role of super agent very well.

Growing up in small Iowa towns before my parents moved to Dubuque, gave me an image of a library at odds with the room before me. It actually felt like stepping into a movie set instead of reality. I was used to jam-packed shelves of nicked wood, mostly oak or varnished pine, with paper mache dinosaurs and castles perched above the stacks, mismatched tables and chairs. Walking through the libraries of my childhood was a history lesson on funding priorities, or lack of priorities, spared for those who valued reading and education and the magic of knowledge.

Here no expense had been spared. Exquisite and rich woodwork in shades of red, mahogany maybe, floor-to-ceiling shelves, hardwood tables and sturdy chairs, not just one set but as far as the eye could see down the large rectangular room. Huge windows cast filtered light through some kind of screen covering. Even the ceiling caught the eye with green glass windows, grille work and embossed cornices.

How could anybody study here? I'd be too busy gawking.

Back to work, Kels. I was here for a purpose.

A quick glance at my new watch — my old one stolen by a band of kidnapping rag-tag soldiers in Sierra Leone — reassured me I was only a minute late.

But the Librarian didn't seem to be in sight. Not the stunning woman I'd seen yesterday, or anyone belonging to the young child's voice I heard over the phone. A few scholars hunkered down at the tables, broken by low book stacks giving each table an illusion of privacy. But no one even bothered looking up as I moved deeper into the space. A burly guard stood just inside the door to my left, my silver ring warning me he was preternatural, his glance more bored than interested, until he nodded his chin toward the far end of the room.

Me? I pointed a finger at myself to make sure he'd really meant the gesture and wasn't just stretching to stay awake. Another stronger nod, accompanied by an eye roll, told me I hadn't imaged his actions.

Toward the back it was.

I paid close attention to my ring as I passed the scattered people at the tables, realizing I'd caught and held my breath until I passed the last one. The ring remained cool on my finger. No obvious preternaturals other than the guard. Didn't mean there weren't other threats in the room, just not any obvious enough that could kill me as soon as look at me.

Wasn't cynicism another word for gaining experience? It was for me.

Just when I was wondering how far I had to walk I was aware of someone materializing behind me. My heart jammed in my throat as I stopped and pivoted.

"I made it," Van whispered, almost on top of me, his hand resting on my lower back. To reassure? Or prevent me from lashing out?

My right hand slapped to my heart before I could prevent it. The whoosh of my words betrayed me. "Way to scare the willies out of me."

"You should be scared, coming here alone. How naïve can you be?"

Nothing like a lecture from an arrogant, full-of-himself male to put some starch in my backbone. "I'm not alone," I said between gritted teeth, keeping my voice low. "You're here."

"But you didn't know if I could make it or not."

True, but I wasn't about to give him the satisfaction of knowing that. His ego was inflated enough. So I fell back on the truth. "You want to find out what's going on as much as I do."

He glanced around but I doubted he was admiring the room as I had been. His look was all threat assessment and, by the frown lines between his brows, he wasn't liking what he saw.

"What is it?" I asked, hoping we weren't going to get thrown out of the room in spite of our keeping our voices low. In a near-silent space, even whispers echoed.

"Only one exit. Behind us. Five individuals between it and us. Shelving too high for you to jump over, which leaves only this aisle for egress."

Egress? It was a good word, just not in the situation. Egress my fanny. An escape route is what he meant but watered it down. He didn't even point out that the aisle had a center partition of shelving with books opened for reading on top, which limited maneuverability even more.

As usual, Van was right. On the other hand, if either one of us stopped until a situation was perfectly safe and secure, we'd never get anywhere and we both knew it.

As if tracking my thoughts, he asked, "You see this Librarian?"

I shook my head, stepping forward. The way I figured it, the Librarian would find me, in whatever guise he/she took. Besides, I didn't want to explain we might be looking for a woman, or a male child, or who knew what. Van tended to get cranky with too many vague variables.

We'd reached the second to the last set of tables when I caught sight of an older man with a stooped back and a head of fluffy white hair. From the side his profile looked a lot like an ancient Einstein.

Catching me staring, the man raised his head and crooked a finger in my direction.

The Librarian?

I nudged Van and turned toward the table, pausing at the closest chair and using it as a barrier between me and the man or whatever he was, his presence warming my ring. Had that happened when I met with the Librarian before? No doubt it was Van's presence now. He stood behind me and to my left. Guarding my back if I was being generous, wondering what the heck I was up to if I was being more accurate.

No time like the present to find out if I'd managed to find the Librarian. And if, for a change, I could get some information that was helpful.

CHAPTER 21

"Am I in the right place?" I asked the elderly gentleman, whispering through dry lips.

"Very good, Miss McAllister. Most only see what they expect to see."

Amen. Something finally went right.

Up close and personal the individual looked even more like Einstein, or as benign a creature as possible, with age spots bracketing his hands, fly-away hair creating a white nimbus around his head, his eyes faded blue and watery. Only his voice, which was the woman's voice I recalled from yesterday, proved to me beyond a doubt that this was the Librarian.

The old man cocked his head at Van. "I'm glad she found you because what I have to say impacts both of you." He waved to the chairs opposite him and we both sat, me directly across and Van in a chair angled for ease of escape.

I had to give it to Van — he hadn't blinked an eye at an old man with the voice of a young woman. A voice speaking at normal volume though no one in the room seemed to notice. I guess being The Librarian came with perks.

"We may speak at ease here," the old man said, "I've created a ward around us."

I wanted to ask if that was like a cone of silence then bit my tongue. Now was not the time for levity. Besides it wasn't levity I was feeling. It was that strained, better-to-laugh-than-fall-apart tension that happened when strung too tight for too long.

"What are you?" Not the first, or the most important question I had, but the words were out before I realized I'd said them.

Einstein look-alike waved one hand as if swatting a fly. "Not important."

He was right.

"Though if I don't answer, you won't focus on what does matter."

That wasn't fair, but I bit back my protest. Call me overly cautious or the need to be forewarned is the need to be forearmed.

"I'm what's most commonly known as a Phoenix."

"Like the bird?" Surprise coated my voice. "The one that can be born again from flames?"

"As usual the myths have the details wrong. At another time I can explain more, for a price, but we don't have much time now."

I folded my hands in front of me, not aiming for a brown-nosing posture as much as to hide nerves. Van raised a brow while glancing at my hands. Nothing escaped him.

I tucked them beneath the table.

"Have you spoken again to the girl?" The Librarian obviously didn't believe in beating around the bush.

"No. She hasn't woken up since she left the hospital."

I could feel the questioning weight of Van's gaze on me. Yup, revealed something new to him.

Tough; he knew she was being protected, that's all he needed to know. Not that I'd communicated with her once, or what she'd said.

"It's imperative you reach her, Miss McAllister."

I thought I showed a lot of restraint as I only released and spread my hands before me. "She's still in a coma."

"Pshahhh," the Librarian muttered. "You are the Guardian. Use your given gifts."

It was tempting to point out that my only gift — turning invisible — was temporarily missing in action, otherwise I was sorry-out-of-luck in the ability department. And what did he mean I was a guardian? Because I watched over Aini in Africa? Or visited her at the hospital? But there was no time to ask as he was rushing on, glancing over his shoulder as if worried someone or something might be coming.

"We must know exactly when the girl turns sixteen."

"Why?" I was glad Van asked it because I didn't want to. I'd had enough potshots aimed my way.

"Do you know anything?" The Librarian's tone sliced and diced. "*If* you studied your numerology you'd know that the number sixteen enables one to overcome obstacles. And she shall face many, as she comes into her gifts. There is no doubt that she will experience trials and defeats throughout her life but also obtain powerful energy manifestations. One being the ability to create portals."

"And that means what?" I asked, adding, "And how is that connected to the Seekers?"

Van really was eyeing me now but I kept my focus one hundred percent on the Librarian.

"I must speak to Fraulein Fassbinder about your education regarding the myths and legends, for you know nothing."

Ouch. No one liked getting a verbal bitch slap, but I held my tongue.

It was a good choice as the Librarian looked around once before lowering his brows and his voice. "The Horned One was once a Seeker in training."

What!

"He did not pass the rigorous testing but possessed enough skills to be retrained as a minion to those hundred Seekers who ruled."

"Ruled where?" I asked.

"Here, of course." I swore his nose pinched, no doubt further appalled at my lack of rudimentary knowledge. "The Seekers inhabited this plane over six thousand years ago."

A flash image of rulers wearing cavemen gear distracted me as I grappled with how long ago six thousand years was, and Van took the opportunity to jump into the discussion.

"What happened to the Seekers?"

"Hubris," came the sharp answer. "Followed by infighting. Death and destruction. They ruled as demi-gods but were never satisfied."

Since this was a scenario often repeated through history I wasn't that surprised, except for one detail. "If the Seekers came from here, where are they now that they are trying to return?"

Van's brow arched either in surprise at my question or that I had enough wherewithal to ask it.

"After the days of darkness, when the Seekers were reduced to less than two dozen, those who became the Long Hunters were able to cast the Seekers into another Realm where they were imprisoned."

"Long Hunters?" Sounded like more trouble to me.

"Those created to counter balance the Seekers. There always must be balance in the Universe."

Finally, something that made sense.

"I hear a *but* coming." I wasn't aware I'd spoken out loud until the Librarian cleared his throat.

"Quite right, Miss McAllister," he said. "A little over a thousand years ago the remaining Seekers escaped. The Long Hunters have been after them ever since."

Didn't sound too capable if these Long guys hadn't managed to catch two dozen Seekers in a thousand years. Except...

"Exactly." The Librarian was doing that creepy follow-my-thoughts thing that gave me the willies. "Just as time took its toll on the number of Seekers remaining, it also ate away at the number of Hunters following them. Plus the Seekers created allies who have been working to bring them back to where the Seekers feel they belong."

"Allies?"

"While they lived here they created preternaturals as well as others with abilities."

"As in designed them?"

"Breeding programs, Miss McAllister. Generations of breeding."

I thought I was going to be sick. What I managed was a scratchy, "Why?"

"To serve them, of course." He shook his head. "They needed minions who would tend to the livestock here."

I didn't have to ask what he meant by that word, as the druid we'd run across in Paris had called humans cattle. So I asked what really mattered to me right now.

"Here?" My throat was so dry I could barely say the single word. "As in this Realm? This plane?"

He nodded. "Precisely. Which is why the Seer is so important."

Suddenly the pieces began to come together. "If she becomes a portal when she turns sixteen..." the rest of the thought didn't need to be spoken out loud.

"Are you saying this Horned One wants to use her or destroy her?" Van asked.

"My initial guess is that he would want to destroy her. After all, having failed to become a Seeker himself, and reduced to an existence in the Underworld, the Horned One harbors intense hatred toward the Seekers, certain ones in particular."

"So stopping Aini means stopping the Seekers from returning," Van said.

"Or the Horned One may want to use her. The one who controls the Seer, controls the portal. The Seekers might be willing to give the Horned One what he sought all those thousands of years ago — the right to become a Seeker himself."

"In exchange for Aini."

"Correct."

"So the Seekers want her as a means to return to this world. The Horned One wants her as leverage to negotiate with the Seekers," I said, getting the details straight in my head.

"Or to kill her outright," the Librarian clarified. "If she falls into the hands of the Seekers, he has no bargaining chip. Better to kill her than allow that to happen."

"And Ling Mai wants to use her to learn more about the Seekers," Van threw out, his voice neutral, but I knew better. I didn't even want to go into why his boss, Kincaide, wanted her. Talk about a hornet's nest of competing agendas, all over one very vulnerable teen girl.

Suddenly I had a new question. "Is this why Aini fell into a coma? Was that manipulated?"

The Librarian nodded. "Though I would need more research to verify it as a fact, I would say it's a logical conclusion. After all, since she slipped into her comatose state in Africa, there was a strong chance your Agency," he looked directly at me, "would have left her there."

"But we didn't."

"Commendable." The smile that crept across his face did not belong to a benign older man. "But shortsighted, as you have now brought the battle here."

"The battle between what the Horned One wants, what the Seekers want and what keeps Aini alive and safe." Then I realized something. "But the nurse tried to kill Aini. Wasn't that at the instigation of the Horned One?"

"Yes. Remember that he seeks control of her. Failing that, he must stop her from falling into the hands of the Seekers. If she does, they have no need of him and his fate, one he's fought against for thousands and thousands of years, will be sealed."

"So if he, the Horned One, was the person who visited Aini in the hospital, why wouldn't he have killed her then?"

"He might have wanted to try to remove her or access her before he resorted to her death."

"And, when the guard interrupted the nurse, she might not have been trying to kill her as much as –" I swallowed at the term the Librarian used. "She might have been trying to access her. Which is why he was killed."

"Exactly." The Librarian nodded his head. The patient professor pleased his dense student finally figured out the right answer. "It is imperative that the Horned One does not reach the girl. She must turn sixteen." The Librarian's voice took on a prissy tone, as if we weren't already aware of that, and hadn't been working to protect her.

The emphasis the Librarian put on each and every one scared me more than Van jumping out at me earlier.

The Librarian continued in his lecturing voice. "The reason the number sixteen matters is that it can be reduced to the single number of seven, with its energies of obligation and responsibility."

Both Van and I must have looked blank as the old man pursed his lips before raising his voice. "She will only come into her power upon reaching sixteen. After that point, she will be harder to use, or destroy, while her warnings will become more specific and useful."

Nice, but not getting us anywhere. I wasn't here to find out more about what Aini might or might not be capable of doing down the road but how to keep her, and the rest of us, alive so she'd stand a chance at reaching sixteen and growing old. On the other hand, since the Librarian was willing to share, I'd be an idiot not to learn as much as possible.

"Warnings about what?" I pushed, now tempted to thread my fingers together beneath the table but holding them visible and still.

The old man leaned forward, his own gnarled fingers twitching. "Warning you all about the approaching danger. The Seekers, Miss McAllister. Those who mean to destroy us."

Oh, of course. *That* threat.

Cynicism was sliding into snark in a big way.

I kept my panic to myself though.

I sensed Van stiffen at my side as the Librarian continued. "The Horned One was created as an ally to be called upon when needed. You managed, though one wonders how, to halt the arrival of the demon Zaradian in Paris, but the Seekers have more than one way to infiltrate and destroy those they see as fodder."

"You mean humans." Van spoke the words so quietly at first I thought it was my own thoughts escaping.

"Of course the humans. Those and any preternaturals who stand in their way."

"Back to the Horned One." I was bound and determined to learn details about the most immediate threat first. "How do we stop him?"

"If he can not use your Aini, he will stop the Seer by any and all means possible."

"But would her being a weapon against the Seekers make her more useful alive than dead?" Van asked.

"In some ways, yes. She can see more than others, understand more than others, and is one of our best defenses against annihilation."

"Yet you say he wants her dead?"

"The Horned One is no friend of the Seekers, but has no need for humans either. He cares not if Aini can protect those who reside in this Realm. If he cannot become a Seeker himself he will thwart the Seekers in retaliation for what they did to him, but only at his hands. No others."

Okay, when phrased like that I was beginning to get the bigger picture.

Swallowing past a sand-dry throat, I summarized so I could make sure I could report the details to Vaughn and the team. "So the Horned One wants to use Aini, if possible, and, if not, then stop her from turning sixteen when she'll come into her powers. But if she does reach sixteen, and comes out of her coma, she can give us more specifics about how to stop the Seekers? The same Seekers the Horned One wishes to hurt but only if he can do so personally."

"Have you not been listening?" The watery blue eyes glared at me. "You *must* stop him from killing her. If she dies, we all die. We will not have the knowledge she possesses if she is killed. She is our most powerful weapon against the Seekers and others. One who rivals my own knowledge."

I was getting that, but shouting we're all going to die over and over wasn't going to help us. Hard, cold facts might. "Again, how do we stop this Horned One?"

"The Horned One is unstoppable," came the so-didn't-want-to-hear answer. If we couldn't do anything, what was the point? Besides, throwing up my hands and shouting "the sky is falling" wasn't my style.

I leaned forward. "Surely the Horned One has some vulnerability?"

The old man sat back, not in a calm way but as if creating space between Van and me. But why?

Waiting tightened every muscle in my body, but if the Librarian needed a minute to figure out a solution to what was looking like an impossible situation, I'd give him the minute. Maybe even two, but he'd better give me something more than doom and gloom. If I wanted that, I could have asked Jaylene to read her tarot cards.

Then I remembered one of the questions I needed to ask. Without saying a word, I rustled around in my day pack and pulled out a piece of paper and a pencil. Even I knew not to use a pen in a research library.

Van leaned over and whispered, "More kindergarten supplies?"

I ignored him. He wasn't being mean. I knew he got a kick out of the fact that more than once on our last mission, I fell back on lessons learned from being a teacher.

Looked like today wasn't going to be much different.

Scribbling as fast as I could, I sketched out the tattoo I'd seen on the arms of two different corpses. Maybe it might help the older man tell us something to avoid there being more victims.

When I was ready to reach across the table and rattle the old man, just to make sure he was still breathing, he sat forward, shaking his head. "There may be a solution but it is risky. Very risky."

Great. So much for getting answers to the hard questions.

I slid the paper toward him, noticing his eyes narrowing.

"Where have you seen this?" he asked, his voice quieter than it had been.

"Two victims. Preternaturals who have been killed since I met you last had this image tattooed on the inside of their arms. I want to know if it means something in particular."

"Nothing good," the Librarian murmured, his voice now sounding more like it belonged to someone older, who'd seen too much pain and brutality to be surprised, yet he was still impacted.

"What does this image mean exactly?" I pushed.

"That the Horned One is already here. The portents indicate that three days before the Seer's natal day, the Horned One can leave his Realm but not before. Once released, his power grows and there will be no stopping him."

Back to the sky is falling. Plus we already had this message hammered home to us. I needed something to learn — something new. Something to help us instead of us simply running around like headless chickens. What could I ask that might help us instead of simply telling us we might as well prepare for Armageddon.

"Something's not right." The Librarian looked closer at the image.

I wanted to ask what but Van jumped in. "If the Horned One is here, why hasn't he killed more?"

"It waits to reach the Seer. Until he can contain, or eliminate that threat, he bides his time." The Librarian's voice chilled me to my bones.

"So if we can keep Aini alive," I said, trying to find the silver lining in what felt like a tornado-gray sky, "at least until her sixteenth birthday, then we might contain this Horned One?"

"Yes, though—"

"I know, I know, we can't kill it." I could only take pessimism for so long. "But we can try."

"Be aware the Horned One will create others to help him complete his task."

I so was not feeling the love from this Librarian. Or maybe he was just a drama queen.

Then I remembered a detail about the image I'd drawn. Tapping the sketch from my side of the table I said, "In both tattoos the face, or where a face should be, was colored in red. Does that make a difference?"

The old man paused for a second before answering, "That can explain why what I'm sensing is wrong here."

"What?" I demanded.

"When two are one they are stronger yet more vulnerable." He looked at me and then Van. "As you both should realize, as love can unite so can it divide."

That had the breath backing up in my lungs. No way have Van or I gone beyond one soul-scorching kiss. We definitely hadn't dipped our toes into the L word territory. Clearing my throat, I kept my gaze from Van and on Einstein.

"Are you saying the Horned One can be killed by someone it loves?" Yes, I was being pushy but no way was I going to return to the Compound with nothing to help Aini.

Van leaned forward, a furrow creasing his brows. "Or do you mean if we can kill the human host body of the Horned One then that might weaken or slow down the bigger threat?"

Why hadn't I thought of that?

"Can it?" I asked of the Librarian who'd been following Van's train of thought more than my grasping at straws.

"The blow can be struck. Not of man nor of woman. Between the end of day and the beginning of a new dawn."

I stole a quick look at Van, hoping this made some kind of sense to him.

The Librarian wasn't finished. "The Horned One can only perish within his own Realm. Here he can be stopped, cast back to where he belongs. But the other ... this could explain where you are involved." The Librarian was looking only at Van before cutting his watery gaze to me. "Two are stronger than one. Together there is a chance. Individually there is no hope."

Yeah, right. As of last night it was as clear as an Iowa summer's day that Van had his orders and I had mine. He wasn't opposed to using me to further his ends and, if I was honest, I'd be feeling the same way if I needed something, for a good reason, from him. No doubt I'd be knocking at his door for assistance if I was in a tight corner. But for now, our orders conflicted.

Van wanted to see Aini to pump her for intel about her terrorist brother. If there really was a brother, maybe given what we'd been learning here now, that could be arranged in exchange for help in keeping Aini alive.

I'd have to check with Vaughn. If Van's Superior was *not* preternatural, then it'd be unlikely he'd jump on the let's-work-together-to-stop-a-larger supernatural threat. But he might be open to protecting Aini if the brother-as-terrorist threat was positioned right.

When had I become so devious? Oh, yeah, about the time I learned how vulnerable human life really is.

"Can you share anything else about how to stop this Horned One?" I asked, feeling like I was splitting threads even as a clock was ticking but not knowing why. Baby steps to achieve a larger goal.

"He's not alive so he cannot be killed," the old man said, but before I could release a here-we-go-again sigh, he added, "If you can remove him from his host, then he is vulnerable. If you can keep him from finding a new host, then he must return from where he comes and you buy yourself time."

At last, something we could work with. He hadn't said we'd stop the Horned One permanently, but I'd take even a temporary win at this point.

"How do we—"

The Librarian stood up suddenly, knocking back his chair in a move that was at odds with his old man's body.

"His servant comes."

Van and I both glanced at the room's sole entrance and exit and in the second it took us to look back at the Librarian, he was gone.

CHAPTER 22

"What now?" I whispered to Van as we both edged closer to the center aisle. The floodgate of adrenaline had already kicked in, priming me to fight or flee.

"We get the hell out of here," Van snarled, grabbing my hand as if I weren't smart enough to follow him. Now wasn't the time to argue though. My whole focus was one hundred percent on reaching the exit before whatever was hunting us arrived.

If I thought that rectangular room was long when I arrived, it was nothing to my impression as I gripped Van's hand. He made no bones about library decorum as he flat out ran down the middle aisle, me right behind him.

My heart pounded, my mouth went dry.

Twenty feet.

Ten.

The doorway dead ahead.

Almost there. That's when the guard who'd directed me to the Librarian when I first arrived stepped into the opening. Blocking us.

"What the—"

Van lowered his head, using his body as a battering ram as he released my hand and increased his speed.

I didn't want to look but had no choice. The second the guard was knocked out of the way, our small window of opportunity to get through the opening and beyond would be within reach.

The guard was built tall, square and solid. Shifter or Were was my guess. Or maybe those were the two creatures I'd run up against one too many times lately, and never in a good way.

Like a locomotive at full throttle Van slammed his shoulder straight into the guard's gut. Even with Van's shifter strength, the other man barely budged.

"Disappear," Van shouted to me, staggering back to position himself for another assault.

He meant turn invisible. Good idea. No could do. Trust me, I was trying in the only way I knew how. My whole life all I needed to kickstart my freaky ability was to feel too much stress, fear or its twin cousin terror. Right now counted as all three and yet nothing was happening. My get-out-of-jail-free, or at least sneak around without anyone seeing me, card wasn't working.

I was trapped behind Van. Book shelves to my right. More waist-high shelving partitions to my left. No weapons.

Van had regrouped and was already charging for a second go, this time lower, aiming for the man's legs.

Smart. I glanced around for something to use as a weapon, anything. The chairs were too heavy to maneuver and there wasn't enough room to use them. No handy metal curtain rods or sconces. I doubted the pencil I had in my backpack would stop whatever the guard was.

I had no idea where the other people in the room had disappeared to, but either they were cowering under their chairs or had been asked to leave by the guard while we'd been talking to the Librarian. Maybe a good thing, there'd be no other deaths than Van's and mine.

Giving up? Or had listening to doom-and-gloom old man zapped my will to fight?

Tarnation, where was my brain? The Taser C2 I'd brought along. Stepping back I rifled through my backpack, grabbing both Taser and cartridge. Here in D.C. even carrying such a weapon was a big no-no. Dying was even a bigger one in my book. Getting Van killed was in the same category.

Injecting the cartridge with shaky hands, I dropped my pack, looking for the best way to hit the guard without taking down Van at the same time.

The Taser had a range of fifteen feet but closer was better as far as I was concerned.

"Back away," I screamed at Van, dancing around behind him, trying not to have him trip over me but wanting to be as close as possible to my target the minute Van got out of the way.

Either he was too adrenaline-charged to hear me or had shut me out, because he ran toward the guard again, both of them now grappling, slamming against book stacks, smashing and rolling to the floor.

Not good. Not good. Not good.

I couldn't shoot. Couldn't get on the other side of them. Couldn't do much except watch Van get his head pounded into the hard stone flooring by Guard Guy.

Every muscle I possessed was locked and loaded, waiting for my chance to act, which is why when I slammed my left funny bone into the aisle divider it didn't register at first. When it did, though, I didn't waste any time.

Using the shelves as steps, I scrambled from the floor to the top of the four-foot stack, stepping over books to the end of the divider, which put me as close as possible over where Van and the guard fought. They'd both had staggered to their feet, Van holding back his wolf self by a shred. If needed he might shift, but only if he couldn't stop the guard any other way.

Each time they smashed against the wooden case I stood on, I had to brace myself. Last thing I needed was to pitch head first into the melee from above.

"Get out of the way," I shouted, not that anyone was listening. It was more like a plea. "Move. Move. Mo—"

There. My chance. The guard had tossed Van backwards, slamming him into the taller stacked shelving on the other side of the aisle, all but burying Van in a pile of dislodged books.

My teacher training was appalled. Thankfully my agent training kicked in. Holding the Taser in a two-fisted stance I stabilized myself, sighted the laser red light, and fired.

The guard jerked, his arms and legs suddenly stiff, his body fully incapacitated as he toppled backwards.

But only for thirty seconds or as long as the Taser held him. Thank heavens I had a version that could hold a continuous stream. Finally, something working for me instead of against me.

"Van," I screamed. "Run. Now."

I had no doubt that went counter to everything Van believed, but bless the man, he scrambled to his feet and scooted around and behind the prone guard's body. Then he circled back, grabbed the weapon from my hand so I could launch myself from the divider, land with a hard thud and roll on the marble floor outside the room, pick myself up and hightail it down the nearest stairway.

You'd have thought Van and I had trained together for years. We hadn't, but I wasn't stupid. With Van's shifter abilities he could catch up to me within seconds, so his holding the weapon on the guard for the full thirty seconds gave both of us the best chance at survival.

I was double-timing down the lower level stairs when Van drew even with me, shouting, "He's coming."

Ignoring the open stares and glares from the library patrons, I only paused long enough to shout at the trio behind the main reception desk as we cut across the front rotunda. "Attack second floor. Call 911."

It might give us a few seconds, or the benefit of the doubt long enough for us to escape.

Once we hit the outside steps Van snagged my hand again, angling us toward the left when I'd been veering us to the right toward the Capitol or Supreme Court buildings.

"Inside," Van said, not even sounding winded though blood marred his face and the front of his shirt. Not enough to attract too much attention unless one looked closely. Good thing he healed quickly or we'd be stopped before we stepped inside anywhere. He meant the Madison Building next door, one of the three locations housing the Library of Congress.

He was right. A short length of sidewalk, across a street and we might, a very slim might, have a chance to duck inside before the guard knew which direction we'd gone.

We didn't have to even get to the front door of the Madison library as a small bronze kiosk was located at the sidewalk just across from the crosswalk.

Racing flat out toward it, we both pancaked against its far side, expecting at any second that there'd be the hue and cry of alarms. Our attacker had all the advantages — being a guard, in uniform, in D.C. — which also meant it'd be a no-brainer for any other law enforcement personnel, of any type, to stop us first and ask questions later. If there was a later.

"Want me to peek?" I said when I could catch my breath. Van stood, shoulder to shoulder next to me, his left arm pressing my right arm against the metal wall behind us, an automatic gesture of protection.

"Should have been here by now if he was coming in this direction," was Van's non-response.

Since I was closer to the edge of the small structure, I eased my head around to see what I could see.

Instead of the guard racing toward us, or even in the other direction, what I saw was a knot of people huddled together in front of the door we'd just exited. Arms were gesturing, some pointing one direction, others already on cell phones.

What was going on?

Van must have caught my hesitation, or relief, as his hand released me and he moved to peer around me.

"Can you hear them?" I asked, knowing he wouldn't get every word but might understand some of the shouts.

"He's dead." Van said, his voice low, his body still braced for escape. "They think he's had a heart attack."

"He who?" I asked. "You mean the guard?"

"Yup." He grabbed my arm and tugged me back onto the sidewalk. "Walk normal. Just two people out on a beautiful late spring day."

"Then wash the blood off your face first."

When had we fallen down the deep, dark hole? I did as he said because Van was right — he often was, which could be frustrating when I had my own agenda. Now I was too dazed to do anything but keep up. The sooner we were away from the Jefferson building, the safer we might be, and we could already hear emergency vehicle sirens wailing in the distance.

Van kept walking, neither of us saying a word until we'd gone several blocks, stepping away from the formal buildings into a street of brick brownstones on the far side of the

Libraries and in the opposite direction of the Capital building. Just past a small church, Van tugged me into the empty parking lot and away from the few pedestrians on the street.

"You want to explain that?" he practically growled, his hand banding my arm tighter than he probably meant it to be.

I shook him off, brushing my hair out of my face before facing him. "Explain what exactly? You were there."

I understood his frustration, but I wasn't about to be the target here. Except he was now looking as much confused as angry.

"Why didn't you turn invisible?"

Okay, he just pulled the rug out from beneath me. "That? Of all the crap we'd just heard, and the fight, and possibly a dead man ... and you want to know why I didn't obey your orders?"

He shook his head, almost vibrating with suppressed emotions, but I wasn't sure which emotions. "Screw the orders. Why didn't you disappear? Get your ass out of the line of fire and escape?"

I didn't know if I wanted to laugh or slug him. I did neither, as I took a step back, inhaled deeply and pretended, just for a second, that everything was under control. Then I took a risk I hoped wouldn't come back and bite me on the fanny. "I didn't disappear because I can't."

There, I'd said it. Gave him the ammunition to use against me with his long-time pal Ling Mai if he chose to do so, and didn't say one itsy, bitsy, tiny word about whose fault it most likely was that I couldn't use my ability. When I needed it. Nope, I could be a cool, calm professional here if it killed me.

"What do you mean you can't?"

"You accept all that?" I waved toward the buildings now behind us. "About what the Librarian told us? About what happened with the guard, who by the way was not a psycho threat when I first saw him? Let's deal with the big issues here."

"This is a big issue." He stepped closer, sucking all the air from around us. His eyes held that golden amber tint that warned me his wolf was fighting for control. The flare of his nostrils, the tightness in his jaw, all signs he was holding his temper by a thread, but I was at a loss as to why.

"What's going on here?" This time I threw my hands wide. "What happened to big picture thinking? Don't we have our hands full with enough problems to blow one issue out of proportion?"

"It's not one issue, it's part of you," he said, his voice calmer now, which actually worried me more.

"So?"

"How long has this been happening? Or not happening?"

"Since Africa," I snapped back. "It's no big deal."

It was, though, and we both knew it. But it was *my* big deal, not his.

"You could have been killed back there." Okay, now we were getting to the real burr up his backside. "If I couldn't make the meeting—"

"Which you did."

"If you hadn't had a handy—and very illegal—Taser on you."

"Which I did."

"If you—"

"Look." This time I was the one who stepped forward, pressing into his space, using my index finger to jab his chest so he'd start really hearing me. "We have some whole, end-of-the-world-problems to deal with. We're both alive. Let's start from there."

He must have reached the same conclusion, or realized there was a time and place to pick his battles, and this was one he wasn't going to win. Not now. He threaded one hand through his dark hair and straightened, back to agent Noziak, not caveman Van.

Good.

I started. "Was that the guard — the one who was chasing us — who collapsed, or whatever happened to him on the library steps?"

"Far as I could hear, it sounded like it was."

"But why?" I muttered, mostly for my own benefit. "One second he's King Kong and then he just collapses?"

"The one break we caught and you're not happy about it?"

"I don't understand it." Nerves still bubbled right beneath my skin. "And if I don't understand it how can I know how to fight it?"

"You mean the Horned One." As usual he followed the train of my thoughts perfectly.

"Exactly. I don't think the guard was the evil being we're seeking."

"Because?"

"We didn't kill him. You fought him but by all accounts he recovered from the Taser and was able to chase us as far as the front steps."

"You sure the Taser couldn't have caused enough shock to damage his heart? The run he must have made compounding the situation?"

I know he was playing devil's advocate because his tone sounded as suspicious as mine did.

"Everything the Librarian said indicated this threat was a little more indestructible than a dinky heart." In fact, my money was on an autopsy showing the guard died of a massive pulmonary embolism. "I'll need to make sure Vaughn gets a copy of the guard's autopsy."

Van stilled beside me. "Don't you mean we? And why Vaughn and not Ling Mai?"

Man was too perceptive by half.

"You think your boss wants to know about some preternatural guard who went berserk after you were talking with some woman/man who calls herself/himself a phoenix?" Yup, focus on the main issue.

"He'll need to know there's more than one threat against Aini." His expression told me one answer, his words another.

"Your boss is...?" I didn't have to spell out the question or the word 'preternatural.'

Van shook his head.

"Then how are you going to explain your meeting me to speak to a Librarian who looked like Einstein spouting threats against mankind?"

The corner of his mouth kicked up, enough to set off that sexy dimple in his right cheek. "I don't have to tell him the details. Only the results."

He'd thrown me, again, probably because I was having a hard time keeping my attention one hundred percent focused on his words and not him. So I'm shallow. I didn't think I was. So maybe it was all this talk of annihilation. My hormones kicking in to do what came naturally — have sex. Not to release stress, though that would have been nice, but to reproduce. Yup, good ol' biology one-o-one. If the species was about to be annihilated, biology revved up the drive to create more life to increase the chances for survival.

Which was a bunch of baloney. Van, all hot and bothered and sexy, was short-circuiting my brain wiring.

"Are you listening, Kels?"

His tone snapped me back to the present with a jolt. "Of course I am."

His grin told me he knew I was lying. So pinch me.

I cleared my throat. "You were talking about hiding the pesky, world-implosion details, and a Horned One preternatural being seeking death and destruction issue, and focusing instead on bringing results to your boss." There, I *had* been listening. Up to a point. "What results?"

His smile deepened. "The results where you bring me back to the Compound with you to see Aini in person."

CHAPTER 23

I'd given up arguing with Van forty minutes ago. Thirty minutes ago, I called Vaughn to back-up my decision that bringing Van anywhere near Aini was probably a mistake. No probably about it. I knew full well Van could hear both my side of the conversation and hers. Vexing shifter hearing.

That's when she told me to bring Van back to the Compound.

What the baloney? Didn't Vaughn know that you didn't just let a member of another agency waltz into the Compound, even if he was related to one of the IR agents? I tried to tell her, in a way that didn't let Van know I was thinking of him as an enemy, okay, not bad guy enemy but more an unknown threat. Or potential threat. Let's face it, Van could wipe out a few of us agents and get to Aini before we could say Jack Spritzeneker.

Still Vaughn said yes.

Didn't mean I liked it, or Van's raised brows that screamed, "I told you so," but I understood following a direct order. I wasn't gracious about it though as we drove in silence until we reached the Compound gates — the guarded gates, though it was only Hercules and Wyatt on duty.

Hercules looked like the still-growing-at-that-gawky-stage teenager he was, and Wyatt, not all that much older, didn't look like a mega deterrent either, especially to a shifter like Van.

These guys were now our first line of defense if any of the bad guys decided to knock on our front door and announce themselves. So far we'd lucked out that none of us had been killed. It was only a matter of time, though, and I could hear the clock ticking.

"Any problems?" I asked Herc, wanting to send him off to play a pick-up game of basketball or do some weight training in the gym. One day soon Herc would grow into the breadth of his shoulders, his height, and lose his endearing gawkiness. Then watch out girls.

"No *problemos*." Herc gave me a comic salute, looking past me to Van in the passenger seat when a grin broke out on his face. "Hi! Nice to see you again."

I'd forgotten Herc had met Van briefly in Paris. They did that male-to-male chin nod thing.

"Don't think because you know him that you'd be able to waltz by him on your own," I said to Van, sounding a little more snarky than I intended, already making a mental note to warn both Herc and Wyatt that just because Van was an ally in Paris didn't mean he still was now.

"Duly noted."

Like I believed him for a second.

Wyatt strolled up then, more swagger in his walk than there was usually, frowning at Van. "You okay?" he asked me, macho bravado in his tone.

"Fine. Thank you." That didn't seem to be enough though as he continued to glare at Van. Not a smart idea. Shifters, even ones in control of their animal selves, tended to take staring as a threatening gesture. Even without glancing at Van, I could feel him bristling beside me.

"We've got to get going." I eased my foot on the gas, thankful that Herc raised the gate and waved us through.

"Isn't he a little young for you?" Van asked as if chewing glass.

"Age wise? No." Even if he was. Experience wise? A lifetime. I didn't say so, because my gut told me that was about to change and very soon. Besides, let Van stew in his own juices for a bit. Turn about was fair play.

Van held his tongue, which surprised me until I caught him scoping out the layout of the Compound, number of buildings, possible usage, presence of individuals milling about. There weren't many, which meant we were more vulnerable than Vaughn would like to admit.

Bad idea. Bad idea. Bad idea.

I pulled in as close to the main building as possible, in large part to hustle Van inside before he memorized the whole set up of the Compound. And trust me, he knew exactly what I was doing.

"The Librarian did say we were to work together," he murmured as he held the door for me to enter what had once been the main house, or more like a manor, on the property.

"Do you follow the orders of every stranger who gives them to you?" I asked, my voice a little too on the saccharine side not to be missed.

He fell into step beside me but I could still see his grin. "You know I've always been game to be with you, up close and personal as possible. That hasn't changed."

I jerked to a stop. "This is so not the time, nor the place, to be discussing anything ... anything ... personal."

"Getting to you, aren't I?" That wicked come-hither grin again, the one that reached all the way to crease the corners of his dark brown eyes. Dare-you eyes, that promised all sorts of wicked delights.

He was enjoying this. What kind of man, or shifter, used the world-going-to-pieces as an excuse to ... whatever he was doing? It wasn't business and that's all I was up to dealing with right now.

I turned to continue walking when his voice halted me.

"Just remember when that kid back there." —he used his thumb to point toward the gate— "decides he wants to stake a claim that you're taken."

I didn't bother answering, probably because sputtering would only let him know how flustered he made me, but turned on my heel and marched down the hall to knock on Ling Mai's office.

Since Vaughn knew we were coming she didn't keep us waiting. Which was good. Hanging around Van Noziak in a quiet, isolated hallway, was not healthy for my blood pressure, for a lot of different reasons.

As if a switch was flipped, Van changed from let's-get-personal to all business once we were seated across from Ling Mai's ornately carved wooden desk. I envied him that ability as I quickly summarized the events at the library and the Librarian's dire words for Vaughn. I followed up with, "We should get the autopsy reports on the guard as soon as possible."

"And you don't think the guard was the Horned One?"

I shook my head. Van kept his silence. "No, but I do know he was preternatural." I glanced at Van. "Shifter?"

"A Were," he said, "but enhanced, which is why he was so hard to take down."

"Enhanced how?" Vaughn asked, a hint of tiredness around her eyes. But she wasn't letting that stop her from extracting as much info as possible from Van, who answered her question.

"Most Weres and shifters are evenly matched strength and agility wise, even if our animal sides are different." He glanced at me, but more as a peer explaining a fine point of law than anything else. "There are exceptions of course, just as there are in the animal kingdom. But when I hit this guy full-on he didn't even rock back on his feet. And I hit him hard."

"I see." Vaughn pursed her lips before glancing at me. "How do you translate the Librarian's recommendation to work with Van?"

Nothing like being put in the hot seat. "Sounded more like a suggestion to me," I hedged. "Maybe because we worked together in Africa."

"It was more than that."

Was Van calling me a liar? In front of my fellow agent and team leader?

He continued, not even looking at me, as if I'd turned invisible. Which I hadn't. Put out? Yes. But definitely visible. "The Librarian tended to be vague on a lot of questions raised, such as vulnerabilities of The Horned One."

"The Librarian indicated that there was a possibility of stopping him if we remove his host body," I slid in, before Van could continue with all doom and gloom. "We need to find and eliminate the host to send the Horned One back to where he came from."

Van nodded. "But he was very clear on the need for Kelly and me to work together to stop him. Or it."

Back to that teamwork thing. Which made no sense.

Vaughn looked at me. "No reason why?"

"No." Not for want of trying. "Which is why I wouldn't take his words literally. More as a guideline. Sort of a team building approach."

Yes, I was laying my explanation on a bit thick, but last thing I needed was to be tied to the hip with Van Noziak.

Vaughn glanced back and forth between Van and me as if weighing and measuring something I couldn't see. I held my tongue when what I wanted to do was shout, 'Did you hear me? Death? Destruction? Ticking clock?' Except then I'd sound exactly like the Librarian, which wasn't a pleasant thought.

Before I could share the intel I'd discovered about the Seekers though, Vaughn folded her hands and spoke. "Kelly, I'd like you to check on Aini, then report for your rotation with Jaylene. You'll be relieving Brenda who's currently with her."

Seriously? I glanced at Van then wished I hadn't as he gave me a remember-my-words look. Good grief, it wasn't as if I was heading out for a tryst with Wyatt. On the other hand, turn about was fair play. If Van could rattle my cage, I could rattle his.

Ratcheting up my smile to a yum-yum expression, I knew when I'd reached the right degree by the narrowing of Van's eyes.

Take that wolf-guy!

Then Vaughn announced, "I wish to speak to Van for a few minutes. Alone."

I rose to my feet. I wasn't stupid, even if I was being sent from the room while the *adults* conferred. That was the part that rankled the most. Van shouldn't even be on the property and yet I was the one being shunted off, not to raise the alarm, but to go about business as usual. Well, as "usual" as needing to patrol the grounds of the Compound could be.

With a stiff nod to Vaughn, and no acknowledgement to Van at all, even though it wasn't that long since he'd saved my life — again — I marched from the room.

Vaughn's order to stop off at Aini's room was really pointless, as the nurse I'd left there earlier was still on duty, paging through a magazine. She looked up and offered a quick smile when I knocked on the door and entered.

I was glad my ring didn't heat up, which meant the caregiver wasn't preternatural.

"Any changes?" I asked, looking closely at Aini who appeared the same as when I left her. I stopped next to her bed and grasped her limp hand, aware of the callouses, the healed scars, the very stillness of it.

"I'm afraid not."

The sigh I released was frustration on several levels. I hated feeling helpless and clueless at the same time. So much rode on knowing Aini's birthdate and on her waking up and the rest of us finding a way to keep her alive.

What had the Librarian muttered? Something about using my given gifts. What a bunch of manure.

I caught the nurse's glance at my left hand, the one I'd wrapped in the cotton blanket covering Aini, squeezing the fabric until my knuckles showed white.

Obviously one of my given gifts wasn't subtlety. I nodded toward the nurse before pressing Aini's hand and releasing it, sending a mental good-bye/get well message and headed out to find Jaylene.

Maybe patrolling around, looking for threats, would be less nerve wracking than the day had been so far.

CHAPTER 24

"Where the hell have you been?" Jaylene snipped the second I found her along a length of fencing on the backside of the Compound.

"What's up with you?" Heck, I was here. What more was I supposed to be doing? I waved off Wyatt who looked like he wanted to hang around a bit longer, but I'd had my fill of males with their own agendas so I all but gave him a direct order to vamoose.

Jaylene shot me the stink-eye, barely waiting for Wyatt to disappear. "You know good and well that we're supposed to pair up, no human without defensive abilities without a preternatural or a human with abilities. Though what disappearing is supposed to do to keep the two of us alive is beyond me. You, I can protect. You helping me? *Hasta la vista.*"

Jaylene and I usually got along pretty well. Better than Nicki and she, or Alex and Mandy, who made a cat fight look benign. But here she was thinking I was going to disappear the minute things got dicey. So not making me feel the love. "Is that what you're angry about? You're afraid I'm not going to watch your back?"

"I'm not angry," Jaylene snapped back, already walking away, her gaze scanning the scrub pine woods on the other side of the fence. "I just don't appreciate my getting stuck here, doing my duty, while you're off playing kissy-kissy with your wolf-man boyfriend."

I had been striding to catch up to her, but her words stopped me cold. "What?"

She glanced over her shoulder. "You know what I mean. Don't play dumb blonde with me."

Okay, I might look like a Barbie doll but that didn't mean I was dumb. Nor did I play clueless, unless the team needed me to, but that wasn't the point. The point was — how'd she know I was with Van and where'd she get the totally wrong idea that we were that close an item?

I rammed some starch in my voice before replying, "For your information the Librarian set up a meeting, and I went, per Vaughn's direct orders."

Jaylene, too, stopped, turning to face me. "And your doggy date?"

"If you mean Van, he's not a dog. The Librarian asked, no, he demanded that Van show up, too."

"I thought the Librarian was a woman."

"She is, but she can also impersonate a he."

"How convenient."

"Look, Jaylene." I fisted my hands on my hips, all the frustration racing through me finally finding an outlet. "If I'd had my druthers I'd have loved to have stayed here, behind safe barriers, spending my time strolling around on a nice spring day rather than fighting off berserk preternaturals and running for my life."

That got Jaylene's goat. She was a fighter, by experience rather than choice, growing up on the rough side of South Chicago, living on the streets. No one implied she was a coward. *No one.* Which is why I wasn't surprised to see her rear back as if struck, clench her hands to her sides and stride forward until she towered over me.

She was all but quivering as she glared down at me. "Safe? Strolling? You really want to say those words to my face?"

The old Kelly, the nice one, the one I'd been before being turned inside out by Africa, would have backed down. I'd have apologized, tried to soothe ruffled feathers, seen things from Jaylene's side. Well, tough kittens. That Kelly was gone.

"Safe. Strolling." I enunciated each word calmly and evenly spaced. The subtext was clear. Bring it on. I was ready.

Not.

I don't know who was more surprised, Jaylene or me, as we stood there, eye-to-eye, even if she was taller than me, both shaking with tension. She actually broke first.

"So melt-butter-in-your-mouth Kelly has grown some fangs." A reluctant smile played around her mouth as she turned, in part to give us both some breathing room. Thank heavens. Who knew what would have happened had we crossed that line. Tensions were high among us all but the last thing we needed was infighting. The very last thing.

But she wasn't finished. "Better be careful when facing larger, meaner, and much more experienced meat-eaters. You don't know squat about what happens to soft, mewling creatures in the real world."

Sticking my tongue out at her retreating back would have been immature and frivolous, but, man, was it tempting.

I hoofed it to catch up with her. When I drew close she grumbled, "This is what we get for *your* messing with the seer."

"Me?" Like I was to blame for saving a teen's life. Or that I'd shaken Aini awake to have her warn us about an impending threat. Jaylene should kiss my scuffed boots that I was around for Aini when the girl woke up. If I hadn't been we'd still be facing the same horrible threat, but without a clue what was bearing down on us.

"You're the one who set off this firestorm," she continued ragging, shaking her head, sounding and acting like a dog who refused to let go of a juicy bone. "Why couldn't we catch a break and just chill for a bit?"

Not that I disagreed with that last part. Jaylene didn't have any idea how a break was exactly what I'd love. Enough time to deal with a few trials of my own. Like what was I going to do about my missing ability? What had the Librarian meant about hidden talents and The Horned One? Best thing that could happen is to have nothing happen on the patrol so I could get back to sitting at Aini's bedside long enough to think through all these issues. And I hadn't even begun to deal with Van.

Keep your eye on the target, Kels, and that isn't Van, no matter how many pesky hormones were singing the Halleluiah chorus.

Just then I caught Jaylene's movement as she pressed her hand to her headset comm device. "Repeat," she muttered, already scanning the terrain. "Got it. Blue-Eyes and I on our way."

Since I was Blue-Eyes, I didn't question, or snark, at the comment. The fact Jaylene used her old pet name for me meant she'd shelved the last few minutes. It was a small win, but I'd take it.

"What's up?"

"Sightings east of us."

"Who?"

"That's what we're meant to find out."

"How many?"

"Small foot patrol."

Tension raced through my nerve endings. "Human?" I asked, mentally crossing my fingers.

"No idea."

CHAPTER 25

The east side of the Compound was wooded on our side of the chain link fencing. Not thick trees, more skinny pine saplings with a rare oak or hickory branching with the neon green of new growth. Outside the fence, an old creek bed, long dried and now filled with rich mulch cut across the woods, leading up to the fencing and a little on our side. A natural way to approach out of sight and low to the ground.

This area was as far away from the main house and buildings as possible while still on Compound land. Someone had done their homework well. It was as if they knew we were understaffed, so, even if there was a patrol, the likelihood that we could get reinforcements here soon enough was low.

I could hear the rapid fire barking of a puppy beyond the far rise. Must be the little girl's, Gabby. The tickle of a breeze whispered past my cheek. Mother Nature and the fear clawing up my spine were an odd mix. Sure we'd added patrols and were watching the front gate but I hadn't really expected anyone to come calling. Until now. Play time was over.

It took us only a moment to see where a section of the fence had been clipped and folded back — big enough for a man to crawl through, small enough to not attract attention unless one was looking for it.

Not good. Not good.

Whoever sliced that fence wasn't playing around. Unless they just came for a look-see.

Yeah, right.

Time to get real.

A quick glance around didn't show us anyone, but that didn't mean a lot. The closest structure was an abandoned barn, big enough for a few horses at some point in time, animals long gone, its weathered wood and tilted walls attesting to its age.

Jaylene radioed to the main house. "Perimeter has been breached. Scan these coordinates for location. No sign of intruders. Checking closest structure — the barn. Send back-up."

She'd already pulled her weapon. I carried a Glock 19 compact, equipped with fifteen rounds and a spare cartridge. Carried but never expected to use it here. The Compound was our sheltered haven, our recuperate-and-relax place. Our home. Since Stone had taught us you never pulled a weapon unless you intended to use it, I knew I'd never think of the Compound as safe again.

Jaylene packed a heavier, longer-barreled Glock 17. Between us we could hold our own in a firefight for a few minutes without reloading, but neither had silver bullets. The old fairy tales had been right about what was needed to slow or stop a lot of the more warrior-like preternaturals — Weres, shifters and vamps. But there was no telling what or who we were dealing with.

"We wait or move in?" Jaylene asked, her muscles tight with the burn of adrenaline coursing through us both.

"Move in," I whispered through parched lips. Last thing I wanted was some of the kids from the Academy, like Sabina, Beau and Herc, to face nasties if we could neutralize them first. There was the flip side of the situation, too. If humans, or mostly humans were after Aini as a means to stop a terrorist threat, it'd be better if Jaylene or I found that out before some trigger-happy teen ended up shooting someone who didn't deserve to die.

Though why another agency didn't just contact Ling Mai or Vaughn directly, work out a mutually compatible arrangement and let us all act like rational adults made no sense. No sense at all.

Infiltrating our Compound was the same as a declaration of war. War meant causalities. No matter how I wanted to spin things, this was not going to end well.

Jaylene nodded, but not before mouthing, "Wink out if we get pinned down. Go for help."

Sounded like a great plan. Too bad I couldn't, nor could I take the time to explain, as she was already creeping away.

She inched to my left, I flanked her right, spreading out as we crept closer to the barn. There were few options to hide once we broke from behind the tree line, with lots of bare ground between where we were and the structure.

Not the best set up for us. If there was someone in the barn, they had all the cover and advantage.

I sucked in a deep breath, then closed the distance, and exposure, as fast as possible. Weapon held close, tucked position a smaller target, breath chugging more from fear than exertion, I flat out ran.

I aimed for a large rock to my right — some cover before a final assault on the barn. Jaylene snagged a spot behind a pile of lumber. Neither location ideal but better than nothing.

"You. Inside. Show yourselves," Jaylene shouted, as if she was used to clearing hostiles from enclosed spaces on a regular basis.

I don't know what I expected — a rush attack, a few shots fired to deter us, something, anything — except a male's laugh.

What the —

The door creaked open as a voice called out, "Jaylene? That you, sweetheart? Hold your fire. I'm coming out. Unarmed."

Sweetheart?

The tension, strung through me so tight I was surprised I hadn't snapped, eased a bit, not in a stand-down-we're-okay way, more in a shaky do-we-trust-what's-going-on way. Unlike the clueless girl in the horror movie who discovers a cat made the noise that scared her silly, right before the monster jumped out from the shadows, I wasn't about to lower my weapon or expect a reprieve. Not yet.

Technically, the man who stepped forward wasn't really unarmed. He dangled his weapon from his right hand, both arms extended overhead. Tall, even taller than Jaylene's six-foot height, and black skin the color of polished ebony, but that's not what was so striking about him. It was his assurance, the raw boldness as if he were stepping into a let's have fun night club, not facing two agents with guns drawn.

"Nice to see you again, Jaylene," he laughed, his attention one hundred percent on my partner.

"F-you and the duck you rode in on, Sweringen," Jaylene snarled, not exposing herself by rising behind her pile of wood. Good thing as I still hugged my ground like the last defensive position it was.

"If I'd known you'd be hanging out here, I'd have hustled over sooner." The man glanced around as if casually checking out the area, but even from my distance I could see the intensity of his face, the tenseness of his muscles. His tone was saying, 'We're all friends' but sort of like a cobra warming up his victim before he struck.

"Throw the weapon away," Jaylene barked. "And call out your buddies."

Sweringen angled his head in a move that might have looked charming, without the gun and breaking onto our land bit, but did as she'd demanded, tossing his gun just far enough to abide by the orders, but close enough he could snatch it in a dive. Very brave or just cocky? Training dictated that once you threw away a weapon you were dead, in spite of what they showed in movies and on the TV. So what was he up to?

"Come on, boys. Meet one of the sexiest women in D.C." His voice rolled across the air, a rich, rumbling baritone. "Jaylene Smart, in the flesh."

So Jaylene had her own secrets on the male-interest department. A quick glance at her warned me that my chiding her about this fact wasn't going to go over too well. If I'd thought she was ready to take my head off before, it was nothing compared to the fire in her eyes now.

Two other men exited the barn, their body language less arrogant, more well-trained tactical experienced, their arms held high.

"That's all of you?" Jaylene snapped, her tone clearly saying she expected a trap.

"Would I mess with you, darling?" Sweringen cast her an arrogant, toe-curling grin.

"In a heartbeat," came Jaylene's whipcord response as she rose to her feet, pausing for a second before shaking her head. "What the hell are you doing here, Mick?"

So she really did know this guy, enough to have him ratcheting up his smile and her to saunter forward, her gun still gripped in her hand but the tension clearly easing from her body.

She didn't glance in my direction as she called out, "Stand down, McAllister. This guy's a bigger threat to your heart than your life."

By the sudden tightening of Sweringen's expression, he didn't like hearing himself being described as basically a benign player. A direct cut to his masculinity. Undercurrents here. Lots of deep ones.

But Jaylene would not be approaching him unless she was one hundred percent sure about her safety, and mine. Let's just hope she was right.

I rose, but slowly, each muscle unclenching until I stood, feet braced, my Glock held steady even if my hands were sweaty, my body language screaming loud and clear that I anticipated a direct attack at any second. That opinion didn't change as I watched Sweringen and his posse all swerve their heads in my direction. Sweringen's eyes tightened even as a small smile kicked up his lips. It was as if he'd found something he was looking for, but not in a male to female way. More a target sighted.

I had no idea who this guy was and no way was I about to lower my guard.

"McAllister?" he asked, his voice still friendly but with a whisper of something else. Something that had the hairs along the back of my neck standing to attention. "That wouldn't be Kelly McAllister now, would it?"

I held my tongue, aware of Jaylene cutting a quick, hard-edged glance my way before responding to him. "What? Not enough conquests, Sweringen?"

He lowered his hands to slap them across his heart. "You're killing me, Jaylene," he murmured. "Didn't we have some good times?"

She shrugged, rather than answered, as I tried to reel in the adrenaline spiking through me with his sudden movement. An action that conveniently meant he was now in a better offensive position. I watched his two friends rock forward, just a smidge, onto the soles of their combat boots. These guys, all of them, were readying themselves. But for what?

Jaylene strolled a little more forward, about half the distance between where I remained and the trio in the shadows of the barn.

"You never answered my question, Sweringen." Her tone now all heat. "What the hell are you doing here? And who are you working for?"

"Obeying orders, darling," he replied, working hard to make it clear he was just like Jaylene. Just one of the grunts caught working for the Man.

"Orders dictating what?"

He rolled one shoulder. "The African girl's a threat. We need to find and secure her before her towel-head of a brother locates her." He glanced at the men behind him before turning back and flashing a big grin at Jaylene. "We're trying to keep you safe."

I just bet he was.

Jaylene was shaking her head but didn't seem as wary as I was. But then she'd hadn't escaped one crazy preternatural already — the day was still young.

Which reminded me. A quick glance at my hand reassured me that I hadn't been imagining the slight warmth to my finger. One or more of these guys were preternatural. How much or what kind I didn't know. Maybe if I stepped closer I could tell how much of a threat they posed. Not that close. I wasn't stupid. Jaylene was welcome to take the risks she was by being as near as she was.

Me, I hesitated. A bunny didn't cozy up to a lion without a very good reason.

"Why didn't you come to the front gate then, Mick?" Jaylene asked, her tone sounding more disappointed than surprised. "You know the concept? Knock? Ask?"

"Seems your director hasn't been as forthcoming as we'd have liked," came Sweringen's answer. He spread his hands before him, a 'What can I say, we tried your way, now we're trying it our way' gesture.

But something was off here. When had Ling Mai been less than forthcoming? Not that she couldn't be secretive, in spades, but she hadn't been around since we learned of the potential terrorist threat and its connection to Aini. Was this guy talking about Vaughn? And when had things escalated to this level?

But like the last two days, there was no time to think through the complications. Not now.

"Guess we'll have to take you and your friends in for questioning then." Jaylene stepped forward and pointed her gun in a gesture indicating arms back in the air, but she was smiling, as if she didn't really see her buddy as a threat. More like she'd scored one on him and wanted him to know it.

I wasn't quite so causal though, realizing only one person, other than we IR agents, was aware that Aini might be at the Compound. Van. And whoever Van worked for.

So were these guys part of Van's team, or were they someone else? I could hardly believe a secondary agency would be as arrogant and desperate to approach connecting with Aini this way. What exactly were they doing? It was broad daylight. Did they want to be spotted? And why weren't they more worried or defensive? It made no sense.

One of the guys behind Sweingen cast a quick glance toward the fence line. The fence and the hole they'd cut into it.

As if I had been slapped upside the head, it suddenly dawned as to what was feeling off. Not Jaylene knowing this guy, but how calm and casual he'd been acting, shooting the breeze, as if waiting for something. Had someone called for back-up before they left the barn? Could that be why Sweringen had exited first, giving his team a few more minutes to call someone else?

That's when I caught the movement out of the corner of my eye.

"Jaylene! More incoming!"

I dove behind my rock as the scene around me exploded. Jaylene raised her gun, laying down a quick pattern that scattered the trio and kept Sweringen from reaching his weapon. Not that he was trying. Nor was she trying to hit them. Just contain them long enough for our cavalry to arrive.

Hurry someone? Two to who knew how many were not great odds.

Sweringen wasn't behaving like an operative under attack, though. He, and his posse, were pelting across the open area. Not escaping but running. Straight toward me.

CHAPTER 26

What the? Firing at unsubs — unknown suspects — was one thing. If these guys had been total strangers, it'd be a whole lot easier to fire to stop them. But—

Both Jaylene and I were shooting to deter or deflect, not to maim or kill. At least I was. Jaylene ducked behind the wood pile again and turned to hold off the threat approaching from the tree line. Four more. Sweringen's team wasn't large but the odds had just increased to seven against two. We were caught between two assaults.

"Wink," Jaylene screamed. "Now!"

She meant disappear before Sweringen reached me.

Trust me, I was trying. Something I never had to do before. Turning invisible had always been my curse, something I tried to avoid as much as possible. Now? Scared out of my gourd, adrenaline slamming through me at mach speed, all the elements were in full force that should have had me vanishing.

Nothing.

When extra abilities don't work, fall back on human abilities. I tightened my grip on my Glock and kept firing. A sudden scream told me I'd hit one of the men, the one just behind Sweringen, who didn't even pause as he continued to barrel forward. The third guy angled to my left, leaving Sweringen aiming for my right.

Scuttling back behind the rock, I froze.

Shoot to kill?

I'd killed once already. Not here — in Africa — and had yet to come to terms with that. To neutralize a threat was one thing, and these guys *were* threats. Big ones, but ... bile choked me. Taking a life wasn't easy. Not like TV, movies and video games made it appear. *Pow.* Another individual bites the dust. They disappear off screen. No, in real life it wasn't like that at all.

Options?

Could I run? Far and fast enough to give our back-up time to reach us? And where were they?

A shout to my left had me scrambling, gun pointed and firing before rational thought stopped me. The man dived, my shot whizzing past his shoulder. Before I could regroup, someone slammed into me from behind.

Sweringen.

My gun flew as I sprawled face forward into the dirt. I twisted, legs kicking, fingers reaching for any body part I could gouge but not making any headway. On my back I was totally defenseless. Sweringen was big, all muscle, and all male. And enraged. Not an experienced fighter who wanted to subdue a woman eighty pounds lighter than him and a good foot shorter, but trying to annihilate me.

I clawed a handful of dirt and pebbles and tossed it toward his face. Followed by a quick, hard jab of my elbow forward, catching him square in the nose. He reared back. An instinctual response and I scrambled, crab walking backward as he smeared blood across his face. I didn't get far before he snagged me and reeled me in.

I choked in a breath as I aimed my elbow bone into his chin, hitting hard enough I could hear the sound of his teeth snapping together.

He reached out, grabbing at my hands, when I saw it. There. On the inside of his arm.

The tattoo. The Horned One. Rude, crude and red.

Time slammed to a halt as I froze. Only for a second, but that's all he needed. My wrists were manacled by one of his hands, my arms stretched over my head and pinned into the ground. He straddled me, pressing down until his face was inches from me. His eyes flamed, crimson red. His breath gagged me — the stench I remembered from before. On the library steps. Sulphur. Corrosive. Overwhelming.

I twisted my head but it was pointless. He laughed. Not the good-buddy chuckle he'd shared with Jaylene. This sounded like it rumbled from a bottomless well.

"You'll learn not to interfere, Guardian," that disembodied voice promised as his free hand circled and banded against my throat. "You'll not awaken her."

Tight. Then tighter.

No air. A pinprick of lights. A roaring sound. Not inside but outside.

Déjà vu. The man on the steps. Choking the life out of me.

My struggle ebbed. This was it.

Van.

Too late.

Sweringen cackled. He'd won and he knew it.

But I wasn't down for the count. Yet. Channeling a few lessons my fellow IR comrades taught me, I used every ounce of energy I had left to raise my knee in one tight, swift upward motion. Bam! Family jewels meet Kindergarten Kelly and not in a nice way.

Sweringen screamed and reared back, giving me room to breathe, releasing his hands to cup himself.

Too late Big Guy!

Someone else shouted, a guttural sound more animal than human as something crashed into Sweringen, smashing him into the rock to my side.

I chugged a deep breath.

Two bodies now, rolling over the top of me. I couldn't crawl away, could barely lower my hands to protect my head. But I could breathe. Sweet, huge gulps of air.

Sweringen and his attacker rolled over and over, freeing me. Not that I could do more than inch away, turtle-style, expecting to be flattened any second. Elbows, arms, legs smacked into me. I was the inert mat in the ring of a boxing match.

Someone grabbed my shoulders, wrenching me backwards so fast I almost flew, landing with a dull thud next to Alex.

"What—"

"Can you move?" she demanded, her attention on the noises behind me.

Best I could do was push to my knees and crawl. Alex growled in my ear. "Get your rear in gear before one of them shifts."

One of who?

That's when the searing heat across my ring finger slammed into me. Preternaturals.

Instead of thinking, I used every ounce of energy I had to jacknife to a crouch. All I could manage. Alex had been concentrating her attention on where I'd been when she twisted, snagged my arm, her grip bruising as she dragged me forward; past the crumpled man I'd shot earlier, his eyes staring sightless at the sky.

Had I done that? Dry heaves erupted in my throat, gagging me, strangling me as much as the hands had earlier.

"Just a little further," Alex promised, not stopping until we were in the lee of the barn. I recognized the splintery, weathered wood as she shoved me against it. Which was smart. I wouldn't have managed sitting upright on my own.

"Who?" I whispered, when I caught my breath, working to get that one word out.

All I received for an answer was a puzzled frown as Alex bent across me, her hands as gentle as she could make them as she pressed fingers against my collarbone and neck.

"Who?" She glanced over her shoulder before returning her attention to my abraded skin. "Van." Then back to business, she added, "Nothing broken. You look like hell and will have a heck of a bruise necklace."

"Are they…" the rest of the sentence was lost in a spate of coughing which hurt as bad as getting the life choked out of me. Almost.

"Are they his teammates?" She spoke out loud my unasked question as her frown deepened. "Assholes."

"So they're not…"

"Hell yes, they are."

That made no sense. Why would Van attack his own men? Why would they attack me if they were trying to reach Aini? Weren't we on the same side? The us versus them side?

Alex hunkered down beside me, which let me know Jaylene was all right. If she hadn't been, Alex would have high tailed it away as soon as she knew I'd live. As if I'd communicated, she continued, "Seems Van's superior must have had a back-up plan if Van couldn't get to Aini through you or me."

I waved my hands toward the dead man on the ground.

"Yeah," she nodded. "Friggin' waste of life."

Easing around the edge of the barn, she fist-pumped her closed fist. "Van's got him, tied slicker than snagging a greased pig in a hog wrestling contest."

Since I'd attended my share of Iowa State fairs growing up, I knew exactly what she meant. Which made it easier to take the next breath. And the one after that. My heart rate decreased to a slow gallop.

That didn't mean I was ready to see Van appear from the front of the barn, Sweringen at his side, arms tied behind him, both men looking the worse for wear. Bloody gashes marred both their faces. The one on Van was quickly healing, as were the bruises. Lucky shifter blood. Sweringnen looked like I felt, rode hard and put away broken even as his wounds were closing before my eyes.

Van's eyes narrowed as he glared at me.

My hand went to my throat before I realized I had no reason to be glared at. It wasn't like I'd called the wrath of Sweringen and his buds down on me.

Alex jumped to her feet as if my alter ego, approaching Sweringen with her hands clenched at her side. "What the hell do you think you were doing? You could have killed her."

Sweringen was shaking his head as if dazed. Or confused. His eyes looked unfocused, no longer that glowing demon red I'd seen earlier, nor did he reek of rotten eggs. In spite of that, I caught myself scooting backwards, putting more distance between him and me. As much as I could manage until I could get back to my feet and run.

Van was bending over, his hands on his knees, shaking his head as he looked at his teammate sideways. "New orders?"

"I failed," Sweringen whispered as if the words were drug from him.

"Failed to reach the girl? Or to kill Kelly?" Van growled.

"Hey, man, I ... I didn't—"

If I could more than croak I would have warned Van not to trust what the other man said, teammate or not, but before I could, Sweringen suddenly stiffened, straightened to his full height, his head thrust back as if pulled from behind. Then he toppled.

"What the— " Van didn't finish as he crouched beside the other man. "Sweringen?"

"Tell him I failed," Sweringen rasped, then twisted, as if in extreme pain.

"Alex, get help," Van ordered, "Now!" His voice rose as he scrambled for a pulse. "Mick?"

Alex made a quick call on her comm set then knelt down across from Van, on Sweringen's other side, the one closest to me. The best I could do was muddle to my knees, not trusting that this wasn't another ruse, in spite of the expression on Van's face.

It wasn't panic raging through him, though that's what I sensed. His actions were calm and controlled, the kind of movements derived from years of training, sort of what you'd see in Emergency Room medics. Not a wasted gesture even as all life drained from Sweringen's face, leaving a still blankness.

I swallowed as I whispered, "Anything?"

Van shook his head, not even glancing at me, or his sister, as he murmured, "I didn't hit him that hard." Then he looked up, and I wished he hadn't. The bleakness in his gaze told me that Sweringen had been more than a teammate. He'd been a friend. Someone close, and Van had killed him.

Unless ... I crawled forward, nudging Alex out of the way as I reached and turned the dead man's arm. Just as I suspected.

"What are you—" Alex started then sputtered off as she caught what I was trying to show her. Twisting Sweringen's arm, it was easier to see his familiar tattoo.

"The Horned One," I wheezed. Then I looked at Van. "You didn't kill him. Whatever took over his body did."

"Doesn't matter," Van spoke as much to himself as to Alex and me. "He's still dead."

There was noise just behind him. Herc, Wyatt, Mandy and Jaylene had rounded up the rest of Sweringen's group, four of them, hands behind their backs, sullen expressions on their faces. It was everything I could do not to walk up to them and slap them silly.

I know, not very agent-like but right then I wasn't feeling particularly agent-like or even nice. This getting attacked every time I turned around was getting old. And hurt like the blazes.

"What do you want us to do with them?" Herc asked, adrenaline clearly still screaming through him. Must be exciting at his age. Better than a video game. He hadn't just lost two teammates, seen operatives die who didn't need to die, wasn't going to send home two body bags to a fellow agency and for what?

Alex stood, walked over to the prisoners, checked their restraints once as she studied her brother, standing a little apart.

I'd never lost a teammate in the field, so I couldn't say I knew what he felt, especially layered on betrayal. These guys, none of them, should have been here, armed and ready to rumble.

A quick look at Sweringen, and behind him, the man I'd taken down, made my stomach twist.

But wait.

I stood, bracing my legs as I grappled for something eluding me.

"Jaylene?"

She turned her head to look at me, only far enough to keep her eye on the four in front of her. "Yeah?"

"How many came in behind us?"

A scowl marked her face. "Four. Why?"

I was already stepping over Sweringen's body, kicking into gear.

"What's up?" Alex demanded as I raced past her.

A good operative would have clued the team in, or been able to talk around the pain banding my throat, the fear jumpstarting my pulse.

"Kels?" Alex shouted at me.

"Count them," I strained to shout over my shoulder. "Call headquarters. Back up needed for Aini."

I could hear Jaylene's oath as she barked out what I'd just realized. "There're only six of these a-holes here. Should be seven."

Bingo. And where was the seventh one?

The attack had been a ruse. The assault on Jaylene and me was a diversion. We'd divided our limited resources to fight off a feint.

Their target all along was Aini.

CHAPTER 27

Spying my discarded Glock, I snatched it up, sprinting like a speed demon. Punching my comm set device as I darted over rocks and around tree fall, I shouted as I ran, "Need help. Stat."

A young girl's voice came over my head set, her voice shaking but clear. "Report?"

"Threat against Aini. Send any backup available. One unsub. Camo fatigues. Assume armed and deadly."

Talking tore at the inside of my throat as I clicked off. My lungs screamed, and my heart rumbaed triple time.

Don't hurt her. Don't hurt her. Don't—

I didn't know if Van or Alex followed. Alex would know where to go, Van didn't, but I didn't pause to look behind me. I don't think I wanted to know if I'd judged him so wrong.

Quickest route from the barn to the hospital wing was diagonal past the training field, hopscotching between a parking lot and the dorm rooms, then hard right before the main building.

I hadn't seen or heard a soul. All out on guard duty, which made sense since we'd just been attacked, but the emptiness cast an eerie silence everywhere. No shouts, no movement, not even some birdsong. The fear and the sweat staining my skin chilled me. Somewhere, up ahead, evil waited. Anyone who went after a helpless child rated evil in my ledger of good and bad. Given what I'd faced since becoming an IR agent, that said a lot.

Catching my side as I raced up to the door nearest the two state-of-the-art rooms used as our medical facility, I paused, when everything in me screamed hurry, hurry, hurry. Running in half-cocked could get me killed. Aini and me both. I had no idea where the seventh man was, but I did know he'd be trained and determined. He could also be a preternatural, which meant he wouldn't be easy to take down alone.

As if I'd ever thought that.

Sucking in a deep breath, I checked my Glock, hit the magazine release, slipped it out and clicked the slide back. Empty. Figured that. Grabbing my remaining magazine, I slipped it into place and snapped it with a muted thud. The movements Stone had taught us until they were second nature helped slow my pulse, calm pounding nerves.

Finger on the frame, I pulled the slide back before I grabbed the door handle. Locked and loaded.

"I'm coming Aini," I whispered, no louder than a breeze, and slipped through the doorway.

Silence. That strained, suspended silence of someone, or something, waiting just beyond the next bend in the hallway.

My muscles tightened, sweat dampening my lower back in spite of the shadowed coolness of the interior. I pushed up the long sleeves of my cotton t-shirt, re-gripped my weapon.

The route to the two rooms, one with double hospital beds where Aini was, the other equipped as a surgery and medical supply center, was twenty steps to the first left, forty steps more. Hard right. Then target dead ahead.

Swallowing back the emotion burning the inside of my stomach and throat, I held my weapon two-fisted style, raised hands, body crouched as low as I could and still move easily, minimizing myself as a target.

Breathe. The one thing Stone had to keep reminding me in training. It was too easy to hold your breath until you got light-headed and passed out. Except for me, I usually disappeared before that happened, which held its own set of ramifications, all of them bad. So Stone drilled me relentlessly before I ever got to the point that terror kicked in and, *poof*, I was gone. Though it still happened. Or used to. Now, when I could have used the ability, nothing.

Right now the panic and fear were there, pounding through me in full force, but so was determination. No one was going to hurt Aini. Not while I lived.

A pause at the end of the first turn, quick peek around the corner.

A body. Crumpled on the floor against the far wall, halfway between the next turn and me.

Ours, not the intruder's. Unless he'd switched out of the camo gear his buddies were wearing and donned a pink hoody, a pair of Basquiat freestyle Reeboks, and was female.

A quick listen told me nothing. Which possibly meant Sweringen's teammate wasn't hunkered down just out of sight. Razoring across the exposed hallway, I crouched beside the body, one hand out to feel for a pulse, my attention still focused straight ahead. There was only a single way in and out of this wing of the building; past where I huddled.

Two fingers to the throat found a thready heartbeat. Alive, but barely. Only then did I look to see who it was.

My heart bellyflopped. Sabina. The teen witch from Paris.

She was barely Aini's age — fifteen. What was she doing … oh, blimey, my orders to send back-up to Aini. Of course. Sabina had been the young voice on the other end of my S.O.S. call. I'd sent her into harm's way and she was just a kid with no training in combat, nothing except for what magic she knew.

I tapped my comm set device to get help for her. The device was dead. Or blocked.

Go for medical care or stop the threat against Aini? I knew the operative was ahead somewhere. No choice. If Aini died we'd all die, including Sabina.

"Hang on, kid," I whispered, close to Sabina's ear, aware of the dampness of blood near her temple. Someone had hit her and hit her hard. For that alone, they'd pay. This messed up op of Van's team had gone way beyond the need to secure a girl against her terrorist brother. If that had ever even been the case.

Guess I should be thankful Sabina hadn't been shot or her neck broken, but it wasn't thanksgiving emotions racing through me as I wiped sweaty hands on my pants legs.

Rising to my feet, I skated around Sabina and wallpapered myself against the nearest wall.

Step. Slide. Pause. Listen.

Each silent footfall bringing me closer to Aini.

Step. Slide. Pause. Listen.

I'd nearly reached the turn when I heard sounds. Bodies scuffling. Metal crashing. A scream.

Someone was fighting down that wing, and the only rooms there were the hospital ones. The nurse? Most likely. Another innocent in the line of fire.

Do or die time, Kelly.

Subterfuge over, I gripped my weapon in shaking hands and went from standstill to adrenaline rush in three seconds flat, scooting around the corner and barreling toward the room holding Aini. The one where the racket was erupting.

I'd never navigated a forty-foot hall as fast as I did that one. My senses on hyper drive. Hearing jacked up. Heart in my windpipe.

Bursting through the doorway, I skidded to a stop, weapon raised and aimed.

The room was large enough for two beds, a bathroom, a sink, and enough equipment to keep a coma patient alive, and not much more. Aini lay in the bed nearest the window and furthest from the door. Between her and me, at the foot of the first bed, a man in camo had his hand raised, the butt end of his weapon aimed at the head of a woman in nursing whites.

"Hold it right there," I growled, sounding as bad-ass as Alex, and that was pretty bad-assed.

He barely glanced my way, but he moved like a lightning bug on steroids, whipping his striking arm down and across the woman's windpipe before I could inhale a breath. Her half-scream was choked off as he slammed her back against him, shielding himself while thwarting me from attacking him or getting to Aini.

"Nowhere to go," I said between dry lips. "Two of your teammates are dead. Don't make yourself a third."

His laugh wasn't human. That was my first clue this was not going to end well for one of us. The second?

The tattoo on his arm.

CHAPTER 28

The intruder wasn't large, a lot of guys trained in Special Forces weren't, at least the types who did more than land, secure and leave operations. The ones who were inserted behind enemy lines for long-term missions, or held a position until more troops could arrive, tended to be lean, mean and driven.

This guy was no exception. "Back off or she dies."

I kept my arms steady, same with my voice. "I leave, she dies anyway."

The smile darkening the man's face told me he had no problem with my assessment.

"Reinforcements are coming," I lied, knowing if Sabina had left her post we were stretched crepe-thin. Surely Alex or Stone or Jaylene might be right behind me. I shoved the idea of Van out of the way. Logic dictated his actions could be suspect if he was involved. Who knew where his loyalties were now that his team had botched their mission so badly. Any other thoughts were wishful thinking.

"More of you sissy girls going to take me out?" the guy in front of me laughed. Not that I blamed him. Right then I was feeling pretty sissy, as well as pissed. Why didn't I have an ability that could help in this kind of a checkmate; Alex's magic, Nicki's strength, even Jaylene's down-and-dirty fighting style would have been nice.

Nada. I couldn't even disappear and dive in low, take him by surprise.

The nurse squeaked, probably because the guy had tightened his hold. The whites of her eyes were widening, sweat slid down her face.

Hold on.

Until what? Talking wasn't helping. Who knew when help might arrive and, if it did, he could still twist and take out Aini before we could neutralize him. So what?

Tap your abilities.

The words of the Librarian, which was about as helpful as raising your hands to halt a tornado.

Missy, Miss.

A young girl's voice whispered across me. Aini?

Could I really hear her or was it desperation screaming through me? Sure sounded like her though. I'd heard Carrie, my dead sister, all the time I'd been in Sierra Leone and accepted it. What was different between talking with someone who'd passed beyond and someone who existed in between, not dead but not here? What could I lose by trying?

Aini? That you?

I didn't say the words out loud, keeping my focus on the man before me, the man with eyes growing redder by the second.

He bad juju, Missy Miss. You go.

So it could be Aini. Was this the ability the Librarian had mentioned? No time to figure out the fine details.

Can't go sweetheart. No matter how much bad magic he's got, I'm not leaving you.

Missy, Missy go pa.

She meant disappear.

If only I could.

Sorry, I can't do that either.

I see you pa. Now.

I didn't have the time, or the attention span, to tell her that I couldn't turn invisible. Then I focused on her words. Aini was a seer, a very powerful one by all accounts. She could see the future. Had she said she could see me wink out? Or was that too close to the present for her abilities?

Aini? Are you saying I can disappear? Right now?

Yes'm, Missy Miss. Go. Now.

Well, Sunday bells, why not try? But how?

Disappearing was always like breathing, an automatic response, not something I thought consciously about. But hadn't there been a few times since working with the Agency that I had to focus on my breathing, make sure I took the next breath instead of wigging out?

Oh, yeah, more than a few times.

Usually I thought nice thoughts to keep from turning invisible. So what if I did the opposite? Focused on what could, what would happen, if I didn't wink out?

The nurse would die. Aini would die. My team would die — all of them. And Van. Nothing could stop the Horned One if...

"What the f—" the soldier before me cried, rearing back as if I struck him.

But I hadn't. Glancing at where my arms stretched before me, gripping my gun, all I saw was the Glock wavering in the air.

Halleluiah and handstands. It had worked!

Fifteen seconds.

One of the scary side effects of disappearing was that I had fifteen, and fifteen only, very fast seconds before two doors appeared before me. One door led to my worst nightmares brought to life. The other door let me experience my death, over and over again. Lucky me. And if I didn't choose one of the doors? My body would be twisted in agonizing pain with the bends.

And to think I was actually glad to be invisible.

Count down to the doors appearing.

Thirteen seconds.

Dropping my visible weapon as if it scalded me, I became totally invisible; using the thud of weapon to floor to help disguise any noise I made launching myself forward. Head low, shoulders first as a ram, power thrust from my thighs.

Ten seconds.

Only way to take down the guy was to slam into the nurse and him in the same waist-high tackle. I hit them both, my hands trying to push the nurse to the left as the operative smacked against the foot of the nearest bed. We all crashed in a tangle of arms and legs.

The nurse screamed like a banshee at midnight in one of my nightmares as I lunged for the man's arm. The nurse had to help herself. Which she did, scrambling as fast as possible from being the meat in the middle of a to-the-death sandwich.

Five seconds.

The guy might not see me but he had no doubts I was there as his training kicked past his initial shock. The more experience a soldier or an operative gained, the easier to slide into auto response. Knee to groin. Elbow to gut or kidney. Fingers gouging eyes.

Except I needed two hands to keep his gun directed away from Aini, from me and the nurse. Talk about a rock and a hard place. Except he couldn't see me. Evening the playing field.

Two seconds. No doors yet, but they'd be there.

He carried a Beretta M9. It fired a 9-millimeter round and, if any of Stone's training held, it had a capacity of fifteen rounds. Fifteen chances to kill someone. One chance to stop him.

All I cared about was making sure that gun didn't discharge. A slug hitting any of Aini's equipment could kill her just as easily as a direct hit. Then the guy only had to keep me rolling around on the floor as she died, painfully, oxygen cut off or any of the other artificial means keeping her functioning, silenced.

Where was the rest of my team? Someone? Anyone?

One second. No door. Not yet.

An elbow slammed into my nose, splattering blood across the both of us.

"So you can be hurt?" he snarled, as if I'd just made his day.

His fighting took on a new dimension. I didn't need Stone's coaching to translate what was happening. Disable me. Free his weapon. Kill the girl.

Smashing between the metal bed and hard linoleum floor seemed to be his most immediate strategy. But I had something he didn't; the knowledge that if I let him regain his weapon I'd be dead. Dead meant Aini was next. Desperation was a very good motivator.

"What the hell are you?" he growled, his strength weakening me. He couldn't see it but I figured both of us felt it.

"Your worst nightmare." I channeled my inner Alex as I spoke so close to his ear he flinched. Then I bit it.

All the way through.

Ewwwww!

Alex would have been impressed. All I wanted to do was gag.

Where were the doors?

They should have appeared by now. Split my concentration.

Phooey! Ignore them! Focus on staying alive.

He bellowed, almost deafening me. Almost but not quite as I heard the thud of heavy boots stampeding down the hallway.

The Calvary had arrived.

I popped back into existence. Avoiding the doors, though it'd been a tight squeeze. Now I'd be blind for twice as long as I'd disappeared but—

Taking advantage of my split focus, the man gave a hard, full twist once more, slamming my back against the floor, now straddling me, gun between us. For the space of a breath I saw Sweringen's face swim before me. No, not his face, his expression, and not a human one.

Skin stretched so tight it looked ready to explode, deep grooves carved in his face, nostrils flaring and eyes glowing red as that stench, rotten eggs, washed against me.

"You can't stop us," he promised, uttered as a vow, his voice low and tinny and sounding nothing like the man I'd been fighting. "The Seer is ours."

Déjà vu all over again.

I so was fed up with bully guys smashing me on the ground and using their size and strength against me. Not. Going. To. Happen. Again.

Straining, I popped my head and shoulders upwards, using my skull to crack against his, hard enough lights and stars circled before me.

He shook his head, hard, then sank forward, all but smothering me with the sudden weight.

Too late, I forgot about the gun between us.

The one that exploded.

CHAPTER 29

The roar of gunfire at close range deafened me, even muffled by our two bodies. I wanted to scream, to scramble away, get out from under that weight, that stench, that sticky wetness spreading across me.

Ick factor times ten.

There was no time to think, only to react as strong hands grabbed the dead soldier's shoulders and tossed him into the corner away from me and Aini as easily as I could toss a crumbled napkin.

My first action? Breathe, as more people crowded into the room. Wyatt called out my name. I didn't catch the rest as Van materialized beside me, a dark shadow blocking the light of the overhead fluorescent lighting. A deep furrow cut the angles of his face, golden amber rimming his dark eyes — a sure sign his wolf was raring to appear.

I concentrated on him as an anchor, the one stable thing in a world that had just tilted. That and the fact I could see. I should be blind. Anything to ignore the fact I'd taken another life.

I didn't kill that man. I didn't. Did I?

Focus on Van. He wasn't the bad guy here. Not this time. Not yet. He was here when I needed him. Again. Focus on that.

"Gotta stop meeting like this." I meant it as a joke, but since I could barely croak out the words my attempt fell flat. Van was ignoring my words anyway, his hands running themselves over me, not in the way I wanted, but coolly, clinically, until I caught the tremor in his voice as he spoke out loud. "No wounds."

Not visible. But I'd killed a man and that always left wounds.

I tried again, low, so only he could hear me as he leaned down to listen. "No need to keep saving me."

"Then keep your ass out of trouble." Guess it was my day for growling men, even though I knew he meant it to sound caring. He had to work on that. Either that or I had to work on my timing. Which sucked.

"Kels?" Alex skidded to the floor beside me. "You alive?"

The jury was out on that one as I could still feel the wetness coating the front of me, still smell the coppery taint.

His blood? My blood?

"Give her some air," Van snapped at his sister.

"She doesn't need air, she needs a medic you idiot."

Lord love a naked chicken, if they didn't stop I'd be in the middle of another free-for-all. "Aini?" I croaked, adjusting their focus.

Alex glared at her brother for a second before rising to her feet and stepping over me. I couldn't see what she was doing but started breathing easier the second she announced, "Looks the same. All equipment working."

Amen. "Sabina? The nurse?"

"Doctor's with Sabina," Van said, his frown easing from lethal to frustrated as all get out. At me, of course. "Nurse is going to be okay. Vaughn took her outside."

Lucky nurse. If I were outside I'd have some reprieve from the intensity that was Van Noziak. Maybe.

Wyatt's concerned face hovered into view. "Do I need to get an ambulance?"

I shook my head, surprised at how much effort it took. But then I'd been attacked twice plus I was distracted. Not by worried Wyatt, or frowning Van, but by the fact that I could see them both. Usually when I reappeared after an invisible event, I'd be blind twice as long as I'd been gone. Not this time though. Why? And what had happened to the two doors?

The blood iced in my veins. As much as I hated my freaky ability, I came to expect knowing what was happening when it occurred. Now? Pink elephants and purple alligators, I didn't need one more hell-in-a-hand-basket issue to deal with.

My turn to change focus, act like an operative instead of ... instead of a shaking, scared-to-my-toes ninny. No matter how I felt.

"Help me up." I raised one hand toward Van, only then noticing how it trembled. So did he.

"You're going to get yourself killed." He didn't move as his tone now sounded ice cold and lethal.

"If I didn't stop the guy, Aini would've died. She dies, we all die."

Two seconds ago, the nicest thing in the world was knowing I was still alive and Van was beside me, not necessarily in that order. Now? Now I wanted to smack him across his over-protective, he-man face.

Who knew anger could work as a cure-all for a pity session?

He must have gotten my message as he rocked back to his feet, reaching for my hand and pulling me up in one economical movement, nudging Wyatt out of the way at the same time. Stone and Jaylene were blocking others in the doorway, acting as a human barricade. No need to fill the room with too many agents jacked up on adrenaline and blood lust.

"All well?" Stone asked, though he could see what the rest of us knew; one intruder dead, Aini safe, Wyatt standing around looking frustrated and wanting to lash out, one agent very glad to lean against Van, just for another second.

Van circled one arm around me. I'm sure it looked comrade-to-comrade to anyone without a clue, as if there were any of them around. Right then I didn't care. I needed to hear his breathing, feel his heartbeat, the heat of his skin telling me he was alive and so was I. Plus, as long as I leaned against him, he wasn't reading me the riot act.

"You look like crap." Jaylene nodded from the doorway. "Better change out of those clothes before you scare the newbie recruits."

She had a point.

Van eyed her. "Could be just what they need." He cast a pointed glance toward Wyatt and, if I had an ounce of energy, I'd have jammed my elbow into his gut. "We're not playing at war games here. Best they know that what they're really facing while they can still get out."

"Would your comrades leave at this point?" I jumped in, looking up at him, which was harder than it sounded with him standing so close. So I inched away, just enough to glare easier.

"No."

"Then don't expect ours to either."

It wasn't a rebuke as much as a get-real-or-go-home statement of fact. His expression told me he didn't like it. Or maybe it was me right then.

"Guess we have one question answered," I murmured, scrambling to ignore the adrenaline still coursing through me.

"What?" Van took my bait.

"The Horned One wants Aini dead."

"Like we didn't know that any way," came Van's curt reply.

He was right, though I wasn't about to share that. Shift focus. To what?

Myself? I no doubt looked like I'd been almost choked to death and raced across the compound to wrangle with a killer who then splattered his guts all over me. Life wasn't fair, as if I needed that lesson hammered home.

I was focusing on something, anything except the dead man crumpled in the corner, the third man who'd died by my hand, intentional or not.

Swallowing to keep the bile from gagging me, I caught a tightening of Van's muscles next to me. He stilled, suddenly on high alert.

"What?" I glanced to see what had caught his attention.

Me. Or more specifically my torso. My blood-stained, gooey yuck of a shirt.

"I'm a wreck, I know it." No way was I going to brush my hands against my tee. Instead I snagged the hem to pull it as far away from my body as possible. That's when he reached over and tugged my sleeves down, covering my arms.

But not before I saw what had staggered him.

My left arm. Inside it, between elbow and wrist. A tattoo.

Not any tattoo, but an angry, raw looking image of the Horned One.

CHAPTER 30

No. No. No. No!

For the second time in a matter of minutes I went into zombie-still mode, the mind-numbing, muscle tightening shock of one too many blows. The kind of blows you couldn't dodge.

"What's up?" Alex asked from behind me, still standing next to Aini's bed. She must have caught on to the sudden stillness of her brother and me. I could hear Jaylene and Stone talking to someone outside the room, in the hallway, the muted beep of Aini's life-support machines, the squawk of Wyatt's comm set turned way too high as he fiddled with it. My mind scrambling to find normalcy. Which wasn't coming.

"Nothing," Van responded to Alex, shutting her out as he kept his pitch-dark eyes glued on me. "Making sure Kelly's okay."

Which I wasn't. Not by a long shot.

If others with this mark had tried to attack Aini, logic said I'd do the same. A conclusion shaking me to my core.

Clawing past the fear galloping through me, I stepped nearer to Van, closing the space until I was sure only he could hear me. "Don't let me hurt her," I begged, my words raw, choked by terror. "Please. Don't."

His hands came down on my shoulder, tightening, as effective as a bucketful of cold water. "Don't be an idiot."

"But—"

"No buts," he snarled, ducking his head until it looked as if he was embracing me, kissing me, not stopping me from spiraling out of control. "Hang on," he whispered before casting one sharp glance over his shoulder at Alex and saying, "I'm getting Kels out of here."

Next thing I knew he was wrapping his arm around my shoulder, banding me against his body, propelling me forward.

Which was good since I wasn't capable of moving on my own.

Who'd have thought, even minutes ago, that I'd appreciate, as in a thank-you-Jesus appreciate, Van's alpha qualities so much.

I didn't say anything, couldn't, until we'd navigated past the huddle of agents-in-training choking the hallway. For a brief second my gaze caught Wyatt's, his questioning, mine no doubt glazed, before I dropped it.

Van didn't say a word until he slammed open the doorway I'd entered just a short while ago.

"Where?" he demanded, ignoring the wash of warmer air over us. Heat kissing my skin but doing nothing for the chill feathering through my body.

Focus. He'd asked a question.

"Where what?" I stammered.

We'd paused, me shaking, him holding me by one arm, the gesture of a peer comforting another. He looked up at someone passing in the distance, gave a silent hey-how-are-you-all's-well-here chin nod, then tightened his grip.

Note to self; Van was very good in a crisis. But I'd already known that. How good would he be if it came to having to put me down like a rabid dog?

"Need privacy," he said, "and something clean for you to put on."

A quick glance at him showed me the golden rim of his eyes. His wolf peeking out.

Of course. Bloody shirt me wasn't making it easy for him to be so close.

I nodded toward the dormitory building. No one should be around there, not now, at least not for a few minutes.

He maneuvered us inside the hushed coolness quicker then I could say Jiminy Cricket, if I could talk around the fist-sized lump jamming my throat.

But Van didn't seem to expect much of me right then. After using a shaky finger to point out my footlocker, he rummaged around, pausing only a split second when he'd snagged a new pair of sin-red panties.

My not-the-kindergarten-teacher panties that I'd bought after Africa and a certain scorching kiss. A girl had to plan ahead, though those plans had just been torched once and for all.

His one eyebrow arched, then he gingerly replaced the scrap of lace and silk as if handling a live grenade. When he found a long-sleeve t-shirt, he rose to his feet, neither of us looking each other in the eye and handed it to me.

"You need help getting changed?"

I might have, but not from him, not right that second. Had I mentioned our timing sucked?

Instead of answering I shook my head, clutching the shirt as if it'd give me some sense of stability. Without thought I said, "Turn around."

His brow climbed so high it'd have been lost in his hair if it'd been a tad longer.

Of course, how stupid could I be? I'd just been tagged to become a minion of the Horned One. The last thing Van could afford to do was let me out of his sight. For any reason.

"Shit," I murmured, a word I never, ever used, no matter how appropriate. But that's what it felt like right then, everything spiraling out of control. For a moment, just one moment, I thought we'd finally been on the winning side of events. We'd just stopped another attack against Aini. That should have been a high-five point in time. Shouldn't it?

Yes, I was being a whiney baby, but that beat screaming at the top of my lungs and tearing out my hair, though I might resort to those any second.

"I could kill her." The words leaked out, past my bone-dry throat. I looked up at Van. "Aini. I could kill her."

"Get it together, Kels." Van took a step back from me, giving us both a sense of breathing room. "You're not going to hurt Aini."

"How do you know that?" I strangled the shirt in my hands. "We don't know what sets off –" I raised my left arm, not able to even mouth the words— "what sets off this thing. Any second I could attack you then go after Aini."

He actually had the gall to crook up a half-smile. "Earth to Kelly. Remember? I'm a shifter. You're a..."

Freak? An armed nuke? What?

As if he'd translated the fright rolling through me at tsunami strength, he shrugged, reached out his arms and stepped forward, folding me into a hug. He wasn't even grossed out by the mess on the front of my shirt. The one I hadn't made a move to remove yet.

"I'll have to tell my team. Protect them against me."

He hesitated then stepped closer. "Let's wait just a bit."

"No." I flung my hands wide as if seeking an escape. I was, but none that he could offer me. "I won't put them at risk."

"Didn't say you'd have to."

"But—"

"Listen up," he said, his voice a rumble through him, wrapping around me. "And listen well. You're not going to hurt Aini. You won't hurt your team. End of story."

"But—"

"I won't let you."

And right there was my safety net. His unstated promise that he'd do what he'd have to do to keep me from an unspeakable act that I'd never survive.

He brushed a gentle kiss across the top of my head. "I promise."

I nodded my head, not able to say more. It wasn't my raw throat holding me back this time, it was tears.

"You believe me?" he asked as I just stood there, a lump of misery.

Another nod, this one accompanied by a sniff.

"We'll work this out. You've got to trust me."

I would. I did. But that didn't mean I was looking forward to hiding one more dirty, little secret.

If I could have managed to say something, I might have, but the door popped open, Nicki poking her head inside.

Van and I sprang apart as if caught stark naked in a compromising situation.

"There you are," Nicki said, swallowing a smile. "We're all meeting in the Conference room."

"When?" I asked, aware I'd need a different shirt as I'd forgotten my hands were just as much a mess with drying blood as the tee I was wearing.

"Two minutes."

"We'll be there," Van said, saving me the effort.

Nicki shrugged as if no concern of hers. I wanted to shout that I was thinking more of a quick shower than humping Van. Neither was going to work.

"You think I can wash up?" I said without looking at him as the door closed behind Nicki. "The bathroom is through that door." I hitched one shoulder toward the end of the room. "No exits. No windows. No—"

"Go." He bit off the word as if I'd thrown his promise back in his face. "We don't have that much time."

I didn't need to be told twice, and I did appreciate what he was doing for me, more than I could ever tell him. But I had an ulterior motive in escaping into the small bathroom. I wanted to see, hope against hope, if I'd been wrong. If there was no tattoo on my arm. No brand of Cain.

Except there was.

With my shirt off, water washing away the drying blood, my heart stuttering, I couldn't avoid seeing that crude image; a faceless head, blood red, thick lines showing horns.

It was real.

I glanced into the mirror, feeling I should look different; marked, damaged goods. Except for being a little paler, I looked the same. It was all I could do not to slam my fist through the mirror.

"Kelly, gotta go," Van called through the closed door.

How much death and disaster could we handle in one day? I guess I was about to find out as I followed Van into the Conference room. The whole team, newer recruits too, were already assembled, although not everyone had taken their seats yet.

A few people acknowledged me with a nod, a smile. Wyatt walked over and squeezed my arm, my left one. "You all right?" he asked, his tone hiding nothing. I could have hugged him for that alone, except I wasn't all right and Van was glaring at me from the seat he'd snagged across the table.

I offered Wyatt a weak smile. "Fine. Thanks."

Hadn't I just had this conversation? Oh, yeah, when I'd arrived at the gates with Van. I was sure that had been in a previous life. The before-I-became-marked life.

He looked like he wanted to say more but a quick look at Van had him holding back instead. A flush climbed his face as he ducked his head and turned, aiming for the back of the room where the newer recruits were clustered.

Van was sitting in one of the chairs nearest to Vaughn, one leg crossed over the other, his hand gripping his ankle. Cool, controlled, in his element, as if he came to IR meetings on a regular basis, or as if his teammate, and friend, hadn't tried to kill me less than an hour before. That and knowing I was a ticking time bomb.

I said nothing as I grabbed a chair further down the opposite side of the table, although I did register Alex's quick frown as she caught sight of her brother and before she slid into the seat next to me.

I wondered if I should warn her I could go ballistic any moment. Or maybe only if I was close to Aini, which I was going to make sure never happened.

As Jaylene entered the room, shoulder-to-shoulder with Mandy, she all but reared back, slamming to a stop. "What the hell is he doing here?" she demanded, her glare at Van sharp enough to slice.

"Jaylene, if you will take a seat, you will soon discover why I asked Van to join us."

Interesting. Although Jaylene didn't seem to think so as she beetled past Van, making sure the whole room knew she wasn't pleased. Several of the newer recruits glanced nervously at one another, not that I blamed them. Jaylene was not someone you wanted on your bad side. In fact, the only one who didn't seem to be bothered by her was Van. He hadn't as much as looked at her, keeping his attention on the wall behind Vaughn, as if the blank space anchored him.

The table was full by the time Herc joined us, his eyes wide, his movements cautious. He looked afraid to set off the wrong person. I understood where he was coming from as I caught myself pleating my hands, in and out, in and out on the tabletop. When I noticed a partial twitch of Van's lips, I quickly jammed them under the table.

Couldn't get away with anything.

I promised I'd trust him. But for how long?

"If we are all here, we'll begin." Vaughn brought us to order, doing a great impersonation of the Director with her tone. "Van, will you summarize yours and Kelly's meeting earlier with the Librarian."

Had that happened today? That was several lifetimes, and dead bodies, ago. No wonder my head was spinning and that was without thinking of my arm. Sort of like having a sudden cancer diagnosis. Knowing there was something inside of me, something I couldn't stop or remove on my own, couldn't control, just had to survive. If that was possible.

So focused on the tangled hopelessness of my thoughts, I missed some of Van's words. Either that or I was getting tired of hearing bad news layered on bad news.

He did a good job of being clear and concise, even about who the Seekers and Long Hunters were, which drew some frowns. Then Van wrapped up with seeing the Library guard dead on the front steps of the Jefferson Building. That part I knew well, remembering the confusion the sight created then, and now, too. And here I'd thought that was the worst the day was going to bring. Naïve, clueless me.

No one said a word until Alex broke the silence when she looked at her brother. "So you tasered this man, then he chased you out the door and died?"

Ouch. I knew Noziaks played rough but he was her brother. Her tone made it sound like he was two on two for killing innocent people. First the library guard then Sweringen. On the other hand, it kept questions about the Seekers minimized, which was good because we still didn't have tons of answers.

"The guard was a preternatural," I interjected, earning a quick frown and raised brow from Van. I knew he could speak for himself, but would forget to protect himself, too. "And I was the one who had the Taser." At least initially, but if the weapon caused a heart attack, it was as much my responsibility as Van's.

Alex threw me a veiled what-are-you-doing look.

Just making things clear.

Alex wasn't finished though. "Still the guard died, much like Sweringen." She sounded like she was working out something that was bothering her. "Both were in a fight, then appeared fine, well enough to walk and talk and then—"

"Exactly." Van looked at Vaughn as if she already knew what he was going to say next. "There was another characteristic between the two. The tattoo."

And now me. Except I wasn't dead. Yet.

"And the man who attacked Aini had the same image," I added, as if I wasn't in the same boat.

"What tattoo?" Herc spoke from down the table, earning a what-are-you-doing jab from one of the new agents-in-training beside him. His frown indicated he had no idea what she wanted. He spoke to everyone. "If we're here it means we need to know. If this tat is a clue shouldn't we know what it looks like?"

"Like this," I pushed a quick sketch I just made toward him, not sharing how well I knew this particular image. "Except the color inside the outline is red not black."

"Mick didn't have a tat like that on him," Jaylene piped up, chewing her lower lip. "Not before and not on his arm." She looked around before adding, "He had other tats but none that were that easily visible."

Oh, crap. That meant he was closer to her than I'd originally thought. No wonder she was po'd with Van if she thought he was responsible for Sweringen's death.

"When was the last time you saw the victim's arms?" Stone asked, putting Jaylene on the spot. But if anyone thought Jaylene was going to squirm, they didn't know her well.

She cocked her chin higher, her nostrils flaring as she looked the agency instructor in the eye before answering. "Two weeks ago."

"I saw him this morning," Van said, his voice as flat as a slab of granite. "And he didn't have the tat then."

Jaylene's expression indicated the last person she expected, or wanted, to back her up was Van.

Vaughn glanced at him. "Were you aware Mr. Sweringen was preternatural?"

Van gave an angry jerk of his head. "No." It sounded like an oath. Then to make things clear to the rest of us he said, "I can scent Weres and other shifters, a few of the lesser demons and a fae in heat. Mick wasn't any of them. If he was a preter, I didn't know it."

"But you two knew each other. Well." Jaylene made it sound like an accusation.

"Yes." Van was back to staring at that empty spot on the far wall. "We were friends, had been for a long time. Mick didn't share and I didn't ask. No reason to. My mistake. Assuming he was human."

"It wasn't a mistake," I threw out, earning a hard frown from Alex, and an even more lethal one from Jaylene, but I wasn't going to let that stop me.

Stone looked at me. "You know if that last guy, the one who attacked Aini, was preternatural?"

"No idea." I didn't say that there'd been little time with that whole fighting-for-my-life bit going on. "I didn't notice my ring heating up."

"So we have five suspicious and sudden deaths," Stone summed up.

"And one attacker with the mark who did not die, as far as I know." Looking at the confused faces, I clarified. "The first attack on me, outside the Library. He had the mark."

"And ran away, so we don't know if he died or not." Van spoke like an operative and not someone hiding a dangerous secret. My secret.

I could learn from his lead if I wasn't feeling so guilty and conflicted.

Glancing at Vaughn I asked, "From what you can tell of the autopsies, were the nurse or the police officer or the library guard the same species?" I knew there hadn't been time to find out about Sweringen and the guy from Aini's room, but I had a theory.

Vaughn gave me one of her job-well-done smiles. "The nurse was an Alvor elf, Officer Packard a shifter, and the library guard a Were."

I looked across the table. "From what Van said his — Sweringen — wasn't a shifter or a Were."

"He could have been something else," Van interjected, giving me a hard look. "In fact it's very likely he was preternatural, judging from the way he fought, a few incidents I can recall from the past. I just don't know what kind. A fae, maybe, or something else I couldn't scent."

"Which means what?" Jaylene sniped.

I knew she was hurting so I let it slide, kept my tone neutral as I answered. "It means that preternaturals are being used as servants for this Horned One. The Librarian mentioned something about that possibility." The fear I'd been fighting to control bubbled to the fore even as I glanced around the table, keeping my voice calm and level. The fact I was now marked must mean I was a preternatural of some kind. But what kind? Which brought me to my second point. "It didn't matter what kind of preternatural being Sweringen or any of the others were, they were vulnerable. And handy."

"You're saying this Horned One took over these bodies?" Alex didn't try to keep the incredulity from her tone.

"From what the Librarian indicated earlier, we might be dealing with something capable of ... I don't know. Controlling another's mind, or just their body." I shifted the conversation just a smidge, from a hunch to something I could back up with a stronger opinion. Besides we were tap dancing too close to what I was hiding. Maybe I was safe, though? I was different, but I'd never set off our silver rings, so maybe I was marked and it wouldn't work. Had I dodged the bullet?

Naïve Kelly back in full force.

"You mean like a zombie?" Herc asked, his voice sounding more intrigued than shocked.

"Yes." I glanced at Van. "Your friend, Mick, seemed rattled or confused before he passed out."

"I saw that, too." Alex backed me up.

"Which means what?" Vaughn asked.

I shrugged, still working out the details. "I'm thinking, and this is conjecture, not fact yet, that if this Horned One can take over others, we might be aiming for a constantly moving target."

Jaylene whistled, her focus on my previous words. "So this means the Horned One is unstoppable?"

"Just the opposite." I looked at Van for confirmation. "According to the Librarian the Horned One can't easily be stopped because he doesn't reside on our plane. But his primary host body can be killed."

Van nodded. "That's right. Kill the host, the person directing the attacks and who is behind using others, and we weaken the Horned One."

"Weaken isn't killing." Jaylene shot back.

"No, but we have a secret weapon."

Jaylene cut her glance at me. "What?"

"Not what, but who." At the puzzled frowns around me I added, "Aini. Once she turns sixteen, the Horned One can no longer stop her. And she's supposed to be able to stop him. Or the Seekers. Or both."

What a mess. On the other hand, I was actually feeling like we stood a chance when Jaylene sat back in her chair, crossing her arms. "Aini? The kid who's in a coma? How the hell do we know when she turns sixteen?"

Talk about deflating my hope balloon even if Jaylene was right.

"I discovered her birth date." Vaughn caught all of us off guard.

"How? She told me she had no family."

"Except for a suspected terrorist brother," Van slid in, muddying the waters. As if we weren't in deep enough trouble.

"You sure there really is a brother?" I didn't want to look at him, not feeling as conflicted as I did, but the words tumbled out. "Or was stopping a suspected terrorist an excuse? A reason for your team to come around here to get access to Aini."

Alex caught my arm, stopping me from saying more. Thank heavens, as it looked like what I'd said had blasted Van right between the eyes.

Sure he was watching my back, but did that mean he didn't get to hear the possible truth? Guess he didn't figure his director, or superior, or whoever he'd been taking orders from would have used him as a red herring, distracting us while his team attacked. And Van called me the clueless one.

"Figure out the brother later," Stone jumped in, yanking us back in line, his attention on Vaughn. "When does Aini turn sixteen, and how reliable is the intel?"

"I spoke to someone from Zimmi who knew her family and her as a child." Vaughn kept her gaze averted from mine. Which warned me I wasn't going to care for the source of the information.

"Who?" Alex asked, giving me a sideways glance as if she too had guessed the informant based on the name of the small town in southeast Sierra Leone.

"Let me presume." Yes, my tone was less than gracious. So what? I'd had more than a rough day and we were discussing the man who killed my sister. Or the sister I thought I had. "You spoke with Gbendi Jebo."

The silence in the room was squeaky tense, most knowing the rumors, if not all the details, about a man I wanted to kill, almost did, would have if I hadn't been turned aside. Probably a good thing as I was getting enough blood on my hands as it was.

"Yes." Vaughn nodded, never taking her eyes off me, as if it was the most natural thing in the world to chat with a man I saw as the devil incarnate, even if he saved my life. My last mission to Africa had been complicated on so many levels I hadn't even begun to pull apart the tangled threads.

"And?" Jaylene demanded, bringing us all back to the most pressing issue, stopping annihilation. "So when's she sixteen?"

"Tomorrow."

CHAPTER 31

"That's good news, isn't it?" one of the new agents-in-training at the end of the conference table asked when the strain in the room escalated rather than eased with Vaughn's announcement. "I mean, by tomorrow won't this girl be safe? And if she's safe, we all should be safe?"

"Not exactly." Alex oscillated her head, a slow, resigned movement, like an ineffectual fan against summer's unrelenting humidity. "But the timing could explain why Sweringen's team so boldly attacked the compound in broad daylight."

"Precisely." Vaughn eyed us one by one. "We're running out of time as our adversary will no doubt redouble his efforts to eradicate our charge."

Who used words like eradicate? And Aini was a person, not a charge.

Focus on the big picture, Kels, the stuff that can get everyone killed.

"So what are we going to do?" I said. Okay, maybe I demanded, but here we were, sitting around the conference room, again, twiddling our thumbs while Aini's life could be in danger. Plus the longer I was in the Compound, the easier it was for me to have access to Aini, with or without Van acting as a guard dog.

"I understand your concern Kelly, and all available guards have been dispatched to patrol the perimeter."

Like that worked so well last time. I didn't say the words, but a quick look around told me I probably wasn't the only one thinking those thoughts. Besides, it wasn't like we had a ton of bodies to stop another breach of the fence line.

"Shouldn't we call Ling Mai and have her come back?" Nicki threw out, earning a hushed silence as we all tried to ignore looking at Vaughn. It's not like we didn't trust her to lead us but like little kids frightened of the big, bad monsters, we wanted our mom — in this case, Ling Mai. Though I doubted anyone would voice any of this out loud.

Vaughn didn't seem to mind the indirect snub as she tilted her head. "Trust me, I'd like Ling Mai here, too."

I bet she would.

"However, she is out of communication and we must handle anything thrown our way."

"But does she know what we're facing?" Nicki pushed. Must be a shifter trait because Van did a lot of that, too.

"She knows," Vaughn answered, her voice calm and level, which went a long way toward diffusing the tension in the room. "And I have no doubt if she could come, she would. But until we hear otherwise, I'm in charge. Any issues with that?"

Way to take the bull by the horns. Who in their right mind was going to take umbrage with Vaughn now? Umbrage? I was even beginning to sound like her. Better get on task.

Nicki wasn't done yet. "So if we don't have our Director can we get some kind of back-up for protection? We can't expect to stop trained mercenaries with a bunch of kids and half-trained newbies."

Good point as all gazes shot to Vaughn.

It was Stone who answered. "A few problems with that." He waited until he had us all by tenterhooks before continuing. "First issue, we can't bring in human help to face off against preternatural threats. It's suicide."

Agreed.

"Plus, we'd risk exposing those among us with extra abilities," Vaughn murmured.

Another valid point.

"Is that all?" Alex asked.

Stone eyed Van then cleared his throat. "The designated back-up group to tag should we need them is EMA."

I caught Van going still, but I wasn't sure why.

"Who's EMA?" asked Nicki.

"The people I work for." Van's answer had the whole room rearing back.

I jumped in where clearly others feared to tread, in part to deflect the animosity flowing toward Van. It wasn't his fault. Really it wasn't. "So we're understaffed for an assault. We have no idea how many individuals can be mobilized to get at Aini, and we also have no idea to what extent they are willing to go to accomplish their goals." I only had to touch my bruised throat to bring home my points as I leaned forward in my chair. I could imagine the bomb I'd set off if I admitted I was the biggest threat of all, being on the inside. One crisis at a time. "And we have no back-up. Can we call on the Council of Seven?"

Yeah, it was a long shot but at least their help would be preternatural.

Stone was shaking his head. "Not possible."

"Why?" If I thought Van was pushy, he was nothing compared to Nicki.

"The Council doesn't have a military or enforcement arm."

"They have assassins," Alex mumbled next to me.

If Stone heard, he ignored her as he continued. "Bringing in preternaturals we don't know puts us at risk if this Horned One can use them."

And we were back to my secret. When in doubt deflect. "What are we going to do then that we haven't already done?"

I wasn't sure I didn't say the words, 'done and failed,' but I could tell from Stone's expression that he was following my thought process.

Vaughn looked in Van's direction. "Van, will you explain your suggestion?"

I didn't have a chance to wonder why all trails seemed to lead back to Van before he said, "My idea's straightforward. I'll return to EMA headquarters."

What? When had he and Vaughn made that stupid decision? Oh, yeah, probably when I'd left him talking with her before the Sweringen attack. I would have thought plans might have changed since then given what happened.

"What's confronting your boss going to accomplish?" Jaylene demanded. Go Jaylene! She might not be a Van fan but no one with any sense of right and wrong wished another to walk into a sure death scenario.

"I hope to discover how far involved my superior is, if the target really is Aini, and what next steps are planned from EMA."

"That's suicide," I managed to say when what I wanted to do was reach across the table and slap some sense into the man. What could he possibly be thinking? "Your people knew you were coming here, so what makes you think EMA headquarters aren't going to assume you know exactly what happened to Sweringen and his men?"

Don't do it. Don't do it.

"I'm aware of that." His voice was as tight as his expression. "It's a risk I'm willing to take."

"It's a stupid move." I didn't even look at him. Van might think the typical, heroic gesture was the right option but he was wrong and going to get himself uselessly killed. "It'd make more sense to have a video conference with whomever this idiot is who's leading EMA."

I know, I know, dissing the head of another agency wasn't going to win me points in the rational and reasonable approach, but I didn't care. I was so angry, and scared, I was practically vibrating.

"If you and Van—" I focused on Vaughn as I waved a hand in Van's direction because I didn't trust myself to look Van's way. "If you let EMA know that Aini isn't here any more — that she's been moved to a safer facility — you can buy us time." I glanced around the table, drumming for support. "We can ask for other assistance to protect the Compound, call in a false alarm to get enough law enforcement hanging around for the next ten hours, just long enough to deter an attack until tomorrow is over."

"You don't think they already have people watching the Compound?" Van said, his voice suddenly weary as if he'd already worked through the extent of the betrayal by his comrades, as well as the superior he trusted. He could no longer avoid what he saw as inevitable. "They're out there right now watching and reporting back to EMA."

He lifted his gaze to mine and it was all I could do to hold against that pain and rage.

"But all we need is some time." I was talking to him, and him alone, now. "Enough time to—"

"To involve innocent humans? Kincaide—" He glanced at Vaughn as if she would recognize the name. My guess was it belonged to his superior. "—Kincaide had to have been desperate to do what he's already done. To be willing to lose the good men he's already thrown away." His glance snapped back to mine. "He's not going to chat with Vaughn. Or anyone else. He's going to act, stop hoping he can avoid fall out, and hit hard and fast. As long as he takes out the target, he'll have won."

I hadn't realized I'd come to my feet, my hands flattened against the table as I all but shouted, "Which makes your grand gesture even more senseless. This Kincaide guy isn't going to let you waltz back to your headquarters and fill you in on his plans when he knows your sister is here." And me, I wanted to shout, but bit back the words. "You're not an asset for him anymore. You're a liability. If he doesn't kill you straight out he'll..." And this is where the words failed me.

I slid back into my chair, shaking my head.

"I know Kelly." He said the words softly, gently, tearing apart my heart with every syllable. Then his voice toughened, his gaze cutting to Vaughn. "We don't have a lot of options. Any data I manage to gather can help you prepare here. If I don't try to get to Kincaide, they'll think you're an easy target. A battle is inevitable. The only option now is to prepare for it in any way possible."

Don't go. Don't go.

Except? If he went, and I went with him, I'd be away from Aini. And maybe having another person, not one of his own agency, might deter Van's boss from immediately killing Van.

"I have an idea," I said, my words lower and quieter than they had been.

Vaughn raised her brows. I got the message. Out with it.

"What if I go with Van?"

"No." The word echoed from Wyatt. Which wasn't helping the situation.

I ignored his shotgun interruption, aware that Van hadn't spoken. This could've been his plan all along. He'd said to trust his lead. So I was. Now only if it didn't get both of us killed.

"I can turn invisible and follow Van into his headquarters, or where he's going. And if he — well, if one of us doesn't return, the other might still get us something. Enough to maybe make a difference."

Alex kicked me under the table, and I kicked her back without ever taking my gaze off Vaughn.

Only Van, Alex and I knew that I'd been wink-out-challenged but I hadn't had time to fill her in on the details. Plus, I wasn't sure my last time wasn't a fluke. Now was not the time to share that little secret either. Not if I wanted to go along with Van. I had to go, to protect Aini, and protect my team. Plus, if I could disappear, I could help Van stay alive.

Van was also the only one who knew my even darker and more dangerous secret, the one burning my arm like a brand. I was beginning to feel like I was back in Middle School where being a girl and keeping secrets, or appearing to keep them, was a full-time occupation.

Van's frown deepened. "It'd be dangerous."

"Of course, it would," Jaylene snorted. "With Kelly along, she might help you escape, or stop someone from straight out killing you. What'ja think, Kels?"

All gazes shot to me. My throat went bone dry. I could no more promise what Jaylene was suggesting than I could fly around the room. But as long as the team, and Vaughn in particular, believed I could act, I'd take my chances. Van and I could work out the details once we were away from the compound. Aini would be safe, and I'd have some more time to talk, or shake, some sense into Van.

"You can come as long as you follow my orders." Van's voice brooked no argument. Part of the show? Or did he really think he got to play Rambo to my Barbie doll?

Bite your tongue, Kels. He found a way to get you away from the Compound and lessen the risk to everyone here. Take the win.

He made to stand up. "While we're sitting around here the clock is ticking. Decision made. I go. Alone."

"Van's correct." Vaughn stepped into the void verbally. "It's time for him to act and us to prepare." She glanced at Stone then at me. "And I support Kelly joining him. Two agents will give both of you a stronger chance to survive and return."

What she didn't need to spell out was how slim the chances were that either of us could do that, but I was going to take my victory while I could. Even a victory based on lies and secrets.

"Two hour patrol rotations twenty-four seven," Vaughn continued. "No one leaves the Compound unless it's a direct order. Herc, you pull together whatever defensive weapons you have available."

"But—" the young boy sputtered as he rose to his feet.

"We have no choice. This is real world testing."

Herc nodded and headed toward the door.

Bless her, Vaughn was being her pragmatic self. The world was shredding around us but she remained constant. What were the chances any of us would live through tomorrow? Miniscule. So of course there was no point to say more.

Van smiled, not a reassuring look as much as a predator preparing for the hunt, and he'd take out whomever he needed to in order to reach his goals. Including me. He nodded once in my direction then headed toward the door. I was too blocked by others to catch up with him, which I think was his intention all around.

Fine, we were going to play it his way, for now.

I moved on autopilot, aware others parted around me as if unsure what to say to me. Yes, there was the whole try and prevent Armageddon, but for me that moment had already happened. Van was going to get himself killed. I'd betrayed my team by getting tagged with the symbol of the Horned One, and the sooner I left my team behind, the safer they'd be.

"I don't think this is a good idea." Wyatt appeared before me, already losing some of the aw-shucks puppy-dog persona he'd had when I first met him.

"I agree with him." Alex had joined him. She at least had reasons, knowing I was giving the team false hope that I could help, or save her brother. I wasn't sure which issue was worrying her more, but I could make a guess.

"Neither of you has any choice in the matter," I said, all hard-core Kelly. Maybe the tattoo brand was giving me backbone where I wasn't used to having a lot. Or maybe I was just getting fed up to my eyeballs with big, bad, bullies who didn't give a flying fig who they hurt or how many.

I brushed past the two of them, knowing full well if I didn't catch up with Van he could be long gone without me, especially if he thought through what it meant bringing me along.

We all faced a foe who would do whatever he needed to kill a girl I'd sworn to protect. Van and I had a snowball's chance in an Arizona summer that we'd get any intel that would help us, and Armageddon waited just around the corner.

Armageddon on steroids.

CHAPTER 32

"If you think you're ditching me, you have another think coming, Noziak," I growled the second I caught up with Van. Something made easier because his sister had already dragged him to a halt. Impressive. I didn't think Alex had it in her. Should have known better.

Van cast me a get-real look over his sister's shoulder, her back to me, her focus one hundred percent on reaming out her brother.

I bided my time. Seeing Van Noziak taken down a few notches might even soften him up for my planned assault. The one where I drilled some sense into him, along the lines of we were a team, not he Alpha, me Omega.

"You're barely recovered," I heard Alex growl, "so what in hell's bells do you think you're going to achieve?"

"Buy all of us some time."

"At the cost of your life?" Alex was playing hardball. No surprise there. It came with the Noziak genes.

"Didn't we have this same conversation in Paris?" he asked, though it really wasn't a question, more like a sneaky, underhanded, turn-the-tables attack. "Right before you faced a druid who killed you?"

She waved her hand, as if dying and being brought back to life were paltry issues.

"If your superior kills you—" Her hands were now white-knuckled, fisted on her hips— "you won't come back."

He glanced over her shoulder at me, his eyes golden rimmed again. Temper made holding on to his wolf side even harder. "It looks like I'll have Kelly along to protect me."

Like he really meant that.

He pivoted to walk away.

Talk about throwing me to the wolves, not his kind of shifter wolf, but the real kind, the chew-me-up-and-spit-me-out kind. Alex.

She glanced at me over her shoulder, her eyes so bleak I wanted to reach out and hug her. Except then I'd have two Noziaks upset with me. Alex didn't do hugs. Van? Man, he did some serious, world-class kissing, that was for sure. But hugs? We hadn't had a lot of time to explore those simple high-five moments of a relationship. The smiles across a crowded room, the looks that said we both were thinking the same thing and wanting to share it, the small touches that meant neither of us wanted to be anywhere else as time stood still.

We might never get the chance either, if Van decided to ditch me on his suicide mission.

Don't get distracted.

Van's back was already disappearing around the corner, so I gave Alex the least wobbly smile I could manage. "I'll watch out for him. I promise."

"And who's going to watch out for you?" she snapped, as I jogged past her.

Good question. Didn't have the answer. Wasn't going to lose my ride.

Okay, so I was a chicken. On the other hand, it was going to take everything I had to travel in a very small vehicle with a very-unhappy shifter. The fact it was my vehicle, and he only seemed to remember that he needed me to get him back to town when he reached it, wasn't helping the situation.

"I'm driving," he announced in that my-way-or-the-highway tone he could get.

"Don't be a grumpy face." I brushed past him before I used my key to unlock the Jeep.

Yes, I was quaking in my boots, and no doubt his special shifter woo-woo powers were aware of it, but give an inch to a shifter and you may as well roll over and play doggie dead. At least that was my theory.

Here's to hoping I hadn't misjudged my strategy, the keep-him-off-his-game-to-get-my-short-term-way approach. Punch too many of his buttons and he could rip the vehicle door from its hinges and throw it, and me, across the parking lot.

He didn't say anything as I crawled in, closed the door and pretended I needed to adjust the rearview mirrors. As if. But it took that long for him to unclench his jaw, walk around the rear and get in the passenger seat. I'd have been happier if he'd stomped, let a little of that male I-want-to-strangle-you testosterone out of his system, but I guess this wasn't my day.

Really not my day as Wyatt was guarding the gate, and he wouldn't open it automatically. Instead he waved me to a halt and gave me a roll-down-your-window circular motion with his hand.

Now I had two males testing my patience to the limit. Had there been a memo sent around and I missed it?

"Yes?" I said in that half-question, half-get-on-with-it tone women can take where it sounds nice but isn't really. "You need something?"

"Not a good idea." Wyatt wasn't even looking at me when he spoke. He was glaring at Van. So did not want to escalate a pissing contest between two alpha males with me in the middle.

I did that two fingers to my eyes gesture, usually employed to get a guy to look someplace other than your chest, and waited for Wyatt to get the message. I had to give him credit, he possessed enough common sense to understand that he was on shaky ground.

His skin flushed as he dipped his head and lowered his voice. "I'm worried about you."

I didn't have the heart to tell him speaking quietly around a shifter didn't make a whit of difference.

"Thank you." I patted the hand he had wrapped over the open window. "I'll be okay. I promise."

"And if you're wrong? You can get hurt and not survive."

I liked how absolutely no one believed my reassurances.

Van leaned forward, his expression as lethal as his tone as he looked around me at Wyatt. "If she doesn't return you're going to die anyway, so there's nothing to worry about."

Sheesh. Men.

"Disregard him," I said to Wyatt, who'd paled. Then I leaned out the window and kissed his cheek. "I'll see you as soon as I can."

The look in his gaze told me we both knew the chances of that happening were slim to non-existent. But he stepped back and waved us on. Last sight of him he was still standing at the open gate, watching us until the Jeep disappeared.

As I was swallowing past the lump in my throat, Van growled next to me. "You do know that if I live, and you live, and he lives, that I'll have to rip his head from his body."

Yup, Jeeps were way too small to travel in with ill-tempered shifters.

This day was going downhill fast.

CHAPTER 33

I didn't recognize the area of M Street where Van told me to pull the vehicle over, which I did, aware of how damp my palms were on the steering wheel. I was glad we'd made it this far as I'd half suspected he'd leave me at the roadside somewhere far enough from the Compound I couldn't return easily. That would have solved his problem — the one where he'd promised to keep Aini and my team safe from me while keeping me safe from what he expected to find at the EMA headquarters.

Rock and a hard place.

The golden light of early evening softened the glass and sandstone buildings in this business-focused sector of town — quieter at this hour than usual, without the bustle of lawyers and lobbyists scurrying between buildings. A few people hustled past, heads tucked, talking on cell phones, hurrying to Georgetown's bars and restaurants, maybe a few heading home. A normal day in an abnormal city.

And Van and I? We hadn't talked over strategy on the drive here. Hadn't talked at all, so I cleared my throat to ask, "We have a plan or are you just going to march in, throw your weight around and hope for the best?"

"What's wrong with that as a plan?"

"Except for the fact it stands the best chance to get us killed, and I won't do it, it might work, but only on a day not ending with the letter 'y.'"

He turned in his seat, so I was no longer memorizing his profile. "Do I detect a hint of sarcasm, Miss McAllister?"

"If you're only hearing a hint, you're not listening close enough."

I could have sworn his lips twitched before he pulled his unshakable, relentless-male-on-an-impossible-mission mask back on.

When the strained silence between us grew until I wanted to choke, and trust me, I'd had enough choking episodes over the last two days, I sighed.

"Thank you," I said, holding out an olive branch.

The look he cast me scalded. "For?"

"For getting me away from my teammates. For protecting them from me."

"And how in the hell am I supposed to protect you if I bring you in there?" he jerked a thumb toward the closest multi-story building.

"I can protect myself."

"In a pig's eye." He turned in his seat, enough for me to see the conflict storming his gaze. "If I asked you to leave, to walk down this street and not turn back…"

"You'd be asking me to abandon my team, my commitment to being an agent. Aini. You can't do that." Then, just in case he was being dense, I added, "I won't let you do that."

He mumbled an oath I'm sure he didn't want me to hear while remaining stone still in his seat, staring straight ahead.

"Look. You don't want me here. I get that. I don't want to be here. But I don't want you to throw away your life needlessly, either. So, I. Am. Here. Deal with it."

He glanced away for a second before stabbing me with a glance that said pay-attention-or-else. "You ever think that your being here is exactly what someone inside that building wants?"

"What are—" then I caught the angle of his glance. My arm. More specifically, my arm with a tattoo.

That's when his words slammed against me. For love of peaches and pears how stupid could I be? I, too, was looking at my arm as I muttered past dry lips, "As in, if I go inside, this … this whatever it is, could be activated?"

"Yes."

Now that right there was the difference between a man and a woman. A woman would have been all about reassuring me, or letting me know they would stick with me through thick and thin, or suggesting a caramel macchiato with extra foam at a coffee shop right around the corner to talk things through and come up with another option. But a man? Here's the cold, logical truth. Face it. Deal with it. Move on.

Once I could get my lungs breathing again I realized there was something to say for Van's approach. If you didn't hide from the worst-case scenario you knew exactly what your choices were. Walk into that building guarding Van's back in any way possible or stay here in the car, cowering.

Except Van had it wrong. My worst fear wasn't becoming a minion of the Horned One, who might or might not be Van's boss. I'd actually been dealing with the fallout of that concept ever since the attack in Aini's room. The fact I was here, miles away from her, gave me some hope.

I safe Missy, Miss.

I jerked. Nothing like a voice out of nowhere rattling tense nerves.

Thank you for letting me know. I'm doing everything I can to keep you that way.

Just the thought I might be hearing her voice gave me more hope.

The worst in the upcoming scenario, creating the rip-my-heart-out-and-pulverize-it-with-fear feeling racing through me that had my hands glued to the steering wheel as if it'd anchor me from shaking apart, was the thought of letting Van stalk into that building, alone. He might think he could do just that. And, if there were only humans there he stood a darn good chance of walking out. But these people were his peers, men he'd faced danger with on other missions, who had shared history with him, who were supposed to be on his side.

That simple fact — betrayal — could mean the rough, raw seconds between hesitating and taking an action that could save his life.

Then there was the possibility of exposing his own boss as the Horned One. Would I be able to go up against Ling Mai; identify her as a threat to the world, and take her out? I'd like to think I could, but I was lying to myself. Once I became an IR agent, committed to following Ling Mai's orders, even when I didn't agree with them, I'd committed to following her. Going against that training, that ingrained loyalty, could destroy a person. Especially a person like Van, who didn't do anything by half measures.

Another reason to follow him inside. Save his sexy hide, whether or not he'd admit to needing me to do that, and protect him from the fallout if Kincaide proved to be the Horned One.

It looked like it was going to be a busy evening.

"Come on," I said, doing everything to make my tone as controlled as I could. "Let's go."

"Still a chance to walk away."

"No. There isn't."

I was out of the Jeep before he could say more, or stop me.

You'd think I had a shifter's strength with the way I grabbed the door handle and yanked the metal and glass door open, startling a man in a suit exiting the building. Kelly Bad-Ass was on the move.

"Wait." Van caught up with me as I stood at the directory reading who all had offices in this building and where they were located. Super heroes in the movies never had these kinds of problems. They could always enter the den of the bad guys, head straight to the right floor, and take them down.

I still wasn't listening to Van as my eyes didn't seem to want to focus. The whole sign was a hot mess blur.

"Kelly." He was right beside me but smart enough not to touch me. No restraint. No reassurance. No nothing.

I glanced at him. "What?"

He did that hand raking his hair gesture then glanced over to the corner. Before I could see what had snagged his attention he said, "Can we head over there? Just for a second."

He was asking me? Not telling me? Who was this Van?

On the other hand, he had a point. Running off half-cocked was suicide for both of us. A moment to get on the same page might keep at least one of us alive and we needed that to alert Vaughn and the others as to what was coming at them.

Start thinking like an agent McAllister — cool, calm, professional. Aini needed me to and so did Van.

I turned and walked stiff-legged to where what looked like a glass sculpture of a sea anemone caught in its death throes was mounted on the wall.

"What?" I said when Van didn't speak.

"If we're going to do this right you have to trust me."

I was here wasn't I? Oh, yeah, that was a clear sign I didn't trust him to survive this on his own.

"Explain." It wasn't a hail-halleluiah-I'll-follow-you-anywhere endorsement, but I wasn't at that point yet. Might never be. Listening was all I could offer here.

"I'm assuming Sweringen might have had time to notify Kincaide they'd breeched the perimeter of the compound. Indicate the team had split up, but not what happened after you engaged with them."

"And that assumption means what?"

"If I'm right, Kincaide knows something's wrong, if he's the guy working for the Horned One. Sweringen's dead, as is the other operative, and those deaths might be telegraphed back to whoever is in control of this op."

"Makes sense. Go on."

"But Kincaide doesn't know that I know everything that's happened at the compound."

"You haven't reported in since when?"

"Since that church parking lot where I told him I was traveling to the compound with you."

"So what are you planning to do?" I asked, wary, worried and waiting for him to spell out his plan, all of it.

"I'm going in with the story I never got in the compound, not with you. That I'd reconnoitered, found Sweringen's team's insertion point but was spotted and shot at before I could follow. Let Kincaide know you all have the place locked down tight and have more personnel than he suspects, operatives who know what they're doing and are not the amateurs he expects you to be."

So far so good. "And you're hoping he'll take you into his confidence then?"

"I'll dangle him a reason to and yes, that's my plan."

"The reason being?" I knew there had to be catch. There always was.

"I'll promise him that I can lead him right up to the gates and get him through."

"And why would he believe that?"

He reached out, his shifter-strong fingers encircling my arm, the one with the tattoo, as his eyes darkened from deep brown to bottomless dark. "Because I'll have you as a hostage."

CHAPTER 34

What the ... before I could react, could speak, he dragged me to the elevators, punched the up button and yanked me inside the metal box. Trapped.

"What are you doing?"

"What has to be done."

He wasn't even looking at me. Nothing softening his face, his stance, the grip of his hand.

This was a joke. Wasn't it? Then why was my stomach knotting? My heart double-timing?

"I'm supposed to pretend to go along with you?" Yes, I was scrambling here, finding the common ground. This was Van. The guy who protected me in Africa. Alex's brother. I knew him. This wasn't him.

Was it?

"There's no pretending here." His words so ice cold a shiver washed through me.

"Talk to me, Van." I meant it. He was scaring me. This was not the Van I knew, and I had to hang on to that thought.

He turned on me so fast I was jerked up against him, but not in a nice, let's-get-together way. This was a total stranger staring down at me, making my throat close up, my legs quake.

"You want to talk, fine. You're an idiot. Thinking you can play with the big boys when we can chew you up and spit you out. You don't even know who you're up against."

"Tell me," I whispered, not knowing where the words came from. I kept waiting for the punch line, for him to revert to the Van I knew. Not this steel and metal stranger without an ounce of compassion anywhere.

"Kincaide, or someone in league with Kincaide, wants Aini. He's tried it nice, which was a big mistake. I promised him I could get in and I did. But I couldn't bring her back here before that idiot Sweringen made all hell break loose. No way to access her then."

No. No. No. Van wouldn't hurt Aini. But could Van have been infected with the tattoo? He wore long sleeves so he could be hiding his arm. He was preternatural, which made him vulnerable. Why hadn't I ever considered that risk? Stupid Kelly. Too stupid to live.

I cleared my throat to respond as if all was normal between us. As normal as possible, since I was, for all purposes, his hostage. Try and reach Van. Remind him of who he was. "Sweringen was your friend. You fought him, to help me."

"If I hadn't, would you be here now?"

He was serious. One hundred and fifty percent serious, and I'd been the naïve idiot who'd been worried about him.

I didn't even answer him as I stepped as far away from him as I could with him still chaining me to his side, so glad when the elevator doors pinged open.

Trust him? Trust him? Trust him?

If I didn't I was so screwed. If I did and he was infected, I was so screwed.

Criminey, what had I gotten myself into?

The gazes of everyone we passed avoided us. This looked like such a normal office — receptionist desk front and center, subdued lighting, a few scattered people wearing business casual. Should I scream? Make a break for it here and now. In public?

Except there was no time. Van was using my shock against me. In seconds he'd dragged me from the foyer, down a short hallway, and into a corner office without knocking on the door.

An older man with that regal, ramrod crispness of career military half rose from behind his desk. From relaxed to full attention in three seconds or less. The second person in the room, one who could be a Van clone — same lethal muscles, burning intensity, shut down expression — twisted, his hands already raised to defend. Or attack.

"Lipwoski," Van said, giving a chin nod. "Leave."

The guy tossed a quick glance toward the older man, who must have made some silent signal because the younger man disappeared faster than my relationship with my parents when I told them I knew I wasn't their biological daughter.

"Noziak," the older man said, easing back into his chair as the door clicked shut behind the departing Lipwoski. "Who do we have here?"

Don't panic. Don't panic. Don't panic.

"Our ticket into Ling Mai's compound and accessing Aini."

Okay, maybe a little panic.

When in doubt, bluff. I stood taller, trying to shake off Van's grip though he wasn't having any of that. So I gathered what wits I could and ignored Van, speaking to the other man. "I'm guessing you're Kincaide."

He inclined his head, although I caught that he didn't take his predator-eyed gaze off of me for a second. Oh, yeah, this guy could so be the big, bad ass running the operations. But was he the Horned One? "You have me at a disadvantage. I'm afraid I don't know who you are."

My, my, my, weren't we all being so civilized and socially polite here.

"Kelly McAllister." I bit out each word, suddenly realizing why historically so many tribal people feared giving their real name to strangers. It meant giving power to the other. And I had no doubts this man was used to wielding power. My warning ring wasn't any help here as Van's proximity made it heat, so I didn't know if this Kincaide was preternaturally dangerous or just dangerous dangerous. Like one option was better than another.

This was clearly a man who could kill without compunction and order other men into battle. I should have listened to Van, the other Van, the nice one, who warned me that coming here was a big mistake. I was out of my depth, drowning before three sentences had been spoken.

Van broke the strained silence. "She's the one who found Aini. Brought her here. Spoke to her when the girl woke for a few minutes at the hospital."

I looked at him, trying my hardest to still believe this was all a ruse; if it was, Van wasn't giving me any indication. Plus he was sharing a whole lot of information I'd think he'd want to keep hidden if Kincaide was the Horned One.

Could be a mistake. Could be a mistake. All a big, fat mistake.

"So, you're that one." Kincaide leaned back in his chair, a pose that should have suggested casualness, but didn't. Not by a long shot. Not if you saw the cruelty of his lips, the empty soullessness of his eyes. Shark, crocodile, raging lion eyes. And what did he mean by that one? Was this man the reason Sweringen attacked me? And the words of the other man? The one who died in Aini's room. There will be no stopping me.

For the first time since the hooded man attacked me outside the Library, the enormity of what we were facing to protect Aini washed against me. This man, this Kincaide, wasn't going to stop until he possessed the teen. I was a pawn to be used in a deadly, murky game. Nothing more.

Surely Van wouldn't toss me to this creature?

Except he already had.

"Fill me in, Noziak." The gaze cut to Van, giving me a chance to inhale short, shallow breaths.

With a succinctness I could admire, in another situation, Van spelled out what had happened at the compound, leaving out little. I knew it'd been a mistake to allow him inside. Hadn't I told Vaughn that?

Fat lot of good it did me now.

"So Sweringen and Peterson failed," Kincaide murmured, not a smidge of remorse or compassion in his voice for the lives lost. Compartmentalization to the nth degree. Or a sociopath. That I could believe. "Yet you still think there's a chance to enter the compound, extract or eliminate the girl without too many more causalities?"

The way he spoke frosted my blood even as I struggled to hear something more in his words. It was there. A tone? A secondary agenda? I had no doubt his primary goal was Aini. That wasn't it. He wanted something else, though. But what?

"And you." He turned toward me. I refused to flinch or quail, but it was getting harder by the second. "Are you the one the Librarian mentioned?"

I looked at Van before I could catch myself. He'd gone even more still. Not glancing at me. I got the message loud and clear, I was on my own.

"Mentioned how?" I managed. Was the Librarian working both sides? Selling what he or she knew to the highest bidder? Come to think of it, I never had paid her.

His smile turned to a smirk. "No time to prevaricate, Miss McAllister. The one who sees is always paired with one who protects. The Guardian. I'm asking if you are she?"

Oh, boy, was he way off base. I caught myself shaking my head before I could answer. What had Van just called me? An idiot. Naïve. Clueless. I could barely keep myself alive, and this big honcho guy thought I was the protector.

"What are you hesitating about, Miss McAllister?" he asked, his tone lethal.

I hadn't exactly been hesitating, just grimacing for a few seconds as I pulled at my arm again. But Van wasn't budging. Then I realized what shaky ground I was on. If I admitted the truth — that I was a nobody, with few discernible skills and absolutely no abilities to protect Aini, no more than any other IR agent possessed — would Kincaide order me killed and attack the Compound anyway? Most likely.

So what were my options?

Play for time. The goal was to identify the Horned One and to keep Kincaide from grabbing Aini until she could turn sixteen. Then she might be safe. Or safer.

I had no doubt Kincaide was in league with the Horned One. But was he possessed by him? If we … if I didn't identify the true Horned One, not only could I kill an innocent man by mistake but let the Horned One go free. I might not like Kincaide personally, but that didn't earn him a death sentence. So buy some desperately needed time.

How could I chew up precious minutes? It was a heck of a gap between now and when dawn arrived. And no telling if Aini had to only reach the day of her birthday and not the hour. With the way my luck had been these last two days, we'd need the exact hour and minute, and she was probably born late tomorrow not early.

"I'm waiting, Miss McAllister." The bite of his words said he wouldn't be waiting much longer. "If you are the Guardian, you can lead me to the girl."

"Why would I put an innocent at risk?" The question exploded before I thought it through. Pissing off a potential psychopath was never a good idea.

"You have a choice. The girl or Washington D.C."

I glanced at Van, but he was staring at Kincaide.

"You heard me right, Miss McAllister. One life or the greater D.C. area. Six hundred thousand, not including the tourists and visitors."

The way he said it, as if discussing the weather, chilled my blood.

"I'm the Guardian." The lie escaped me. "I can take you to Aini."

Now it was Kincaide's turn to pause. He glanced at Van. "She telling the truth?"

Van gave a stiff shrug then added, "She's an innocent. Doesn't know how to lie."

I know I was taking a risky chance but maybe it was the only chance Aini had.

"Van doesn't know everything," I said, licking my lips, sensing more than feeling Van's sudden attention. I was now being in the position of ignoring him instead of the other way around. Touché Wolf-Guy. Two could play close-to-the-chest games.

Kincaide steepled his fingers beneath his chin, his elbows planted heavily on the arms of his chair. "Explain."

"Van doesn't know that I've been able to talk with Aini since she's left the hospital."

Kincaide's brow twitched. "My understanding was that she's still in a coma."

"She is." I plowed ahead. Chess had never been my strength. Neither had high stakes poker. Didn't mean I couldn't learn, and fast. "But I've been able to communicate with her. Mind to mind."

"You expect me to believe you?" His tone indicated the chances of that.

Bluff. Bluff. Bluff.

"I don't really care what you believe." Channel my inner-Alex. I'd never be a witch but I was learning, and fast, how to be a bitch with the best of them. "You kill me and you destroy any chance you have of questioning Aini."

Not for a nano-second did I believe he wanted to know about her terrorist brother, if the man even existed, but it'd been clear all along that there was something he wanted from her. That was the subtext I'd sensed earlier. He still might kill her outright if he could do nothing else, but the reason he hadn't thrown everything he'd had at the compound earlier was because he didn't want to risk killing her until … until what, I didn't know, but the conversation with the Librarian gave me a hint. I could sense the heightened anticipation flooding through him.

"Why should I want to speak to the girl?"

Oh, he was good. Just the right mix of disinterest and ennui coated his words. My years of coaxing information out of scared, reluctant five and six-year olds were about to pay off. Two could play the word subterfuge game.

"I don't know why you need to talk with Aini. Nor do I care." I managed a rock-hard ripple of my shoulders, hoping it looked a whole lot more casual than it felt. Time to sweeten the pot. "All I know is that I can speak with her. Plus, I'm your only chance to get back into the Compound easily and access the girl."

Kincaide glanced at Van. "This true?"

Keeping his eyes straight ahead,Van said, "I know she can get us back inside." He paused, then added, "And the Librarian did mention Miss McAllister needing to use her special abilities regarding the girl."

Kincaide's reptile gaze swung back to me. "And these abilities include mind-to-mind transmissions. How convenient."

This is where things got tricky. If he didn't believe me, there was no reason to keep Van or me alive. If he did believe, I'd bought us some precious time.

"What do you have to lose?" I interjected, a hint of a sneer in my voice. I doubted this guy had a lot of people who called his bluff and was counting on that approach helping me. "Send

me back to the Compound, or close enough I can communicate
with Aini, and I'll show you what I can do."

"How close is close enough?" he asked.

Got you, you bastard. He might sound uncommitted but the
very fact he was weighing my statement gave me hope.

"I don't know." Truth lined my words because it was a fact.
"I've never tried talking with her from farther away than the
front gates."

Van glanced at me but said nothing.

"Noziak?" Kincaide barked.

"Yes, sir." Van snapped to attention.

"Take her to the blue room. Send in Lipwoski and
Hammond."

"Yes, sir."

He was on the move, tugging me along with him before I
could figure out if my gambit had paid off.

The man I'd seen before was waiting right outside the room.
Van jerked his head toward Kincaide's office. "Old man wants
you and Hammond. ASAP."

Lipwoski didn't ask questions as he pushed a comm device
on his shoulder and disappeared into the room. I never saw the
second man arrive as Van steered me down a side hallway to a
small room that had the feel of an interrogation space; pale
blue colors, a huge mirror on one wall, a scarred table and
metal chairs dead center. If the color was meant to soothe, it
failed.

"Sit." Van snarled, almost throwing me into the chair before
he marched to the mirrored wall, looking into it and keeping
his back to me.

If I'd been the totally clueless ninny he had called me, I
might have started asking questions, pushing for answers,
demanding an explanation for such high-handed, heavy
behavior. But even an idiot could guess there was someone or
more than one person behind that glass, waiting, expecting to
learn if Van and I were captor and captive or peers executing a
plan.

Heck, even I didn't know.

So I held my tongue, feeling the strain in the air, the
heaviness weighing around us both. I'd grown up in tornado-

country and recognized the sensation, where the air goes calm and still — silence quiets the birds as they disappear to their nests. After a few minutes, the very air changes, and a line of inky, thick clouds swell on the horizon — clouds warning that they aren't fooling around.

That was Van's look reflected in the mirror, the distorted, strained look of a man at war with himself.

Or maybe that was naïve Kelly wanting to believe he really was a white knight and not a dark warrior.

"Show me your arm," I said, the words torn from me.

He glanced my way, his only movement, before he ignored me.

I'd take that as a no. But why?

Before I could ask again, or launch myself on him, the door slammed open. I jumped. Van, of course, didn't.

It was the Lipwoski guy. "Come on."

I couldn't help it. I glanced at Van, no doubt a silent question wreathed my face. You? Or me? Or both of us?

Van answered by stepping forward. Since Lipwoski didn't bat an eyelash, I had my answer.

I stood, smoothing my hands down the front of my pants, drying the sweat from them although the room hadn't been that warm.

"Where are we going?" I asked once I reached the door. Like a prisoner suddenly released, I somehow felt safer in the closed, small room than facing the unknown outside. A new man was already disappearing around the corner, Lipwoski and Van not far behind him when my question, or the fact I wasn't moving, stopped them.

Lipwoski cast a what-the-hell glance at Van as if asking, 'Is she always a PIA?'

Van gave a silent shrug then snapped at me. "Come and live. Stay and die. Your choice."

Given the options, I straightened my shoulders, raised my chin and marched forward. Van waited until I was even with him before he again grabbed my arm. His hold not so tight this time, but clearly a restraint.

If, and it was a big if, we survived whatever was going on, Wolf-Guy and I were going to have a serious conversation about communication.

Yup, that was me, overly optimistic Kelly ignoring the fact I was leading the bad guys right to Vaughn and my fellow agents and I didn't have a clue how to warn them.

CHAPTER 35

There were eight of us in the elevator. Van, me, Lipwoski and I guessed the man named Hammond. Kincaide was there, too, which surprised me. The other three looked like thug killers and the fact my preternatural detector ring was searing my finger meant I was most likely the only human in the group. Or mostly human.

The ride was silent. Deadly serious silent, until we reached an underground parking facility and joined up with three more teams jumping up our numbers to more than I wanted to consider. Twenty-five? Thirty? Not looking good. Next thing I was being hustled into a black SUV. Van was directed to the passenger seat. When he paused before opening the door the one called Hammond jammed a Taser into Van's back and zapped him.

Van arched as the current slammed into him.

"Nooooo!" I shouted, fat lot of good it did. The back door snapped open and I was shoved into it so fast I barely heard the click of silver handcuffs encircling Van's wrists and a hair-chilling laugh from Lipwoski beside me. "You didn't think we'd trust a shifter now, did ya, Noziak?"

I didn't hear Van's reply, if there was one, as Hammond shoehorned him into the front seat then turned to glare at Lipwowski.

"Knock that shit off, Lipwoski. Kincaide won't like it."

"What he don't know won't hurt him."

I was sitting behind the driver, shaking, but if I thought my position could give me a strategic advantage it took less than seven seconds before the man beside me, Lipwoski, pulled out a weapon that at first glance resembled a transformer toy.

By the time Hammond had started the vehicle and shifted it into reverse, Lipwoski had folded out then snapped open a folding vertical fore grip, an integrated telescoping buttstock, and pistol sights that flipped-up to rifle sights/BUIS. It wasn't only the power of his gun, it was the ease with which he used it.

Nice — if I was the one holding it.

As it was, my throat went dry even as I mouthed off. "Boys with toys?" I said, raising a brow.

The smirk Lipwoski gave me did not bode well for Van or me as he raised the weapon, sighting it on the back of Van's head. "An HK MP7 PDW at SWAT Round-Up," he said, like that meant anything. The fact Van froze did, though, that and Lipwoski's next words. "On full-auto, I can shoot multiple-shot strings at 900 rounds-per-minute. And I have silver bullets." He followed up by quickly clicking a magazine into place, clacking home the bolt with authority and chambering the first round. "Either of you two try anything, anything, you're dead."

Subtlety didn't seem to be Lipwoski's forte. I glanced out the window, pretending disdain but in reality buying myself a few moments grinding my teeth to get my racing heart under control.

Lipwoski had us, and both Van and I knew it. One of us sneezed and the other was dead. Right then I didn't know if that'd even bother Van but it was acting as a great deterrent to me. No point in trying to wink out before we got too much further. If I did Van was dead. The only question was would I die before or after him? I might turn invisible but a bullet shot into where I was sitting would still kill me.

By the time the driver revved us up the exit ramp, five big, black SUVs slid into position behind us. Not an unusual sight in D.C. — the caravan itself wouldn't earn even a few curious glances — which left me desperately running through scenarios to get us out of this situation.

A little over an hour later I was still running possible plans, counting each mile as we got closer to the Compound, the road a secondary one, winding and empty of traffic as the SUV's headlights cut a swath of incandescent light across stands of piney woods and the periodic farm-style house. Night had fallen, thick and black here in the Maryland countryside.

That's when I got the brilliant idea of trying to contact Aini telepathically as we drew closer. Talk about feeling like an idiot as I sent out S.O.S. messages using only my thoughts. I finally gave up caring if I was an idiot. Or if I could contact her, but my theory was to create some distance between Kincaide, his assault team, and my friends and teammates inside the Compound.

After another ten minutes my signals felt more like praying. Begging for an impossible miracle. Something, anything that might help.

When I actually heard Aini, I almost jumped. "I's here, Missy, Miss."

"Stop the car," I whispered, not wanting to scare the guy with the gun, but needing my focus to keep in touch with Aini.

"Why?" Lipwoski demanded.

"I've got her."

He eyed me as if I was trying to run a fast one past him. Not this time, but give me an opening and it was payback time. Right now I just wanted this assault team slowed down, buying some time to get to my team through Aini.

Talk about a snowball's chance in the bad place. Except this was the bad place now.

"Please, just stop the car. It's hard enough communicating this way without bumping along the road." Technically the road wasn't that bumpy but trying to hold a dialogue this way was like patting your head while rubbing your stomach while navigating a high wire across the Grand Canyon.

The fact I was scared witless wasn't helping. Nor was that free-floating-I'm-about-to-get-sick feeling in my stomach.

Lipwoski radioed to Kincaide, and a few moments later all the vehicles pulled off the road into the rutted driveway of a private residence. The older home looked hunkered down for the night, and I hoped it stayed that way.

"Try anything and you're dead," Lipwoski made very clear, his tone smug.

"Got it." I reached for the door. Before my hand closed around the handle, Lipwoski's nifty little gun was jammed up against my temple. Van rumbled in the front seat as I slowly, very slowly raised my hands and swallowed the bile in my throat. I also mentally spoke to Aini.

Can you hear me?

Yes, Missy Miss. You scared?

Very. Can you wake up? I need your help to warn the others. Tell them to flee. Now!

It was their only chance. There were not enough of them to halt Kincaide and his personal army. They had to escape and take Aini with them.

Don't know. I try.

Please. Try as hard as you can.

"Just wanting some fresh air," I whispered, aware the quiver in my words didn't have to be faked. "Don't blame me if I throw up on you here."

Another lesson learned from my kindergarten years. Vomit, or the mention of vomiting, was a great way to clear a space.

"Hammond, keep an eye on him," Lipwoski barked to the driver as he used his gun to nudge me forward.

In slow motion, I gently opened the door and eased myself out. Right into the muzzle of another gun-toting thug's weapon. These guys were serious or liked lording it over helpless hostages. Cooler night air washed against me as dozens of fireflies tangoed past. Somewhere nearby an owl hooted. Didn't some Native American tribes believe the owl was a harbinger of death?

Aini? How're you doing?

Hard, Missy. So tired.

I understand. I wouldn't ask if it wasn't important.

Kincaide appeared from around the rear of the vehicle, his expression closed except for the bullish tilt of his jaw. "You've contacted her?"

"Yes." I stood, surprised my legs would hold me, but they did.

"Good. Now ask her exactly what I ask."

I managed a stiff nod.

"Tell her I want to know where the clavis of Dryghtyn is?"

"The what?" I wasn't being dense but grabbing at what might be my only chance to learn what Kincaide wanted and why. The Librarian had mentioned Dryghtyn, but not a clavis. Hopefully Kincaide's answer would tell me once and for all if he was indeed the Horned One.

"Don't be a fool, Miss McAllister," he said. Guess my opportunity for clarity was closed, but I wasn't about to give up easily. Too many lives were at stake.

"I can't help you if I don't know what I'm asking for."

It was lame, but I was desperate.

Kincaide paused, his face blank until he gave a slight shake to his head and appeared to come to some kind of conclusion. "Not that I believe you but you should surely know Dryghtyn's the primeval force out of which everything in the Cosmos is formed." His voice had taken on the tone of an evangelical believer. Not what I needed, but at least he was talking. "From Gods to the smallest speck of dust in the Universe, we all owe our being to Dryghtyn."

Of course we did. Not.

Normally I wasn't snarky, respecting others beliefs and truths as important to them, if incomprehensible to me. But for the love of monkey brains, was this guy out of his mind? He expected a young girl from Sierra Leone to be able to answer such an out-there question? I didn't have a clue what a clavis was, but my best guess was it was something tangible, something Kincaide wanted. Probably a power item.

"Ask her," he growled, as if I was intentionally dawdling. I wasn't, not this time, but every second I could give Aini might help pull her out of the coma. She just needed enough time to alert the team to the danger waiting twenty minutes away. Us.

I stilled myself, quieted my quaking and closed my eyes. Didn't know if that was going to help but staring into the barrels of a bunch of weapons pointed at me wasn't.

Aini? You still there?

Nothing.

Oh, oh, not good.

Aini? Kind of need you here?

"What's happening?" Kincaide demanded. Obviously not the most patient of men.

"Give her a second." I kept my eyes closed to ignore him as long as possible. Aini?

I's here.

Thank heavens. I guess I sighed out loud as Kincaide spoke up, "What's going on?"

My eyelids snapped open. "Can you just give me a moment? I haven't even asked her yet."

"If you think—"

"I can't possibly think, much less hold a conversation with all the interruptions," I bit back. "It's your call. You want me to ask your stupid question or not?"

Even in the weak glow of half-moon above I could see the rage wash across Kincaide's face, making him look almost demonic. Still he managed to speak with iron control, "I'm not a patient man, Miss McAllister. Don't push me too far."

Trust me, I wasn't.

Squeezing eyes shut, I tried again.

Aini?

Yes?

Someone here wants to know where the clavis of Dryghtyn is. Do you know what he's talking about?

Bad juju, Missy. Very bad. You speak with the Horned One.

There's a huge gap between suspecting bad news and confirming it. I'd just been catapulted over that chasm. My heart jumped first as I wrestled my head into reminding me I had a job to do. Learn as much as possible and warn my team. Mouth dry, the thudda thud of my heart screaming through me, I pushed past the fear.

How do you know he's the Horned One?

Only he speak the sacred words.

What sacred words?

Aini paused before starting up.

Dryghton, the Ancient One. From the beginning and is for eternity, male and female, the original source of all things; all-knowing, all-pervading, all-powerful; changeless, eternal.

In his name one beseeches.

In the name of the Lady of the Moon, one bows.

In the name of the Lord of Death and Resurrection, one begs.

We, who are nothing, in the name of the Mighty Ones of the Four Quarters, the Kings of the Elements, protect us.

Bless us who are doomed to die.

Jiminy Cricket!

My eyes snapped open. Not because I wanted them to, but I wanted to make sure the world as I knew it still existed. Which should have reassured me but didn't, not with the cold cascading through my body.

"Well?" Kincaide took my action as permission to pounce on me.

I cleared my throat. "Do you know anything about a moon lady or a lord of death and destruction?"

His smile warned me I wasn't going to like his answer, but he didn't answer me directly. Instead he asked, "What did she say about the clavis? I need to know where it is?"

I shook my head, not in a negative as much as a resignation. Instead of immediately jumping to what Kincaide wanted, I pushed my own agenda.

Have you been able to warn the others, Aini?

No. Sorry, sorry.

Poor kid, I could hear the same despair in her voice as was washing through me.

Maybe if I found out where this thing was I could better keep it from Kincaide. A long shot but better than nothing.

How about the clavis? Do you know where it is?

Non notoso, Missy Miss.

What don't you understand, Aini?

Why you want know about yerself?

What?

He speak of you, Missy Miss.

CHAPTER 36

Fuck a duck!

"What?" Kincaide shouted at me, though he was standing right beside me, leaning forward, as if pushing to know what I'd just learned.

I so wasn't any clavis. Nor did I want to be.

It is as it is.

I took Aini's words to mean it sucked to be me.

Warn the others. Please Aini. Prepare them.

There was no answer as I swallowed so deeply I was surprised my Adam's apple wasn't in the soles of my feet. "She says it is unclear."

"What's unclear?" Kincaide's spittle hit my face. Not a happy camper, and an unhappy camper in charge of too much fire power was a very dangerous proposition.

Stall. Find a loophole. Think.

"She says..." Tiger bells, what could deflect Kincaide? We only needed enough time to reach midnight and a new day, "...she says the clavis is near, but is still hidden."

"What the hell does that mean?"

I shrugged, though it felt like a steel beam was rammed through my shoulders.

"It means you stand to get what you came for," Van said, shocking me as I hadn't even been aware he'd left the rig. He looked at me, his expression unreadable. "Can you reach her?"

He meant Aini. I shook my head. "She's stopped talking."

I didn't see Kincaide's hand coming. A hard, open handed slap that punched me back into one of the thugs behind me, my lip split, blood pooling inside my mouth.

Van growled, though he didn't move.

Kincaide turned on him, as did half a dozen weapons. "When I want your opinion, I'll ask for it."

Van spoke anyway. "You lose her, you lose your way to communicate with the girl."

A braver person than I was as I wiped what blood I could off my mouth and regained my feet. I held my tongue. Van made a good point, and probably saved my life, as I could all but see steam rising off Kincaide. So close but thwarted.

"Give me one good reason I shouldn't kill you here and now, Noziak?" Kincaide taunted.

I was the one who answered. "Because the Librarian said Van needed to be kept alive. He and I come as a team, whether we want it or not." I put as much disdain into my words as I could. Hard to do as my lip and cheek were already puffing up.

Believe me. Believe me. I promised Alex I'd watch out for her brother. I gave her my vow. If he turned out to be what he'd appeared, a betrayer, let Alex deal with him.

Kincaide glanced at me, a look so lethal I'm surprised it didn't vaporize through me.

"Bring her," Kincaide barked at last to Lipwoski who grabbed my arm, squeezing so hard I knew he wanted me to whimper or cry out.

Think again, pig.

"Hammond, you stick to Noziak like white on rice. Got it?"

I refused to exhale, a dead giveaway that I'd been holding my breath. Van and I would be kept alive. For now.

Kincaide wasn't finished marshaling his troops. "Peters, your team takes the flank. Brennan and Murphy, circle round the back. Sweringen managed to infiltrate from there once, if you wait until we raise the alarm at the front, you should be able to get in. The rest of you come with me."

Before anyone moved, he stepped closer to Van, raising his gun to Van's chest. "You," he said, eyeing me, "you have one chance to save his life."

Kincaide meant me, but in case I was clueless, Lipwoski jerked me closer to where Van stood, barely breathing, holding himself still, his gaze lasered on his boss. I sure wouldn't want to be in Kincaide's shoes with that look, but if Aini was right, and I had no reason to doubt her, then Van was the one in the most danger here. Not because of the gun but because of who Kincaide was.

"What do you want?" I whispered, not having enough air in my lungs to ask more.

"Where in the compound is she?"

"Aini?"

Kincaide slammed his gun against Van's chest.

"Okay, okay." Fear propelled my words. "Long, low building, east side of the Compound. Red brick." I was talking about the dormitory but only Van knew that. I crossed my fingers that he'd have no reason to reveal my lie.

"How many entrances?"

"One."

"Guards?"

"I don't know." His hand twitched. "There should be a nurse. Possibly the doctor. Maybe one other."

Kincaide paused. A bully playing chicken as he laughed, a low, curling sound sliding down my skin, before he raised his hand, all cool and collected. "See, that wasn't so hard," he said.

Bastard.

Van hadn't moved a muscle, as if used to being threatened by a Horned a-hole on a regular basis. Maybe he had. What did I know?

"We move in from here." Kincaide, waved his free hand forward. "Team 1 with me."

Great. We were a good couple of miles as the crow flies from the Compound. In the dark. Without lights, it'd be a hard slog. At least for those who didn't have preternatural vision, something most of this group looked like they possessed, as we took off at a fast clip. Sight and stamina.

I hadn't told them exactly where Aini was, but if any of Kincaide's team managed to get past the Compound's outer perimeter, the wrong intel might give Aini a few minutes, that was all.

Being this clavis thing or person wasn't going to help Aini. Maybe later, if we got out of this situation alive it might, but right now it wasn't helping, so it was time to ignore it and get back to the most important issues. Stop Kincaide and his men from breaching the Compound's perimeter. If not possible, do whatever was necessary to keep him from reaching Aini.

My only chance to help my team was to connect with Aini, force her to warn them as I tripped and stumbled my way closer and closer.

Each step took me nearer to betraying my friends.

Closer to letting the Horned One succeed.

To killing Aini.

CHAPTER 37

We were coming in from the direction I'd been jogging through earlier. Was it yesterday? Or today? My how time flies when you're scared to death. Not. Especially not when bringing a boatload of trouble down on the only people left I really cared about.

My mentally calling to Aini with each step hadn't produced anything. Not as much as a whiff of her voice. But I did hear another sound. A familiar bark, bark, bark.

Gabby's puppy, acting like some big ferocious Pit Bull.

Great. Last thing we needed. Kincaide was about as stable as quicksand, he didn't need noise alerting Gabby's family to a squad of men in dark clothing sliding through the night.

"Shut it up," Kincaide growled to someone behind me.

"It's only a puppy. It'll quiet down in a sec." I used my best don't-be-an-idiot voice, picking up my pace to move us beyond Fang's territory.

But I wasn't quick enough. As if called, the clueless puppy wrestled its way through the underbrush, running full tilt toward me.

"Go home." I leaned toward him, whispering as loud as I could as I flapped my hands in a shooing motion. "Go away. Now!"

"Enough, Kelly." Van warned me off, but I ignored him. Fang wasn't his pet. If anything happened — Gabby would be heartbroken. I had to shoosh the dog away.

Kincaide pulled up short. I hoped the sight of the ball of fur would reassure the man there was no threat, but I'd forgotten Kincaide wasn't a man. That was if there was any humanity left in him. And that was my problem. Could I, when the time came, kill both Kincaide the man and the Horned One inhabiting him? Wasn't Kincaide as much a victim in this situation as I was? Killing the Horned One, no problem. Killing Kincaide? Could I live with that?

Yes. If this bastard hurt the dog, there was no going back.

Kincaide raised one hand, pointing at the puppy as I lurched toward it, meaning to scoop it up in my arms — my desperate kill-the-dog-kill-me protection plan.

Lipwoski's iron grip stopped me. Jerking me backwards a good two feet, leaving Fang squatting back on his hind legs, trying to figure out the game we were playing.

I shouted, not caring if the whole country heard me. "Run!"

Lipwoski guessed my action as his hand clamped over my mouth, digging in. Deep. No amount of struggle making a difference.

That smell, the rotten egg one, tainted the air as Kincaide smiled.

No. No. No.

Nothing. I couldn't do a damn thing.

Fang whimpered, cocking his head as I squeezed my eyes shut.

Please. Please. Run. Escape. Please.

No. No.

Words scarred my throat. He didn't have to hurt Fang. Didn't—

There was one sharp bark, cut off, then silence.

"Bring her," Kincaide ordered, sounding so smug I knew there was no hope for Gabby's puppy.

I pulled out of Lipwoski's grip and threw myself toward Kincaide but someone grabbed me from behind, lifting me off my feet. Kicking. Rearing my head back. Nothing helped. Nothing.

I couldn't focus beyond the blind fury driving me.

Even realizing it was Van pulling me away, creating distance between me and my target.

Tears bled down my face, choking me.

"Stop it, Kels," Van growled near my ear.

Instead of a response, I slammed my head backwards, feeling the smack when I hit his jaw. His hands tightened. A vice, one kept me pressed hard against him. The more I struggled, the stronger he held.

"You'll wake the family," he whispered at last. "He'll do to them what he did to the puppy. You want that?"

The words slammed against me. The truth deep within them.

Kincaide would — he'd kill Gabby, her mom and dad. All of them without a second thought.

My struggles ceased, but not the grief, soul deep. There was no reason, no sane reason to hurt the puppy. Gabby would be devastated, never knowing what happened. But Van was right. Whatever Kincaide used to be, he wasn't anymore. Only a monster remained.

I chugged in breath as Van eased his grip, leaving me standing on shaking legs.

"Don't do anything stupid," he said, but there was no heat there.

"He's not human." My voice was low, tear-choked and guttural.

"No. He's not."

I looked at where Kincaide stood, a deeper darkness in a dark night and shook against the shudder ripping through my body.

Bastard. Killer. Murderer.

"Move out." I heard what wasn't said. I'll let you live this time, McAllister, but don't push it. What I did with the dog I can do to you, too. I need you for now, but not for much longer. Don't forget that.

Van released me and stepped back. I didn't even glance his way as Lipwoski grabbed my arm, tugging me forward. I averted my gaze from where Fang had been, choking on the screams still burning my throat. But there wasn't anything left. Nothing but a smoking circle, about the size of a small puppy who hadn't hurt anyone.

Stumbling as Lipwoski dragged me forward, I made a vow. No longer was it enough to protect Aini. Now I was going to make sure Kincaide paid for what he'd done.

If he'd been human once, he wasn't now.

CHAPTER 38

By the time we came into sight of the main gate I wanted to throw up. Not very agent-like, but there wasn't an inch of me that wasn't bruised or running on muscle-burn alone. That and revenge.

I hated them. Hated them all. But mostly Kincaide.

Like a bull's eye target, all I could see was his rat-face and smell the sulphur.

Don't think of the puppy. Don't. Think of payback.

The last mile Lipwoski yanked me along. Every time I fell he jerked me up, wrenching my arm from its socket. I chugged air like an asthmatic going down for the count. My muscles quivered, pushed to their limit. My thoughts screamed, Aini, to no avail.

It wasn't the distance, in the dark, though that wasn't easy, or the pace set by guys, or preternaturals, with a whole lot more stamina than I had. It was the anger chugging through me over Gabby's puppy. That and the layered effect of the day. I'd lost track of whether today was the day I was attacked at the Library the first time or the second. Sweringen's assault and the one in Aini's room hadn't happened all that long ago, though it seemed weeks. Not according to my body's response now.

When Kincaide finally raised his hand to halt us, only determination kept me upright. That and watching Van, who hadn't even broken a sweat in spite of the challenge of navigating with his arms shackled behind him. If he could deal with Kincaide, then so could I.

Sometimes naïve, wishful thinking was the only thing that got me through the bad times.

He cast me one veiled, quick glance, one that had my breath backing up, the little I could inhale. I swore his eyes spit fire before he focused on the activity around the front gates. The guards there had been doubled up. Which meant Aini hadn't woken up and warned them.

They were doomed.

Fury burned through me, directed at Kincaide and his men. But that wasn't going to help anyone. Especially my team.

Instead of tying myself into more knots, I focused on the Compound entrance. Four guards were better than the usual two, but it also meant four were now vulnerable and probably unprepared to deal with a direct assault.

Who was on duty? Hard to tell from here, especially with sweat blurring my eyesight. Swiping one hand across my face, I rested hands on my knees, figuring it wouldn't hurt to let the jerks around me think I was broken, or close enough. If they saw me as a victim, they might, just might, make a slip that could let me disappear and escape.

Van Noziak was on his own. If he was going to play his cards so close to his vest, then he'd have to deal with the fallout. It was all operatives cover their own sixes.

I sent out another message to Aini.

Nothing.

Okay, so no help there, either. What next?

By squinting I recognized Wyatt as one of the guards at the gate. Herc was another, maybe Beau, a wicked powerful magic user. Unfortunately he was as raw as the first sunburn of summer. He hadn't even been around a week and here he was, pulled into a military operation with deadly consequences. Poor kid.

We weren't close enough to hear anything the guards were saying, at least those of us without preternatural hearing, as Kincaide had stopped us at the edge of a line of old growth trees and waist-high brush. He pointed toward a shallow gully hiding a culvert paralleling the roadway beneath us, down a slight sand and pebble incline. The culvert abutted the asphalt roadway and beyond it was cleared land up to the gate and fencing. Maybe twenty feet of open ground.

Lipwoski slammed his hand to the back of my head, pushing me forward onto my hands and knees. I cried out, or tried to, except a dirty hand jammed into my mouth, pulling my head back even as I fell forward.

Gagging, I struggled to breathe, not to escape, as the barrel of a gun indented my right temple.

"Make another sound and you're dead," Lipwoski growled in my ear, his breath hot against my skin.

If, no not if, when I got free, I was going to make Lipwoski pay, too.

Revenge was my new motto. One I was embracing with a vengeance.

I saw Van tense as Kincaide looked over his shoulder, silencing us both. Only when he was sure we'd obeyed his orders, as if there was any choice, did he make hand gestures indicating two at a time were to move out, down the slope, and spread out in the culvert.

Risky, as the wrong step could dislodge a small landside of pebbles, altering the IR agents on duty. There were few night sounds brushing past on the light breeze, far off the grind of a big rig's motor, but other than that, just silence. As if the darkness held its breath.

I watched the guards, mentally screaming at them, though I couldn't mutter a thing with Lipwoski's beefy, dirty hand gagging me. I didn't want them in harm's way. But just like my communication with Aini, nothing happened.

Kincaide trained his agents well: each duo snaked along, silent as the night around us. Lipwoski released his hand as I sucked in a deep breath, hoping and waiting for Van to raise the alarm as he inched forward with Hammond. They broke past the brush, now darker silhouettes against the inky darkness, the floodlights from the Compound casting elongated shadows behind them.

Any second. A misstep. Kicking a larger stone. Something to alert the IR agents.

But nothing. Ghost-like, they moved forward, leaving Lipwoski and me to go next. My heart splintered, accepting at last that Van really had turned on us, on me. The rat bastard coward. How could he?

Before I pulled my anger around me as a shield and moved ahead with my captor, Kincaide stepped forward and brushed against me. "Make a mistake and Noziak dies," he promised, sounding as if he wanted the excuse.

It was all I could do not to snarl back. Van made his choices. He could more than take care of himself. Why should I waste one more second worrying about him?

Because this was not like him. The Van I'd seen in Paris and Africa went out of his way to care for those he saw as under his protection. Okay, maybe I wasn't in that category anymore, but he wouldn't harm his sister. Would he?

I grimaced when I wanted to growl, but I trusted Kincaide's threat.

I know, I know, Van had washed his hands of me, but there was enough of the old Kelly left, the one who believed most people were fundamentally good, wanted to do the right thing even when it was hard, and could be counted on when the chips were down, to hope for the best. That Kelly, the naïve one, was grasping at straws, justifying Van's actions. I trusted Van. Okay, I wanted to trust him. I used to trust him, and if I was wrong? I glanced at the guards, two young kids and Wyatt, who had no idea how much of a world of hurt was coming at them.

Please keep them safe.

And Van?

Please let me be fundamentally right about him, too.

Only when I was sure I could move did I raise myself to a half-mast crouch and start inching forward. My most immediate goal was simple. Not get myself or Van killed until I was in a position to really make a difference for my fellow teammates. This far away I could be silenced with no one the wiser. A little closer and maybe, a big maybe, I could save a few lives.

I hadn't been trained as a stealth fighter, so if they didn't want me to avalanche a bunch of gravel down the slope, then they'd just have to wait for me to plant each step cautiously before I took the next one.

Besides, it meant I was eating up time. Not enough to keep Aini safe but I'd take what I could.

Lipwoski was all but vibrating beside me, knowing if he pushed me too fast it'd backfire. Didn't mean he wasn't happy to jam the butt of his rifle in my back like a cattle prod as often as he could. Every time he did I came to a full stop until he got the message. The way to keep me moving was to stop treating me like I was a cow needing to be prodded on the way to the slaughter house. Apt as that description might be.

I'd won my small victory, but I was still going to be one huge bruise tomorrow. If there was a tomorrow.

By the time I slid into the gully, I swore I could hear Van release a sigh of relief. Not likely, as his back was toward me and as rigid as it had been all night.

Bent double, I couldn't see anything except the lip of the road. We were spread out in a scraggly line, bunched shoulder to shoulder. Van was on one side of Kincaide, I was on the other with Lipwoski sandwiching me in.

What now? Was Kincaide going to charge the gate, risking all of us while hoping he could take out the guards before they alerted the others? He might throw us away but I doubt he'd do the same to himself. No, he wanted to create a diversion, get more IR people here, so his two other teams stood a better chance of infiltrating.

No chance to wink out. We were so close, Kincaide's men could feel where I was. Cry out? Alert my teammates? I might be close enough if I made enough of a ruckus. I stilled myself, sucking in a deep breath to shout a warning, but even before I could utter a peep I could hear the rat-a-tat of assault weapons off to my left.

The diversion had commenced.

What the? Peters, was that what Kincaide called the other team leader? Not that I cared but somehow it was easier to believe my people stood a chance against someone I could call by name. Thin straws grasped, but going all 'we're lost, we're lost' wasn't going to help either.

At least the IR gate guards now knew something was happening. They'd be better prepared since they weren't so in the dark.

Yup, more of that naïve thinking.

Shouting erupted from the front gate. Were people being pulled from there to reinforce whatever was happening along the left perimeter?

Any second I expected Kincaide to order an assault, to lay down a spread of gunfire, enough for the guards to duck for cover or run. My breath was coming in short, hard pants, fear jamming my lungs, tension locking my muscles. At this rate I was going to hyperventilate or pass out.

As I struggled to slow the hurtle of my heartbeat, Kincaide reached forward and fisted a hand in my shirt, yanking me toward him, his whisper like a shotgun blast to my strained nerves. "Do exactly what I say and your friends might live. One shot, one kill. Got it?"

Wasn't that military jargon for — each of Kincaide's men had an IR target in their sights? If I screwed up, they'd die.

I nodded. There wasn't enough spit in my mouth to do anything else.

"Noziak," he spoke to Van, his voice that harsh, strangled threat, "Hammond has your friend here lasered in. You make a wrong move, and she's toast. Got it?"

Van's frown had me wanting to back up but he gave a curt, tight nod.

Kincaide no longer was looking at either Van or me but toward the Compound as he raised one hand. "We move forward."

What? Move forward where?

Kincaide dragged me up and over the lip of the road, jerking me beside him, a little in front. A human shield? Probably, plus he could control me better up close and personal. His right hand banded my left arm, his left hand held his weapon. Another of those nifty H&K specials Lipwoski had. My luck was getting stuck with the one commander who could fire left-handed.

Van walked slightly before his handler, making it look like the two of us were together, which we were, but not in the way it might appear. The don't-shoot-us-we're-friends way. This was ingenious. By the time we got close enough that Wyatt,

Beau and Herc could sense we were more captives than team members with friends, it'd be too late.

With the pole-mounted security lights illuminating the front entrance, I felt like we were walking toward the Pearly Gates, all light and bright and promising safety and respite.

Wrong.

In the one guard house, a box really, that was rarely used, I could see a single silhouette. The other box on the opposite side of the gate looked empty, so someone had enough smarts to not be a sitting duck.

All be as it meant to be, Missy Miss.

I stumbled, hearing Aini's voice loud and clear, Kincaide's grip the only thing keeping me upright.

Aini? That you?

Silence.

Aini, please did you warn them?

Nothing.

What kind of help was this stupid new ability of mine if it didn't work? Lord love snakes and salamanders, doing nothing wasn't an option.

The single outline of a person hadn't moved but a voice called out. "Halt, right there."

It was Alex.

No! No! No!

Kincaide stopped, raising his weapon. I wondered if Alex could even see it bracketed by Van's and my bodies? What had Lipwoski crowed about? Multiple-shot strings at 900 rounds-per-minute.

Alex, Wyatt, Beau and Herc were dead. No matter what.

Reality slammed into my gut like a concrete block.

Only one thing to do.

CHAPTER 39

Those were my friends at the gate. To survive, knowing I got them killed, was not an option. The new Kelly book of rules.

Saying a mental goodbye to anyone who cared if I lived or died, I did the only thing possible. I threw myself backwards, doing a body check toward Kincaide instead of away from him, careening into Van and taking everyone by surprise. Especially me as I winked out.

Kincaide stumbled backwards, tried righting himself but I wasn't having any of that. With my free hand I clawed at his eyes, hearing the blast of his gun tear through the night. He'd been primed to fire. My only hope was the rounds went wild. Anywhere except at the gate.

I might have bought Alex a moment or two, not much more as Kincaide's team in the culverts started firing.

One shot, one kill.

Please let them survive!

If my team was behind cover they couldn't be killed. Right? Yeah, like wimpy plywood offered much of a barrier.

Kincaide had a lifetime of fighting experience, and he wasn't afraid to hit and hit hard. One second I was in control of the situation, the next slammed flat on my back, my jaw and head ringing. He might not be able to see me but that didn't slow him. Not at all. He slashed out at where I should have been and connected. Hard.

He leveled his gun, not at the gate, at where I was.

I'd like to say I was brave, facing death head on, but I wasn't. Fight or flight wasn't an option, so the only thing left was freeze and die. I squeezed my eyes closed and waited for the blast.

Instead came a grunt and cry.

Before I could look, a heavy body slammed on top of me. Kincaide. A shape hurtled past so fast it was more blur than shape. Van, running not toward the gate but outside the fence line, toward where the second group, the larger one, was attempting to infiltrate the Compound. He kept to his human self but his wolf part was clearly driving his power and speed.

He wasn't a bad guy!

Halleluiah and amen.

If I wasn't scrambling to shove Kincaide off of me I'd have pumped my arm in an IR team huzzah. But I didn't. Kincaide might be on the ground but he was far from immobilized.

"Move. Now. Now. Now. Team Five. Forward." He reared to his knees, shouting into his comm mic.

What team Five?

No time to think as I rolled away the second I could free myself. I rolled and rolled until I smashed into Hammond's still body. The one lying sprawled in the road, his neck at a twisted angle.

Do not gag. Get away. Live to gag another day.

By now Kincaide was roaring to his feet, making him the only target visible to my teammates.

Fire. Fire now!

Why weren't they? Why?

Oh, yeah, not being able to see me, but knowing I was out here, held them off. Something that wasn't bothering Kincaide's men in the least. They were keeping up a steady stream of fire, pinning down my team.

Big problem was Kincaide and I were between his men and the gate. This is exactly how friendly fire kills people. On the other hand, if they hit Kincaide, my job would be done.

Except ... that's when I saw it. Several bullets actually plowed into the man, but except for small twitches, he kept on moving. Bullet-proof vest? Or did being the host to the Horned One make him invincible to gunfire?

Not good.

I slithered across the tarmac at an angle, hoping Kincaide's men weren't firing as low as I was keeping, hoping more that I could make a trajectory away from the gate and then circle back. Waiting, every second, for death to slam into me.

I also kept expecting the two doors to appear now that I was invisible; the doors that forced me to choose one more nightmare. But they didn't. Not sure why, but if this was my silver lining, I'd grab it.

Glancing over my shoulder, I saw that Kincaide stopped, legs planted wide on the roadway, sweeping his weapon in a focused arc toward the gate. He was laughing, a high, maniacal sound chasing goose bumps across my skin. No one could survive that kind of gunfire.

No one.

My team still hadn't fired. Hiding or…

Save yourselves. Do something. Anything.

If they couldn't, I could.

Crawling back as fast as I could to where Kincaide stood, I latched on to his ankles with both hands and pulled from behind, toppling that asshole face forwards.

I hoped I broke his nose.

He couldn't see me, but knew something had taken him down. I scrambled, not away from him but in front of him, before he could get that wicked weapon showering another round of bullets where he thought I'd been.

How could I stop him?

His men were already climbing over the lip of the gully, taking advantage of no gunfire from the Compound. Since Kincaide's men couldn't see me I used my position to literally pull the legs out from under one or two before they caught on to what was going on. It felt real good to upend Lipwoski, who toppled across Kincaide, who didn't hesitate to thrust his gun into the man's gut and fire.

No one even blinked.

If I had any doubts about who, or what, Kincaide was, he'd just blasted them. Literally. Run with the devil and pay the consequences.

I expected to see Kincaide scramble to his feet and lead with his remaining guys but he didn't. He remained crouched on the ground, twisting away from the gate, staring down the road.

What now?

To my left, Alex's head peeped around from the remnants of the gatehouse. I could see her but she couldn't see me. Now was my time to crawl toward her while Kincaide remained statue still and his crew looked leaderless.

I had no idea how I could remain invisible for so long but I was taking the win.

If I could get to Alex, I could alert her to the threat against Aini. Though they didn't have enough people within the Compound to hold off the other two attacks and form a perimeter around the teen.

One problem at a time. Gate first.

Kincaide had been stupid to attack the front gate with as few men as he had, though he didn't strike me as the foolish type.

On the other hand, he'd just thrown away lives. That defined an idiot in my book.

Already the man closest to me was hedging back toward the culvert, leaving a blood trail from a nasty wound in his leg, as I crab walked in the opposite direction, keeping my head and body as low as possible. No one consciously wastes bullets firing at the ground. At least that's what had saved me so far.

What felt like a lifetime later, I reached the gate, breathing hard and afraid any second I might reappear. When I did, I'd become blind. Last thing my team needed was a sightless fighter who was more liability than asset. I'd reappeared earlier today and there'd been no problem, but I'd had a lifetime of expecting blindness; I wasn't going to let one fluke episode train me otherwise.

"Alex," I whispered, trying not to scare Herc who was flat against the ground opposite Alex's position. Wyatt was huddled on the other side of him. Beau lay flat on the ground behind Alex, the whites of his eyes betraying his fear even as he gripped an assault rifle so hard I was surprised his fingers didn't leave indents. Last week he'd been practicing for football tryouts. This week? He had no idea what he was getting into. Neither did Alex and I or we'd never had have him return to the Compound with us.

Five of them — two only teens, three untrained, and Alex — that's all, holding off a direct assault.

"That you, Kels?" Alex's voice jerked me back to the here and now.

"No, it's the Easter Bunny."

"Watch it McAllister," she snorted, sounding relieved and fed up at the same time. "I've hunted rabbits for dinner."

Point taken.

I scooched closer until I was right beside where Alex hugged the ground as there wasn't much left of the guard shack. "I'm here," I whispered.

She didn't flinch, but then she was a Noziak, and they were bred tough.

"Van?" she asked, betraying where her fears lay. Mine too, but that wasn't going to help either of us.

"Headed toward the barn. Another larger group infiltrating there. Need back up around Aini."

"Need back up everywhere." The words were curt even as she passed along my intel into her comm mic. Enough to make me happy. Or relieved.

Now to solve the Kincaide problem.

I held one hand to get her attention, though it might have worked better if I was visible.

"Is that—" she gave a chin nod toward Kincaide, rallying his men in the middle of the road, not worried about hiding or protecting his assets. They were clearly all expendable.

She didn't have to finish the sentence. "Yup. Kincaide aka the Horned One," I confirmed. "And scarier than a serial killer on speed."

"At least there's only a few of his men acting as back up here. If we can take them out, that'd leave him stranded."

"Exactly what I was thinking. Got an extra weapon?"

"Take mine." She shoved her Glock in my direction.

"What are you going to do?"

This time she was the one who raised a hand, more a finger to make her point. "I can shoot or I can use magic but not both at the same time. You can only shoot."

Made sense. I glanced at Kincaide. "You notice the bullets aren't phasing him?"

"I was hoping we were just piss poor shots."

"I wish, but I'm afraid it's something more."

"You sure?"

"Not a hundred percent but enough to not trust a kill shot as our best chance to take him out."

She eyed me. "What happened to the Kelly who saw the positive side of things?"

I thought of an innocent puppy and raised my gun for an answer. Then got back on task. "Can you and Beau execute a binding spell? Freeze him?"

"We can try."

Good. Things were looking up. From totally no-win to a slim chance.

That's when the slow rumble that I'd been aware of for a few minutes broke through to me.

"What's that?" Alex asked, raising her head to see further down the dark road.

I didn't have to look. I knew.

Team Five.

I cleared my throat before I could get the single, death-knell word out. "Reinforcements."

CHAPTER 40

"What the—" Alex started before cutting herself off and barking into her comm set. "Four, no five, maybe six Hummers coming into range. More could be coming."

"Of course they're with the bad guys."

She nudged where she thought my shoulder was. "Got a count?"

"Give me a sec for a tally. It's not like they're wearing phosphorus numbers on them."

I'd been mumbling to myself as the first vehicle pulled up about seventy feet away, just outside the range of our Glocks. Several bodies hustled out, crouched low, taking advantage of their vehicle as a screen.

"Five to six guys in the front rig. Multiply that for number of rigs and I'd say minimum of twenty-five." I hesitated, then added, "but I'd bet there are more."

"Yeah, that's what I was afraid of." She kept her voice low so as not to panic the kids huddled behind the other security box. Beau said nothing, which meant he'd already learned how to not flinch at bad news or was too in shock to realize what the arriving men meant.

We could hear the slap of boots against asphalt, low murmur of male voices, the rustle of cloth as the incoming men spread out behind the Hummers, down into the culvert, up the slope into the deeper brush cover. They moved with stealth, precision and training; fanning out in a matter of seconds.

We were so screwed.

"Probably have longer-range weapons," I said. "We're outmanned and outgunned."

"Any good news?" Alex snapped, fear riding her voice.

"Give me a sec. I'm thinking." I didn't tell her I was also panicking.

Obviously Kincaide had his own plans, as he stood up, widening his stance like a gunslinger at high noon with all the firepower on his side. Then he started that laugh. That low in the throat rising to a high keening gloat; a scratch along a chalkboard noise.

I wanted to stop him for that laugh alone.

His few men who'd slunk back into the darkness stepped forward.

If there was one thing I couldn't stand was smug bullies. "Pull Wyatt and Herc back," I ordered, though no one had put me in charge. "You and Beau keep your heads down. "

"What're you planning to do?"

"We can wait here and have them run over us, or I can take the battle to them."

Alex managed to snag an invisible handful of my shirt, which was a lucky grab given she couldn't see me, and jerked me to a stop just as I was rising to run forward.

"Don't be an idiot. Give the rest of our team a few minutes to get here."

"We don't have a few minutes and everyone's engaged." Yes, I was snarling but I was also watching Kincaide's men spread out, clearly not intimidated by what they saw of our defense.

"I'm the only one who can stay out of sight long enough to possibly take Kincaide out."

"And if you can't?"

"I'll know I tried."

She released my shirt, reluctantly, but freeing me to complete what needed to be done — a suicide mission.

"You get yourself killed Kels and Van'll come after me. Just remember that."

I didn't have the heart to tell her he might not be able to. He was only one against half a dozen trained operatives. But I didn't have time to worry about him. Not now. Especially since my own thoughts twisted my gut. I also ignored the fear screaming through me.

"Here." She reached down to her ankle and pulled out a long dagger. Her anathema blade. "Take this, too. As a back-up."

Which really left her defenseless.

She cut off my protest before I could speak. "I've got Beau. And Herc has some of his devices."

"If I can't kill Kincaide, I want you out of here," I growled, not trusting her magic or woo-woo, prototype defense weapons. "Got that?"

"Who made you Queen?"

"I did." She couldn't see me. Couldn't see that my strongest weapon right now was bravado. Couldn't see my hesitation as my shoulders tightened, bile bubbling in my throat.

I didn't want to move forward. But more than that, I didn't want my friends to die.

Focus. Most immediate goal was to take down Kincaide. Cut off the head of the monster and maybe, just maybe, his men might back down.

And here Alex thought glass-half-full Kelly was a thing of the past. So did I.

"You freeze Kincaide," I murmured, already to my knees. "I'll disrupt his men as much as possible until we can stop him."

"Stupid plan," Alex said as she waved Herc over. A brave kid willing to dash from his side of the gate opening, but maybe he was still at that age where he thought he was invincible. Or that this was a video game without real casualties.

I wish.

Before Herc could trample me, I scurried to my feet. Only Alex's weapon wavering in both hands showed, so I shoved the knife under my shirt, the Glock I held tight against me, praying that with the light behind me it wouldn't be visible until it was too late. I inched forward, quaking in my shoes but knowing we, no I, didn't have a lot of options. Kincaide needed to be taken down.

I doubted anyone could really see me as I moved into the open but still I held my breath, making me light headed. Once I pulled up the Glock and started using it the bad guys would be noticing me then. Noticing and doing everything in their power to take me down.

No gunfire from the men entrenched in their positions. Yet. But I knew that was going to change real soon.

"You two pull back and find cover," Alex shouted to Wyatt and Herc. For a second I thought I heard Wyatt talk back, then I blocked him out, focusing my whole attention on marching toward Kincaide, step by step.

I didn't wait until I was on top of him to shoot, aiming for his shoulder, or legs, where he wouldn't have body armor. If I had to kill him I'd face that. A small, naïve part of me still wanted to believe there was a difference between Kincaide the man and Kincaide spawn of the Horned One. I hadn't yet crossed the Rubicon of whether I could kill the latter and save the former, but after watching what he'd done to the puppy … So maybe I had made my choice. Right now all I wanted was him out of commission and to know if he could be stopped by bullets.

It took less than three shots to confirm my earlier fear had been right. Bullets bounced off him without even a dent.

Criminey and fuss buckets.

No one wore full body armor and moved the way he could move. All my test seemed to accomplish was to alert Kincaide, and the men closest to him, that he was under attack from someone or something they couldn't see. Invisibility gave me some protection but not a lot as several weapons swung in my direction.

I dove to the side, my default response to fire power.

Now Alex. Freeze him!

Alex wasn't waiting for my permission to commence operation stop-him-any-way-we-could. A pulse of magic washed over me, so intense it slammed me forward, almost upending me from my knees onto my face. I staggered as it knocked me further sideways, which gave me the chance to live as bullets started strafing where I'd just been.

Keep nimble and moving. Already I was scrambling to end run around Kincaide, coming between him and his reinforcements in the Hummers. I didn't want to assume all his men were there by choice. Attacking a private residence on

American soil was not something the average soldier would do easily. Unless Kincaide told them there was a very good reason to do so, such as stopping a terrorist threat aimed at D.C., but that still didn't mean they deserved to die because of following the wrong guy.

I made each shot count as I aimed, fired and moved, aiming for legs. Three of four guys crumpled before Kincaide barked out what I expected was an order. It wasn't. It was some kind of chant.

"Enemy Mine. Hell I call.
Night black. Sin red.
Torments of flesh I command forth!
Boils and blood appear.
Tear asunder.
Dukes of darkness, Kings of hell
Smite mine enemy. Once. Twice. Thrice."

The last words hadn't even finished before I'd slammed to my knees, then the asphalt, writhing, clutching my stomach. My gun slipped from my fingers as an army of biting, stinging seizures tore across my flesh. Chills raced across my skin and sweat broke out.

I tore apart from the inside out. Pain erupted in pulses, each punch stronger than the last. I wanted to beg for mercy, but all I could do was whimper. Nothing more would come as I bit my lips so hard blood pooled in my mouth.

So this was death? Worse than any of the nightmares I'd experienced behind my doors. All I could hope, pray for, was that it'd end. Soon.

Not going to happen as I heard that laugh of Kincaide's. Low building to high. Non-human. The sound of nightmares. He had no idea where I was, but he'd brought me low, so low scraping bottom would be up. Dying would be a relief.

Alex's binding spell hadn't even slowed him. We were out of options.

Kincaide's men behind me were moving closer, firing as they came. Like a light winking out the pulse of magic Alex had been using was cut off.

Curling like a pill bug was all I could do.

Missy Miss they coming.

Now? I can't help you, Aini. Nothing ... nothing ... left.

Silence. As if my whole world dimmed to nothing but pain.

This was how it was going to end. Not with a shout of defiance? A fight well fought? But on a mute whimper. And one image. Aini. Alone. Far from her home. Trusting that strangers would help her. Strangers like me.

She was even more vulnerable than I was.

Like anything I could do was going to make a whit of difference.

Another jolt of pain, enough to clear my head for a nano second. Clear and remind me. Aini would certainly die if I didn't try.

Hold on, Aini, I silently screamed, pulling to my knees. Hold on.

Like a penitent begging for mercy, I knelt-walked toward Kincaide. Pain twisted my spine forward, forced blood up my throat. Didn't matter. Aini needed me.

Just then a large shout erupted from the guardhouse as someone came hurtling forward, his weapon thrust forward, the deep chug, chug, chug of his Glock firing, his determination echoing through the night.

Wiping sweat out of my eyes, I raised my head enough to see Wyatt playing GI Joe, or Rambo, or some Super Hero. Except he wasn't.

"Get back!" I screamed, though it sounded more croak. Waving my invisible hands didn't help. "Go back."

He was only a man.

"Go!" I sobbed the word. "Please."

When the first bullets tore into him I could see the shock scream across his face.

Time slowed as one, two, then more, lots more bullets plowed through him, tearing him apart. Stomach, chest, neck. Blood geysered even as he kept pumping forward.

Words jammed. I couldn't escape watching, helpless, one hand stretched toward him as if it could push him back, reverse time, do something. Anything. Nothing.

Momentum crushed him onward, arms windmilling, mouth open in a silent cry. He slammed onto the asphalt, close enough splatters of his blood sprayed me, still warm.

"Wyatt," I stretched for him, my single word a torn, ragged whisper. I wanted to shake him, to throw myself over him, protect him. But it was too late. His sightless eyes stared into mine, ripping through me.

Noooooooooooo.

The darkness of the night wrapped around us, muting all other sounds though I knew there were screams. Alex's. Mine. And more gunfire. My hand grabbed Wyatt's arm as I dragged myself forward. Dampness coated my fingers clutching at him as my tears escaped. As useless as I was.

I brushed one hand across his hair, but there was no soothing. No going back. No fixing any single action that brought us to this.

"I'm sorry." I leaned toward him, brushing my lips across his forehead. "I'm so, so sorry."

CHAPTER 41

Reality slammed into me with the force of a Mack truck. First the sounds torquing around me; auditory overload made me want to slam my hands over my ears. Then the smells — Wyatt's blood, sweat, that egg-sulphur stench. And then the memories — the attack outside the library, Sweringen, Van letting me believe he betrayed me.

And here I was, in the middle of senseless death and pure evil. I looked up, seeing Kincaide. No, not Kincaide. Stop thinking of him as anything remotely human. He was the devil. Nothing more.

Evil.

What had Fassbinder said? The bringer of souls to the underworld. Not a guide or a mentor but ripping them from life simply because he — it — could. The Horned One who meant only more death and more destruction. Unless I stopped him.

How?

Screams of rage and frustration boiled inside me. A caldron of misery. How was I supposed to do a damn thing against a demi-god? Bullets didn't phase him. Alex's magic didn't reach him. What was left?

That's when it hit me. I was slumped there, in a pool of regret when I realized I was no longer wrung out with pain.

Wyatt had broken the spell the Horned One had cast. He'd saved my life.

And I was whining.

"I'll find a way." My words were lost in the shouts of Kincaide's men around me, of IR reinforcements arriving at the gate.

If I didn't want my team to end up like Wyatt, I had to get off my butt and do something.

What had the Librarian mentioned eons ago? Two are stronger than one. Together, there is a chance. Individually, there is no hope.

"Van," I shouted, aware I was betraying my position. Since I wasn't twisted like a stale pretzel, I could move, scuttling backward, giving myself some room between me and the Horned One. "Van."

I'd keep screaming until he appeared or I couldn't cry any more.

Two can stop him. Two, not one. Van and I were supposed to work together, not apart. I hoped that's what the Librarian meant.

Enough dead bodies littered the roadway that I couldn't maneuver unless I stood. Smacking into Lipwoski's corpse I paused, staggering to my feet, but not before I eyed a wicked looking assault knife sheathed along the length of his leg.

My brain kicked into gear, rusty and slow but engaged. If a bullet couldn't take down Kincaide, maybe a knife might. Or slow him down?

Lipwoski's weapon was too large for me and somewhere I'd dropped Alex's anathema dagger. It wasn't large, or fancy, and I wasn't even sure how sharp it was, but it was a weapon. If I could find it.

Plus it held magic. Didn't know how much or if it'd make a difference, but I wouldn't know unless I tried using it.

Scrambling like a desperate mother looking for her screaming child's pacifier, I twisted right and left before I spotted Wyatt's body. There. On the other side of him. Alex's blade.

What had Stone taught us about knife fighting? Other than to avoid it as too close and personal for women not trained and experienced.

I was barely trained but gaining experience by the minute.

Use the whole body, not just the knife hand. Disable another's weapon by going for a quick wrist or arm slash. Aim for arteries. Blood loss can take down an enemy as surely as a direct blow to the heart or vital organs.

No more calling for Van as I scooped up the weapon and pivoted to move into Kincaide's space.

I was on my own. My assets? Invisibility that had lasted longer than I'd ever pushed it before, making me light headed with the strain. A ceremonial knife, which I hugged close against me like a talisman. Kincaide was distracted; focused on the increased activity at the gate. His team holding back, waiting for something.

Biggest asset? Nothing to lose.

CHAPTER 42

Each step closer to Kincaide made the sulphur stench thicken until I was breathing only through my mouth and even that didn't help. I wasn't rushing in. There wasn't enough left inside me to hustle, much less pounce.

No, my plan was bare bones basic. Shuffle forward, slow and sure, looking for whatever window of attack I could find and give it my all. I might get in one or two slashes. That's all. They had to count.

Kincaide faced away from me, toward the gate, just standing there as if expecting little resistance, no need to hide for this guy. Shouts and movement increased behind me. His reinforcements marched forward, using darkness as their only cover. Once they got closer and started laying down more fire power, it was over.

Another step forward, coming around Kincaide's side, his profile half in shadow from the vapor lighting overhead. That smug I'm-winning grin tightening my muscles for a final push.

That's when the silver grey wolf sprang, so silent I never heard him coming.

"Van," the single whispered word a plea as he slammed into Kincaide, taking him down.

But not out.

Kincaide roared, not in pain but in triumph, as he struggled to his feet, his hands buried so deep into Van's fur they had disappeared. I could only see what they were doing, clenched around Van's throat, holding snapping teeth back, rattling Van's wolf body as if shaking a stuffed toy. Kincaide's eyes gleamed orange-red, an unearthly yell erupting from him.

Van's shifter form was larger and denser than the average grey wolf. Kincaide must be holding a good hundred and fifty pounds of snarling, lethal predator, and acting like it was a stuffed toy.

Alex shouted but it sounded far, far away. Everything down a deep, bottomless tunnel.

I staggered forward. Punch drunk. Wyatt's blood made my grip on Alex's dagger slick.

Van's growls were lessening. Like Fang's puppy growls.

"Not going to happen."

I lurched around to come up behind Kincaide. Shouts exploded from the gate. Screams from the other direction. Kincaide's men shuffling back.

A respite? Or false hope?

Focus. Aim for Kincaide's back.

Now. I raised the knife over my head. One chance. Only one.

Was any part of him still human? Didn't matter any more. If I had to kill an innocent man to stop the Horned One I'd have to live with that.

With a cry and a lunge, I put everything I had into raising my arm for a downward thrust.

That's when the doors appeared, calling me.

CHAPTER 43

Fifteen seconds.

My window of time before I had to choose a door. Not one of two but one of three. What horror could be behind door number three?

A raw laugh tore from me. Who cared? I'd be dead by then.

Thirteen seconds.

Momentum drove me. Along with fear.

Eleven seconds.

I plunged the knife in deep with everything I had.

Van hung like a limp rug from Kincaide's hands as the dagger slid through cloth and skin and nicked bone. Down, down, down it went, from shoulder to rib cage. The weight of my entire body dragged at it, pushing deeper, so deep I might come out the other side.

Kincaide's yell increased, changed timber. He tossed Van aside. Still I hung on.

The tattoo on my arm burned. I'd actually forgotten about it. Please, please, please. Don't let that be a huge mistake.

Nine seconds.

Like a gyro on speed, Kincaide spun and spun. I wrapped my legs around his legs and wouldn't let go.

This was for Aini. For an innocent puppy. For Van.

Damn Kincaide. Damn him to hell.

Acid seared my skin where I'd been marked.

The doors slammed open.

Can't let go. Can't...

I wrapped my legs tighter around Kincaide's, tripping him, sending us both smashing on to the asphalt.

Blood, his blood, greased my hold, forcing me to push harder or lose the knife, the tat burning deeper.

Men's voices stormed around me. Gunfire. But less now. Someone shouted. Alex? Jaylene?

Kincaide was weakening. But so was I.

The doors pulled at me. Didn't matter.

My body spasmed.

Kincaide gave one last violent jerk, flinging me from his back. I smacked into the pavement with a dull thud. My head bouncing. Twice.

Darkness swept over me. But not until I saw the evil in Kincaide's orange-red eyes dim.

Dim was good. Die was better.

CHAPTER 44

Sounds swelled around me, my chin rubbing against asphalt grit.

Was I dead?

The smells hit me first. Cloying scent of fresh blood. Lingering whiff of sulphur. Trickle of a late spring night breeze.

Then came the sounds, like the opening of mall doors on Black Friday, an ebb and tide of voices, some female, most male, cart-wheeling around me.

Right in front of me sprawled Kincaide's still body, blood pooling across his back and down his side.

We'd done it. We'd won. Hadn't we?

A pair of buff-colored rough-out boots bit into the pavement near my face. "You alive?" Jaylene demanded as she scrunched down, her hand chomping down on my shoulder.

"Ow!"

Articulate, I wasn't. In pain, I was. My response seemed to be enough, though, as she shouted to Mandy. I must have popped back into existence, but I wasn't blind. How long had I been out?

Next thing I knew my teammates flanked me, pulling me up in as gentle a manner as possible. Which didn't say much. I hung like a stuffed grain sack as they towed me toward the gate area. Or where the gate had been. Now it was a gapping hole.

"Van?" I whimpered, flinching with each step forward. "How's..."

"Girlfriend, you've got to look out for you. Wolf man knows how to take care of himself." Jaylene chuckled, so I assumed she meant he was still alive.

Relief flooded through me. That was good. Real good. If he lived, then so could I.

"Don't know how you did what you did," Mandy murmured while shifting her arm underneath me, absorbing most of my weight, "but you took the bad guy out."

I tried a smile that came out more as a grimace.

They pulled me up beside the rear wheel of a vehicle, easing me to the ground until I was propped in a sitting position. The view sucked. Bodies scattered in the darkness. Most wore the EMA uniform. I refused to look too closely though, averting my gaze from where Wyatt had fallen. Even one senseless death was painful. This? This was stupid, no-point carnage.

Mandy squeezed my shoulder before heading back to where Kincaide's body rested. For some reason I kept expecting him to rise again. Maybe one too many zombie movies. That or I didn't really trust him to stay dead.

I caught myself rubbing my arm, where the tattoo was. Now, it itched like a day old rash. Too chicken to find out if the image was gone, I let my hand fall, taking tally of the other aches and bruises, as if I'd been side-swiped by a dump truck. I also shoved away questions about that third door I'd seen. All that mattered right now was I lived, and so had Van. I'd deal with everything else later.

Out of the shadows Alex headed my way, her steps slow and deliberate, looking as wrung dry as I felt.

I called her name, but it took several hoarse shouts before she shook her head and focused on where I rested.

"You look like hell," she mumbled, sinking down beside me.

"Right back at ya."

That earned a weak smile.

"Is Van…" I couldn't form more words. Yes, Jaylene had hinted that he lived, but there was alive and there was barely hanging on. From what I'd seen of Kincaide's action, I was afraid of details.

Alex looked straight ahead, her voice thick with emotion. "He'll make it. Damn shifter blood. Never thought I'd be happy he has it."

Only then did I start breathing.

"You stopped Kincaide. You bloody well stopped him." She glanced at me as if seeing me for the first time. "Way to go, Kels!"

"Oh crap."

"What?"

"I lost your knife. It's..." I chin pointed toward the EMA director's still form. "I think it's still in him."

"My anathema dagger?"

"Librarian said the Horned One could only be killed by a blow struck. Not of man or woman." I hissed a shallow breath at the stupid risk I'd taken. "I thought, maybe, your ceremonial dagger was different enough to do the job."

Alex looked at me for the longest time before she threw back her head and muttered, "Saints preserve us from fools and children."

Not what I expected.

She leaned toward me, making her face only a silhouette because of the floodlight behind her. "The dagger didn't matter. What mattered is that you're obviously not human, since you could strike the blow and kill him."

As if the earth shuddered, I sagged against the wheel. Guess good news had to even out bad news. Van living weighed against hearing words I never wanted to hear. I'd fought enough preternaturals to know I never, ever wanted to be one of them. On the other hand, Van was, and he was the most honorable, good person I'd ever met. And Alex wasn't all human. Neither was Nicki. So maybe being not all human wasn't that bad a thing. Just like people, preternaturals came in all varieties. I just had to find out what flavor I was and if that was going to change me any more than being an IR agent had already.

It took a second before I realized I could live with that. I released a sigh that came out as a simple, "Oh."

"Mega oh." Alex glanced up as Mandy and Jaylene came staggering back toward us with Herc. He looked as whipped as Alex.

As if answering my unspoken questions, Mandy hunkered down beside me. "Alex, Sabina and Beau combined their magic enough to bind or blow back most of the assault here. Herc followed up with a few of his containment weapons. Then when the Horned . . the head guy bit the dust, it was as if most of the life went out of the troops assaulting in the secondary locations."

"Aini?"

"She's okay. No one got as far as her."

I closed my eyes.

"It was close," whistled Jaylene. "Too close."

And she didn't even know about the threat to D.C. from Kincaide. How was the team ever going to stop the Seekers if a second tier didn't-make-the-cut demon just about took us all out?

Another thought to shove to the side. Or wait until we had enough of a breather that I could share with the team.

"Any other casualties?" I asked.

"Only Wyatt as far as I know," Alex murmured, though I could hear the bitterness, the anger in her tone. "Lots of wounded."

"Stone has set up a make-shift triage center near the dorms," Mandy said, rising to her feet. "Let's get you over there. Or we can head right to the showers while there's still hot water."

"Showers sound divine." I pushed myself to my own feet, pretty proud of the fact I could, even if I had to pause to make sure my legs held. I took another glance at the bodies — Kincaide, Lipwoski, Hammond. What was going to happen to them?

"Stone's taking care of the details." Mandy clearly tracked my thoughts.

With a final head shake at the shame of it all, I turned to follow her, finding myself asking, "You're sure about Aini?"

"She's safe," Mandy reassured. "Missed all the fun."

This kind of fun I could do without, too.

CHAPTER 45

Less than an hour later I passed Alex as I walked down a shadowed hallway. The shower made me feel human again, even as I grappled with the fact I clearly wasn't. The tattoo was gone, only a faint scarring remained. I could live with that. There was something else I couldn't live without though.

I'd killed Kincaide, human and Horned One. One goal met. Now I had another agenda. One based on knowing how fragile, how precious life was. It was time to take my future in my hands, accepting that every moment I lived could be my last.

Mandy had shared that Van remained in the Compound, healed in body. It was what she left out that bothered me. A smart woman would have crawled out of the shower and into bed. Right now I wasn't feeling too smart.

I needed to see Aini, too. First Van though. There was too much between us that needed to be resolved. I'd sent out a mind pulse to Aini earlier, right before the showers but there'd been no response. I hoped that meant she was fine, just resting. Mandy said she was okay so that would hold me.

"You speak to him." Alex came marching down the hall, brushing past my shoulder, her words harsh and strained, her gaze straight ahead. "Maybe you can get through to him." Then she stamped away as if she'd pronounced a death sentence. I wished I knew whose.

With more nerves than I wanted to admit, I accepted that I had a choice. Go toward Van or run as fast as I could in the opposite direction. I could see Aini first, then Van.

Coward.

I couldn't turn around, not right now and leave what was between Van and me unfinished. I'd come too close to losing him to know that it was time to get out of the fetal position and take the moments of grace I'd been allotted.

My palms sweated, my breath backed up in my lungs. I had no idea what to expect if I walked through that closed door, the one beckoning at the end of the hallway. A real door this time and a real man. A man torn by betrayal. Oh, yeah. A man hurting. A man who was no doubt beating himself up more than anyone else ever would. That's the kicker, because accepting that he was doing just that drove me, too.

There was no turning back. Not for me. Not now.

What if instead of Kincaide lying dead beyond the gates, it'd been Van? Was I going to keep running away? Waiting for permission? Afraid of the risks? Wishing for more time to take baby steps toward what I'd been afraid to act on until now?

I'd been raised to be a good girl. To follow the rules. To think before I acted, until I could talk myself out of anything and everything. But nothing prepared me for this. If I had a thousand more days to feel the sun and the wind and the possibility of more, I would hesitate. I'd hold back. I'd do what I'd been taught I should do.

Now?

Sucking in a breath that splayed my heart against my backbone, I raised my chin. I was not running away. Not this time. I was going to reach for all I could, make the most of the moments remaining, one second at a time. Time to burn the rulebook and find out how bad this good girl could be.

CHAPTER 46

Each step mimicked the solid thud, thud, thud of my heartbeat. Raising my hand to knock on that closed door made my decision for me. If he said go away, would I? If he didn't answer, would I accept that as a final decision? If he...

Forget this. I grabbed the doorknob, ignoring the cool slide of it beneath my palm, the slow buzz of exhaustion beneath my skin and threw open the door.

Where were the sound effects when you needed them? Inside me cymbals clashed and oceans roared. At the very least I expected fire works. Instead I was met with silence. A yawning, gaping vortex of silence.

Van stood across the room, at the lone window, one that looked out on the roofs of the nearest buildings, in the distance a half-moon crept earthward, dawn hiding just beyond the horizon. The room swam in shadows, clinging desperately to the last shreds of moonlight. Between him and me hunkered a bed, a very plain, very normal, even boring bed. Nothing to rev my heartbeat or tighten my nerves to the breaking point. But it did.

I glued my gaze on Van, ignoring the bed and the possibilities, the ones it represented and the ones clawing through me.

I'd come to offer comfort. That was the last thing on my mind now.

He hadn't moved, hadn't as much as blinked as he stood, facing away from me, his hands jammed into his pants' pockets. I could read the tension in his back, every muscle clenched, his very inaction a mockery of the emotions pouring through me. Volatile, scalding, desperate emotions clawing for release.

I cleared my throat, the sound an explosion through the strained silence. "Alex said you were brooding."

So I sucked at small talk. I was impressed I could speak at all.

He lowered his head, shaking it as in disbelief, or maybe with a silent groan. At the best of times Van Noziak wasn't an easy person to know. He let you see only what he permitted you to see. Charm, frustration, determination. But now? Now control radiated from him like the heat from an inferno.

Yet he said nothing.

Like a rubber band held under pressure for too long, I waited, afraid to move, not knowing if it'd be toward him or slamming the door behind me.

"If you came for an apology, I'm sorry."

Oh, criminey. "Don't be an idiot. That's not why I'm here."

At last he turned, only his head, glancing at me as if not really aware I was there or what I was doing.

That made two of us.

Shadows danced across his profile, sharpening the angles of his face, the darkness of his eyes, the steel edge of his jaw. The look of a hero. Or a fallen angel.

Nerves rumbaed beneath my skin, waiting. For what? A smile? A nod? Something telling me I wasn't alone here. My want wasn't in vain? That I wasn't making an absolute, sorry fool of myself.

So what?

Say something. Anything.

When he spoke at last, I could feel the rumble deep in my chest. "What do you want?"

"You."

And there I stood, emotionally bleeding, waiting for this fearless, fire-eating, stubborn man to acknowledge my words, the cost of them, the promise I offered.

But when did Van Noziak do what I expected?

His nostrils flared as if racing hard, the skin across his cheekbones tightened, the pupils of his eyes enlarged.

"You don't know what you're saying." His words came bleak and guttural. Then he turned his back.

That was it? I came to him and he shut, no, he slammed the door in my face?

"Who are you to tell me I don't know myself." I marched so fast and furious across the width of floor I was surprised the linoleum didn't erupt in flames.

He didn't expect me to grab his arm, to tug him toward me, to face me. Not an easy feat with a shifter, or a smart one, as up close I could see the golden band around his pupils, his wolf straining to break free.

Tough pinkies.

"You listen, and you listen closely, Van Noziak." I tightened my fingers on his shirtsleeve, to keep them from shaking, or from me stabbing them into his chest. "You're the one who's always said there was something between us. Here's our chance to find out. What are you going to do about it?"

His muscles tightened beneath my touch, from solid to stone. He all but growled, "And what about tomorrow? And the day after it?"

I snorted, throwing up my hands. "What kind of chicken-liver excuse is that?"

He stepped forward, swallowing all the air between us, his eyes glowing golden. "This is not you, Kels. This is survivor's rush driving you. Adrenaline after-burn. Any solider getting through battle expects to feel this."

"And?"

"And I want more." He softened his tone but not its impact. "I could have gotten you killed today. I'd made a call and it was the wrong call. My actions almost cost you. I did that."

"But you didn't. I'm here."

"Not good enough. You trusted me, and I let you down."

I threw my hands wide. "So you're going to play the I'm-not-noble-enough card? We both made mistakes. Will do so again. This isn't one of them."

"You sure?"

"I wouldn't be here if I wasn't."

His brows arrowed together, the lines bracketing his mouth deepening as he said, "I don't want a pity fuck."

Curling my hands into balled fists at my sides, it was all I could do not to pound on him. Except I knew what he was trying to do in his misguided-Noziak way. He was still playing protector. Lone wolf tarnished-shield. What he couldn't admit was he was as unnerved by what churned between us as I was. Had been since I'd first laid eyes on him.

"I'm not asking for tomorrow." I whispered the words, feeling them tingle against my skin. "I'm not asking for forever promises. I know we probably don't have them." Could almost guarantee that given what we both did. But I meant what I said. There was no L word, no vows, or pledges except those that can be given between two with limited horizons.

Stepping closer, I laid my hand against his chest, aware of the heat of his skin, the pounding of his heart, echoing my own. "All I want is the here and now. Can't that be enough?"

I leaned my forehead against him, aware how rigidly he clasped his arms at his sides. "Please don't make me beg."

"Damn you." His words said one thing, his actions another as he wrapped those strong arms around me with the gentleness of a man afraid of himself.

I raised my head, accepting his pacing. For now. Feathering a kiss across his jaw, I listened to him suck in his breath, still his body.

Van Noziak, you break my heart.

Nibbling the corner of his lips, those sinful, sexy lips I'd dreamt about too many nights in a row, his muscles tensed. A good kind of tense. A dangerous kind.

His hands slid to my shoulders, my upper back as I raised on my tip toes, brushing my tongue across his lips, my hands to his back, feeling the tension, the restraint.

"You know what I am," he whispered, a final warning shot.

"A pain in the ass?"

I could taste his smile as his fingers dug into my arms.

"You had your chance to run, Kels."

CHAPTER 47

Van wanted slow. I wanted him. Now!

Like everything else between us we muddled, tripping over our own feet, our eagerness, as we tangoed toward the bed. I slid my hands beneath his shirt, aching to touch skin to skin.

He paused, the back of my thighs brushing the bed, my nails already scraping his back.

"You've been hurt." He offered it as an olive branch, one last reason to step away from the chasm.

But it wasn't going to work. "So have you, Noziak."

"But I'm a…"

"Shut up and kiss me."

And he did. Long, slow, deep kisses melting me from the inside out. Mother of Angels this man could kiss.

His hands worked their own magic. Teasing and tantalizing, sliding beneath my shirt, cupping my neck to angle my head for another of those soul-robbing kisses. Tongue. Touch. Want. Need.

I wanted more. Lots more.

Fumbling, I tugged at his shirt, pulling away from him long enough to shove his sweatshirt over his head. He tossed it to the side with a growl then nibbled at my lips as his very sure, very nimble fingers undid my shirt buttons, one by one, with agonizing slowness. If I'd kept my t-shirt on he wouldn't have been able to tease me like this.

He was going to kill me.

He tore the last buttons. So I wasn't alone in my need.

As the cooler room air chilled my skin, he tumbled us both back onto the bed.

I wasn't cool any longer.

Somewhere, way in the back of what was left of my functioning brain, I knew shifters ran hotter than humans. Van was like a heated blanket surrounding me, protecting me, warming me. Who knew warmth could be so sexy.

My tongue tangled with his, mimicking what I wanted from him, but he had his own agenda.

Why wasn't I surprised?

He pulled back, levering up on one elbow, his hand brushing tangled hair from my face, calluses whispering across my skin.

"You're sure?"

I reached up, clenching both hands in his hair to pull him down until my whole world was framed by the deep chocolate, golden-rimmed desire in his eyes. "Fuck me. Now."

He got the message.

Every ounce of focus and ferociousness that made him a warrior also made him a lover. Clothes were tossed aside, cloth ripping, his hands and lips and body memorizing mine. Gone was the gentleness.

Finally.

I strained toward him. My back arching, my body quivering. He parted my lips again with his own, his wicked tongue promising as his hands slid down my sweat-slickened body. Down. Down. Down.

Till he reached between my legs and started stroking. I exploded like a tinder dry forest meeting an inferno, my screams swallowed by his smile.

But he wasn't done.

He angled over me, his arms rigid, his body more heated than mine, his expression promising as he rose and then lowered himself, stretching, filling, claiming.

I sighed as he inched in. Then grabbed his buttocks and pulled.

We went over the top together.

CHAPTER 48

Lying there on the crumpled bed coverings we hadn't even bothered to shove aside, our bodies satiated, skin still damp, breathing slowing, he glanced over at me. We were both on our backs, neither able to move, to do more than look at one another. A wicked smile played around those wicked-good lips.

"What?" I asked, finally able to speak.

"I didn't know you knew the f-bomb."

I raised up on one elbow, surprised at how comfortable I felt with him, both still naked, the morning sun bathing the room in a golden glow.

"I know a lot more other words, too." I found myself teasing, glad that, at last, I could disconcert him. "Want to find out what they are?"

His smile morphed from startled to intrigued as the lines around his eyes deepened. "You're a tease, Kelly McAllister."

I leaned forward until my tongue tickled his ear, close enough I could whisper words I'd always wanted to use but not to just anyone.

His response was immediate as he twisted, pinning me back on the bed, his eyes darkening. Against my leg I could already feel his member quickening.

But before I could respond, show him my words were more than syllables, a solid knock beat against the door.

We both glanced that way.

"What?" I snarled as Van reached for the spread, pulling it across the both of us just in case someone incorrectly translated my demand into permission to enter.

"Team meeting in five minutes. We have problems." It was Jaylene's voice, focused and to the point. I could hear her footsteps receding even as I glanced at Van, took in his knit brows, the tightening of his features.

He swore a short, pithy oath I'd never heard as he jackknifed to his feet.

I guess our moment was over.

"No, it's not," he said, as if reading my thoughts. "We've only just started. Soon as this meeting is over we're out of here. Three days. You. Me. A hotel room. Got it?"

No point in telling him that the moment we left this room our lives were no longer our own. We both knew it.

We dressed in silence. I tucked my ripped shirt into my pants and hoped no one would notice. As if the whole Compound wasn't aware of where we'd been and what we'd most likely been doing.

Oh, well. If bad girls could do the deed, they could hold their heads high, even if my face was flushed and there was a hickey or two on my neck.

I think I could get into being bad.

Right before I took a deep breath and tugged the door open, Van pressed the flat of his hand against it, giving us a few seconds more of privacy.

He lowered his head and kissed me. A claiming brand that curled my toes and had me forgetting Jaylene's words.

"Remember this," he whispered as he raised his head. "We're not done here. Not by a long shot."

Clearing my throat, I nodded. No words would come. If they could, I had no idea if I'd be agreeing or begging.

Jogging to keep up with his faster pace, I cast a quick glance back toward Aini's room. Guess I wasn't going to check in on her for a bit. First thing when the meeting ended I would. A promise.

By the time we reached the Conference room I thought I had my game face on. If I didn't the solemn expressions flashed my way would have sobered me up pronto.

I slid into my seat next to Alex. Van across the table. So close and way too far away.

"What's up?" I mumbled, aware of hushed voices around me asking the same question.

Alex shrugged, her gaze avoiding mine.

Soon, I could see, we'd have to have a little discussion. I wasn't going to hurt her brother. Not in my game plan, and the sooner she understood that the sooner we could get back to normal. Whatever that was.

Vaughn came in last, her shoulders so rigid I'm surprised they hadn't snapped. As she took her seat, all sound ceased. My throat went dry then closed up as her gaze swung to mine.

"Have you tried to contact Aini since last evening?"

"Yes, but I had no luck." I could feel the kaboom, kaboom of my heart revving up. "Why?"

"Will you try?"

What kind of answer was that?

Sucking in a breath so deep I almost coughed it out, I closed my eyes, making sure my last glance was anchored on Van. Then I stilled myself.

Aini?

Nothing.

Are you there Aini?

Quiet. Except for a very faint, far away sound, like the stirring of the evening wind through aspen trees.

What was going on?

Aini, if you can, speak to me. I need to know you're okay.

Silence.

My eyelids jerked open. "What's happening?" I was halfway out of my seat, heading to Aini's room when Alex's arm restrained me.

Vaughn glanced at Stone before looking back at me. Then she looked around the table. "I heard from Ling Mai this morning."

Several of us leaned forward.

"She's with the Council of Seven and they've received a message."

For love of popcorn just tell us.

"One of their most powerful mages confirmed that the Horned One has left this world to return to his own."

Wasn't that good news? I eased back, aware my muscles still were primed, ready for fight or flight.

Jaylene, bless her heart, spoke for all of us. "That's what we wanted, wasn't it?"

"Yes." Stone spoke. "But he didn't return to the Underworld alone."

My skin went cold. Across from me I caught Van's movement but didn't look his way. Not until I could breathe again.

When I finally moved I saw all eyes on me.

Stone's voice was not the gruff, take-no-prisoners drill instructor as he said, "The Horned One took Aini with him."

CHAPTER 49

Voices were raised all around me, questions tumbling over questions, as I pressed my palms flat against the table, as if that would stop my world from spiraling.

"Explain." The single word escaped from me, like a child crying in the night. Silence slammed into the room with me as the focal point.

I raised my gaze to Vaughn's. "How are they sure?"

Stone went to answer until Vaughn stopped him with a touch to his arm. "She deserves to know the details," she muttered, then spoke to all of us. "From what the mage reports, the Horned One was able to grab Aini's soul before he departed."

"How?"

"Why?"

Jaylene and Alex looked at each other as their questions bumped against one another.

"How, is probably because Aini was in an in-between state." It was Alex answering, which made sense because of anyone in the room, she understood the other realms that existed parallel but separate from ours. "In a coma, Aini was vulnerable. Neither here nor gone."

"Now you tell us?" I snapped, mad more at myself than her, though my tone didn't indicate that.

"Hello? Trying to stay alive?" came her whiplash response. "You were the one in touch with her. Why didn't you know?"

"Alex." Van's voice shot across the room, zippering Alex's mouth, for the moment.

Trouble was, she was right. I should have known. Called out to Aini more often. Checked in with her. Something.

"Have we checked her room?" I clutched at straws.

"Yes. No change in her condition," Stone answered.

That could mean—

"The machines are the only thing keeping her physical body alive. Stimulus elicits no response from her."

So she could be gone. Taken? But how? I killed that rat bastard. If I looked, I'd still see the blood soaking my skin. Then it hit me.

"The third door," I whispered, remembering those horrible last minutes.

"What about a third door?" Vaughn nudged.

I looked at her. "There, at the end, three doors appeared while I'd been invisible, not the usual two I see."

"What's the third door mean?" Nicki asked, glancing from my face to others, as if any of us had answers.

"I don't know." I shrugged. "It could have been a portal from here to the Underworld. I just don't know."

Vaughn cleared her throat. "According to what Ling Mai has gathered from those old enough on the Council to recall the old tales, as long as Aini has not reached the moment of her birth she can still be coerced into giving the Horned One what he wants."

"Which is what?" Alex asked.

"Your guess is as good as anyone's," our team leader answered.

This was not good. Not good at all. But what could we do? "We defeated the Horned One here, and his human receptacle is dead." I thought that sounded better than repeating what we all knew. That I'd killed Kincaide. "So I thought he couldn't return here. Isn't that what the legends said?"

"Fraulein Fassbinder should be able to confirm that, but yes, I think that's accurate." This time it was Vaughn leaning forward. "But that doesn't mean he's not dangerous."

"Meaning?"

"You should remember that the Librarian mentioned The Horned One was a failed Seeker."

Now that she mentioned it, the words came back.

"So?" I knew I sounded like a petulant child but couldn't help it, not with my blood running cold. "If the Horned One is gone, and can't get back, he shouldn't be a threat. And the whole terrorist brother bit?" I kept my gaze averted from Van's. "I'm assuming that was a smoke screen just to get to Aini. So what's the issue?"

"You're right. There never was a brother, Ling Mai confirmed that. And, while the Horned One might not be a direct threat, what about what he could compel Aini to do?"

We were all staring at her now.

Alex jumped in. "Such as?"

"Before turning sixteen, Aini can be used."

"To get to the Seekers?" I said, working at the possibilities.

"According to Ling Mai, that's what the Council fears."

"If Aini did contact a Seeker, doesn't mean they can get to this realm. Does it?" Nicki jumped to the worst-case scenario. The one we were all ignoring.

"What if it does?" Stone was the calm voice of reason.

"Then we fight them if they come." Nicki all but spat the words.

The sad, strangled laugh that wanted to escape remained lodged in my throat. Had she already forgotten last night? We'd barely hung on, and stopped Kincaide by fluke. "We're not ready to face anything more powerful than what we just did. Not yet," I murmured, feeling every ache and bruise. "Neither can we ignore the possibility that we might not have any choice in the matter if the Horned One gets his way."

Nicki all but growled. "Can't the Council do anything? They're preternaturals. They should have more firepower than we have."

"They do." It was Van answering. "But they have no provision to raise what amounts to a standing army."

"Why the hell not?"

"Think it through, Nicki," Vaughn soothed. "Last thing humans want is a preternatural mercenary group, trained and ready to fight. Until this Seeker threat, there's been no need to even consider such a dangerous option."

Nicki sat back against her chair with a hard thud. Once again we all remained tongue-tied, grappling with our own thoughts, aware of how fragile and vulnerable humans really were. Except not all of us were humans.

"We're positive about Aini?" I asked again, my hope a fragile thread.

"We brought in a Necromancer to confirm," Stone said. "She's not there, Kelly."

There were such beings as Necromancers? Like that, or anything should surprise me by now. Heck, I was the clavis, whatever that meant. Except I know in my gut what it meant. It meant I was tied to Aini, just as she was tied to me.

"So the Horned One was trying to get Aini all along to use her, not kill her." I spoke the words aloud to fill the hole that had opened up inside me. "But what if we bring her soul back into her body? Before she wakes up?"

"What are you thinking?" Vaughn lasered her penetrating gaze at me.

"Do we know the exact time of Aini's birth?" My thoughts were still so tumbled it was hard to get a bead on what was driving me. So I was winging it.

Vaughn opened a file on her desk, scanned what looked like an email before saying, "She was born at 11:08 p.m. Sierra Leone time."

"Which is what in our time?" I asked, feeling urgency whipping me.

"Seven p.m.," Van answered, not surprising me in the least. Of course he'd be able to calculate time zones with ease. "It's nearly 5 a.m. now, which means we have roughly 14 hours before Aini's actual birth time and date."

"So what?" Jaylene jumped in. "Did you miss that part that they were in the Underworld, wherever the hell that is?"

"I know where it is." Alex's voice right next to me made me jump.

Vaughn was already shaking her head. "You're not thinking what I think you're thinking."

"Why not?" Alex straightened her shoulders and got that stubborn Noziak tilt to her chin. One I recognized, which boded well for what I, and it appeared, she was thinking. "We've had to go to the other side before. Once to save Franco.

Once to battle a Djinn. If Aini's in the Underworld, I can find her."

"And if she's not?" Van's tone sounded like he was grinding glass.

"Not your call," came Alex's reply as she turned to look at Vaughn. "If Ling Mai gives the go ahead, I'll go after her."

"Not without me." The words were out before I could think them through. Like an electrical current whipping through the room, all gazes turned to me. Only one mattered. Van looked like he couldn't figure out who to throttle first, his sister, or me.

"Wait just a—" Alex started but I cut her off.

"If you can get me to the other side, I'll be an asset." I didn't want to go into the whole clavis thing, but this is why it mattered. "If I'm close to Aini I can reach her. Connect with her. Let her know we're coming, which might give her just enough hope to keep her from..." I let the words trail off. No need to spell out what she was facing. We'd all battled Kincaide's Horned One. No telling what it meant to face a wicked nasty demon, maybe the biggest demon in the Underworld, on his home turf.

"I'll come, too," came a third voice in the room. Mandy.

"No way." Alex shook her head so hard her waist-length braid whipped behind her. "Last thing we need is a soul catcher."

"Technically, I'm a Spirit Walker," Mandy replied calmly, something she didn't often do when talking with Alex. "And I can be of help."

"Doing what?" Alex scoffed. "Advertising for any souls wanting a free ride out of their realm to this one?"

She didn't take the bait as she kept her voice calm, her hands loose in her lap. "If you're guiding, and Kelly is acting like an antenna seeking Aini, who'll be watching your backs?"

That had Van's growl deepening but Mandy had a point. No telling what kind of energy Alex and I would need to expend just to find Aini. If we could.

"This harebrained idea is nothing but a suicide mission." Van's voice dominated the room, making it too small and cramped. "Better to prepare yourselves in this Realm where the battle will happen."

"And leave Aini?" I asked, hanging on to the real issue. "Abandon her?"

"She's gone, Kels. Nothing you could have done to change that. A poor soldier fights the last battle instead of gearing up for the next one. The only one he can control."

Van's words, the gentleness in which he spoke them, ripped across me. Easy enough for him to wash his hands of Aini. One more casualty. But she was more than that. She was a real person. Part child, part woman. I'd promised her I'd watch out for her and she trusted me. I'd failed her already. Was I going to turn my back on her now?

"The Librarian called me her Guardian," I said, enunciating each word, a death knell echoing through the room. "I can't guard her from here. If Alex can take me with her—" I glanced at Alex who gave a brief head nod. "—and Mandy is willing to help." She offered a tight smile. "Then I'm going."

"With my permission," came a familiar voice in the doorway.

Ling Mai. She'd returned and spoken.

Looked like I was heading to hell.

CHAPTER 50

Van caught up with me in the courtyard after the Conference broke up and after he had argued, again and again, against the mission.

"Why?" he demanded with a harsh, guttural tone as he grabbed my arm.

The wealth of questions in that one word spun between us. Why go? Why volunteer for a no-chance-in-Hades assignment? Why leave him?

I focused on the first issue, pushing the others aside with a ruthlessness that surprised me, even as grief twisted through me. "I owe Aini. She needs my help."

"That simple?"

Heck, no, it wasn't. Everything in me screamed against leaving. There was nothing I wanted more than to stay here, stay with Van, let him wrap his arms around me one more time and say everything will be okay.

Instead I cleared my throat, swallowing against my words.

"Some things are simple. This isn't, but we both know I have to go."

I turned away from the bleakness in his gaze, the tears acid-etching my own eyes. Logic said one thing, my heart the exact opposite.

This wasn't fair. I'd used up every last ounce fighting the Horned One only hours ago. And now? Last thing in the universe I wanted to do was follow him into his lair. There'd be no coming back.

But if I let those words, those fears escape, I just might stop. The only gift I could give Van now was my certainty. Even if it was a lie.

He didn't want me to go. I understood that. I really did. But like him I had chosen an ugly job that had to be done. That was the bottom line.

I could do this mission. He couldn't. If the tables were turned he'd expect me to accept his choice. His duty.

No matter how it tore me apart, tore the two of us apart. We'd had our moment, it had to be enough. An unfulfilled wish and a dream. Never enough, but it was all we were given.

He paused, his face tightening, matching the loss in his gaze before he spoke. "And if I ask you not to go?"

Don't do this. Not to you. Not to me. Asking the impossible was not going to make it any easier to follow his sister to a place I did not want to go.

"You won't ask that," I said, my words choked.

"Like hell I won't."

Anger. Anger I could deal with. It was easier to fight Van's anger than his pain. He'd already been betrayed by his commanding officer and had yet to deal with that fall out. Last thing he needed was to think was I was abandoning him, too.

"This is no longer about us," I said.

"Everything's about us from now on out."

He was tearing me asunder. Ripped apart and bleeding from within, I'd still have to go.

I quieted my voice. Ice to fire. "If the roles were reversed, what would you do? Knowing there's a slim chance, but still a chance, to save an innocent girl and maybe the world at the same time?"

"Not fair, McAllister."

"Fair has no place in a war and that's what we're fighting."

He looked like I'd hit him. It was the truth and we both knew it. I had to go. He had to stay. Tears jammed my throat, but I swallowed them, tasting of bile. Neither of us needed them.

Our time was running out. The threat I chased wasn't going to go away. Not without a fight. A to-the-death battle.

For a second I thought he'd say something more, reassure me, even hug me, but that wasn't to be. Not as anger and frustration bubbled through him. I could see it, in the angle of his jaw, the way he rocked forward on his feet.

Then he turned and walked away, taking my broken heart with him.

I could have called him back. Offered false promises.

But I didn't. Instead I squared my shoulders and wiped my eyes with my sleeve. I had a job to do. Time to find Alex and go after Aini.

Time to follow through on my vow.

I'm coming, Aini. Hold on.

The End

DID YOU LIKE
INVISIBLE SECRETS?

Thank you for reading about Kelly McAllister in this novel and I hope you enjoyed her story! Let the world know by posting a review on Goodreads or Shelfari. Write a Customer Review. You = Awesome. Me = Grateful.

I also love hearing from readers! Find me on Goodreads or Facebook or Twitter!

Questions? Comments?

Help make the next edition of this book even better. If you've found a pesky typo in this book, here's your chance to let me know. Email suggestions to:
Assistant@MaryBuckham.com

WHAT READERS ARE SAYING ABOUT INVISIBLE RECRUITS

"Not since Kate Daniels and Mercy Thompson have I fallen in love with a female character like I have with Alex Noziak." ~Urban Girl Reader.

"This is a definite must read for anyone who enjoys a bit of a thrill, a good laugh, and great characters with attitude." ~ Parchment Place

"I ... encourage those of you who like action, magic and sassy heroines to snatch up this series." ~ Romancing the Genres

WANT TO READ MORE ABOUT THE INVISIBLE RECRUIT TEAM? CHECK OUT:

INVISIBLE PRISON (novella)
On her first days with the Invisible Recruit Agency, Alex Noziak learns she's not the only recruit with secrets to hide. But hers could get her kicked off the Team even before she begins. Or they could get her killed.

INVISIBLE MAGIC (full length novel)
On her first official mission for the Invisible Recruit Agency Alex Noziak discovers that to save the innocent she must call

upon her untested abilities. But at what cost? She has nothing to lose, except her life.

INVISIBLE DUTY (novella)
The mission sounded easy for Alex Noziak, part witch/part shaman. And easy is what she needed. But in the heart of Africa, she finds something so deadly it will test her in ways she never expected.

INVISIBLE POWER (full-length novel)
When Alex has a chance to save her brother and expose the Weres who held him hostage, she must make a hard choice with lives at risk, including her own.

INVISIBLE FATE (full-length novel)
Forced to choose, will dark magic be the only path. Hidden from a world unaware of magic, a recently and only partially trained group of operatives known as the Invisible Recruits are the only ones willing to stand between mankind and those powerful preternatural factions seeking to change the balance of power and gain world domination.

Be the First to Find Out When the next books in the INVISIBLE RECRUITS series come out.

Sign up for my newsletter on:
MaryBuckham.com

The Kelly McAllister books

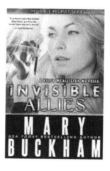

INVISIBLE ALLIES (novella)
Juggling with the side effects of her developing powers, patience isn't Kelly's current strong suit, especially around Alex Noziak, once a best friend, who has become a constant rub since realizing Kelly has an interest in Alex's brother. Now

they're stuck together on an off the record assignment. Two IR operatives should be able to track down a runaway witch in a small Missouri town without breaking a sweat, but even if they survive working together Alex is hiding a secret that might rear its deadly head and get both of them killed.

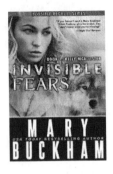

INVISIBLE FEARS (novel)

He's a preternatural fighting for the humans.

She's a human fighting for the preternaturals.

Kelly McAllister's Invisible Recruit mission in Sierra Leone is to locate and secure a threat to humans and preternaturals. Van Noziak is also there, with his own secret mission, one that's on a collision course with Kelly's. In deepest Africa the race against a deadly bloom reveals secrets, exposes fears, and forces unlikely alliances.

INVISIBLE EMBRACE (novel – coming 2015)

ABOUT THE AUTHOR

 A USA Today bestselling author I started my career writing romantic suspense novels. Nothing like bombs and gunfire making a relationship more complicated. Between publication dates I was also fortunate to become a writing craft instructor, offering live workshops around the US and Canada as well as online workshops to writers throughout the world. As fun as the travel, and getting to know so many writers of all genres was, my first love has always been fiction. Thus the Invisible Recruit series was born and took off running!

I love conflict. On the page. The conflict between dark magic and white. The conflict between beings created with different needs and wants. Witches. Mage warlocks. Shifters, Weres, and demons all trying to co-exist against their natures. Bring it on!

I'm a huge paranormal and fantasy lover. Especially Urban Fantasy and any paranormal fantasy series that allows me to throw myself into magic and mystery page after page, book after book

The paranormal world of the Invisible Recruits is built on women who must learn to embrace their preternatural talents to fight good and evil. Talents that they've hidden from the human population for fear of being different.

But because I love conflict I've dropped these women into a world where magic and fantasy exist side by side with humans intentionally kept in the dark about Shifters, Weres, warlocks, witches, and especially about magic.

Throw in a strong dose of romantic suspense, emotional relationships to add more conflict, and paranormal beings you've never heard of before, and you'll know why readers can't get enough of this fast-paced paranormal thriller series.

www.MaryBuckham.com
www.InvisibleRecruits.com